MW01121736

RETURN FROM EXTINCTION

a novel by
Brandon Helms

Dedicated to my wife, who was with me the whole journey. I would be nothing without you.

© 2017 Brandon Helms

CHAPTER 1
A HEARTFELT GOODBYE

"Money? Well, you can keep your money. Power is what I'm after. Funny thing about power- one moment it's in your hands, the next, it's in mine." The man said.

He was tall, with graying hair and a certain pallor to his skin. He was perhaps forty, yet had no laugh lines at all on his face. It is often said that one's life story is written in the face and eyes. This man's life story looked to be one of cunning looks, wicked grins, and corrupt smiles. Thick black-framed glasses magnified his eyes and made them look as though they could pierce directly into the soul.

He spoke with a german accent that, despite its chilly intonation, still held a disingenuous charm, like a sort of Hitler if you didn't know better. He was dressed in an off-blue dress shirt and checkered brown tie, which went below a black sweater. Over all of it he wore an unbuttoned black suit jacket, as if announcing to the world that he would conduct whatever probably wicked business he had come to conduct as he pleased, and he would expect the universe to bend to his demands. He was no stranger to power.

"Sir, the transplant, um,... donor, is almost ready." A hospital nurse said, passing by the doorway.

The man had an exceedingly rare cardiovascular condition which required a fresh heart from a very specific genetic match every few years. A significant portion of his immense wealth was devoted to trying to find a solution to his condition, but with no solution yet in sight, these barbaric heart transplants were necessary for his survival. And survive he would.

He glanced through the tinted green glass into the adjoining room. There was the 'donor'. A relatively young man compared to himself, with a wife and two children, although none of them were with him in the room. The promise of money to lift his family out of their crippling poverty was enough to convince this man to make this sacrifice. Every penny he made at his dirt-poor job went to the family scraping by and desperate attempts to save his wife through the latest experimental treatments. She had an incurable form of pancreatic cancer, and would surely die, the doctors said. But he had to try, try to save her. And so he sacrificed.

The donor was writing a letter, probably a last goodbye to his family. It was ironic how, in the man's eyes, the donor's heart would ultimately only lead to heartbreak for his family. The donor had kept this venture a secret from his family, for their sake as much as his. He had asked them to wait in the adjacent waiting room without telling them why. As per the agreement, when the deed was done, the donor's family would be presented with the money, and they would have a chance at a good life. The man had no intention of delivering on his promise, however. He would take the heart and keep the money, too. Eggs and promises are easily broken.

He looked on as the donor paused to pull out a photo and look at it lovingly. It was a young boy and girl, likely his children. Next to it he laid a portrait of himself and his family together. The caption read *The Storm Family*. The donor caressed the portrait of his family. If their circumstances had worked out for the better, surely they would have been able to live life happily together, growing old with each other. But these were not better circumstances, and they would not grow old together.

The donor carefully placed the letter and the photos inside an envelope and sealed it. He handed it to a waiting attendant. The man watched through the glass as the scene played out wordlessly, like a silent movie. The donor's lips moved and he spoke with gestures of the hand, but no sound could be heard. His words would be lost to history. As the donor left the room, the attendant brought the items directly to the man, as he had been ordered beforehand.

The man unceremoniously tore open the envelope and skimmed through the letter. He laughed. He folded it back up and put the bundle in his own pocket. This was one for the archives. He coughed suddenly and violently into his arm. When the coughing fit was over he was surprised to see blood on the cloth of his suit jacket. The transplant couldn't come soon enough. He whispered something into the ear of the attendant and the attendant nodded solemnly and left quickly.

The little boy in the other room sat in silence. His little sister played with her toys, oblivious to anything that might be going on around her. He felt that something was wrong, but he could not figure out what. Maybe it was just the way the overly-bright lights of this rich people building seemed to shine like a spotlight on every stain and patch on his worn out clothes. He brushed some dirt off self-consciously. Or maybe it was the way the clock on the wall screamed out an endless rhapsody of ticks and tocks until it was like a song played too many times on the radio, driving the listener to insanity. A nurse entered with a subdued expression.

"I'm afraid that your father has passed away." She said, with the practiced somberness of someone who delivers bad news for a living. The young, now incomplete family sat in stunned silence. The boy's mother broke into tears. His little sister was still off in her own world playing with her toys. The little boy felt a tear streak down his face.

Tall, black-clad men began pulling his mother and sister away, and one came for him. Without thinking, the boy bolted out the door. Everything was a blur— the sounds of people yelling, the sights and smells, none of it made any sense. He found himself collapsed against a tree some time later, alone.

But he would try to be strong.

ABOUT 20 YEARS LATER....

CHAPTER 2
SALVAGING

"Isn't it odd to think that we could die at any moment and never expect it? I like to think I would have some feeling beforehand and know it was coming. But we wouldn't. One moment you'd be here, the next, not so much."

Gye's attention was only half on the words of his friend. Marquis Parcell always seemed to be talking about either nothing at all or altogether too much at once. It was better to pay him only half a mind, as it seemed to even out over time.

"Aren't you just a ray of sunshine today? Now hurry up with that detonator. The competition will be here any minute, so let's not hand them any victories." Gye said.

The ancient, sandy village surrounding them in the midst of a desert stretching for miles to the horizon in every direction was decrepit and falling apart, but appearances could not be trusted here. There was more value to be found here than Gye's entire home town.

"You ever think we might be doing the wrong thing?" Marquis asked.

"You having second thoughts?"

"Eh, no. I just mean, maybe… this isn't what I envisioned when you asked if I wanted to make a business out of adventuring."

Gye considered this for a moment. Marquis had never quite been supportive of, as Gye liked to say, using every tool at one's disposal to emerge victorious. But in the salvaging business, where a good haul could net half a million credits or more, there was no room for getting soft or growing a conscience.

"Are we in this together or what?" Gye demanded.

Marquis sighed and then acquiesced.

"Of course we are, Gye. To riches and glory."

"To riches and glory!" Gye repeated back, more enthusiastically. After this mission Marquis could do what he wanted, assuming all went to plan. Gye hoped he would stay with him, though. Finding a partner who was both trustworthy and competent in this business was nigh near impossible.

Marquis connected the finished detonator and admired his handiwork. The competition they had been tipped off about would surely arrive within minutes. When they did, they would find an enticing wooden chest sticking out the doorway of one of the old dwellings. Likely they would be immediately drawn to open it. Once they did, they would be greeted by a rather nasty explosion. Not enough to kill, of course, but enough to dampen their enthusiasm and send them home if they had a lick of sense in them. It struck Marquis that it was quite possible that the competition might very well not have any sense at all, and continue searching the place like raccoons digging into trash. Something about the quest for riches made men's eyes glaze over with lust, and all wisdom recede from their faces. Perhaps soon he would be rid of the whole business.

Gye signaled to the waiting all-terrain Jeep to pick them up. Aside from himself and Marquis, two other men routinely made up their band of thieves. Thieves? Yes, perhaps that was the best word for it. But to steal from the dead was of as little consequence as romance, in Gye's eyes. Both the riches of dead and romance of the living were alike to him in that they seemed pointless. Not that he didn't partake of either.

The wind kicked up some and they had to cover their eyes as they got into the waiting Jeep. The driver, a middle-aged hispanic man named Rafael, grinned as they entered. Beside him was the navigator, James, a catholic hispanic. He spoke no english and communicated through Rafael.

"James thinks you're cutting it a bit close," Rafael said with a toothy grin, after a quick exchange in Spanish. To Gye other languages always seemed to cascade out the mouths of those who spoke the languages like water down a drainpipe. The Jeep headed for a spot to view the unwelcome competition without being seen. Rafael and James both wore dark khakis and airy t-shirts. They were much more smartly dressed for the job than Gye, who wore heavy blue jeans and the type of blue button-up shirt a cowboy in the wild west might wear in one of those old photos. He was a handsome man, tall, with wavy dirty blond hair and blue eyes. His grizzly beard seemed to add half a decade to his age, which was why he wore it.

Marquis' had no beard but had a confidence in his own existence that Gye could only envy. He had to fake his own confidence. Marquis' mop of wavy blond hair seemed to reflect the constant gentle smirk he wore on his face. He had several tattoos of various esoteric meanings on his arms. Gye, on the other hand, did not have any tattoos. He was afraid of needles.

The dust was kicked up into a frenzy by the blades of a helicopter. The Jeep was out of view of the helicopter as it landed. Gye tucked a pistol into his belt and jumped out of the Jeep. They were behind one of the village dwellings that had probably been home to a family many hundreds of years ago.

As the helicopter wound down, five people hopped out of it and had a look around. It didn't take them long to see the welcoming decoy chest sticking out of the doorway.

"Like leading bison to slaughter," Gye muttered. But it was not to be that simple.

The competitors halted abruptly near the dwelling. One of them, who seemed to be in charge, was giving out orders. Gye could not make out what the orders were, but they could not bode well for an easy victory today.

One of them extended a probe towards the decoy chest. A small explosion boomed. The person holding the probe was barely knocked off of their feet by the concussive blast. The leader laughed and gave the order to move on.

"Curses!" Gye muttered. Marquis had the look of disappointment on his face of a man whose dreams of escaping a prison had been dashed by an attentive prison warden. The likelihood of escape was dropping like the drops of rain that used to tease the ground with the idea of respite from drought in Gye's hometown. Gye saw fortune the same way- something that always seemed to be just ahead of him, eluding capture. He would not let it slip easily from his grasp this time.

The competition could not win and get away with the haul without the use of their helicopter. So they wouldn't, if Gye had anything to do with it.

"Gye, James has something to say." Rafael said. After a few more whispered words in Spanish, Rafael nodded and continued. "He says he can fly us out of here if we want to… commandeer their helicopter."

"And leave the Jeep?" Gye asked.

"Sometimes you have to sacrifice a hog to catch a lion."

"Fair enough. Let's do it. It was last year's model, anyway."

"Of course. The grill was too european for my taste."

"The europeans don't make good cars, good music, or good citizens." Gye retorted.

They waited until the group had disappeared into one of the dwellings before starting off, dashing from sandy dwelling to sandy dwelling towards the helicopter. Marquis clutched the box containing the valuable haul tightly as he ran. Luckily the competition had started their search on the wrong side of the village. Hopefully that fact would buy Gye and his crew a bit more time.

The existence of the village had long been the subject of passed-on tales and legends. The story went that during the Spanish colonization of northwestern Africa, one of the Lords to King Ferdinand had run off with a valuable ancient gold crown adorned with jewels. He had tried to start his own kingdom in Africa but had been overrun by the indigenous people. It was said that the crown passed on to a local leader who had kept the crown safe. The rest was unconfirmed rumor, until now. Now, the race was on to see who would emerge with the crown. Gye and his crew had a head start, now they just needed to not lose it.

Marquis stumbled, nearly dropping the valuable box as he ran. He clutched the box sheepishly and ran a little more carefully. Gye kept an eye on him.

They arrived at the helicopter.

"Almost seems too easy." Rafael said.

As if in reply to that sentiment, shouts were heard from the competitors. Gunshots whizzed through the air, emitting a sickening sound like Gye imagined a paper cut would sound like.

"Go go go!" He shouted as they jumped into the red helicopter. The motor buzzed to life. The red paint on the exterior was peeling and cracked, but the corporate name was still visible on the side from perhaps decades past. It said *Rockenhoffler, inc.*

Gye gave a shout and whoop as they began lifting off. A bullet smashed weakly into the glass, resulting in little more than a dull *thud* sound. They were home free. The competition had been beaten. It wasn't the first time this crew had barely evaded death, but the first time they had done it for any real fortune.

"Too bad we left the champagne in the Jeep, eh boss?" Rafael said. He smiled gleefully. He was the only married one of the group, hoping to strike it rich with Gye as part of his crew and take his wife on the honeymoon he had promised her a decade ago. It looked like he would finally be fulfilling that promise.

"Quite so, Rafael. But a toast nonetheless to you, gentlemen. We've finally struck it rich!" Gye replied. He was ecstatic, but the type of man to avoid showing strong emotion of any kind, sad or joyful. There were smiles all around.

"To you, to us, to adventure, to riches and glory!" He shouted above the sound of the propeller, pantomiming clinking champagne glasses together with the others. They laughed. Rafael translated the celebration into Spanish for James. The sandy, dusty environment below seemed to blur away under the dull buzz of the helicopter.

Marquis' words about the possibility of dying at any moment without foreknowledge came back to Gye just then. Sure, it was true, and terrifying if you thought too long on it. But it was worse, he reflected, to decay in one's shell throughout life in the hopes of preserving a shell worth looking at.

"It's such a pity how so many people are trying only to live long lives rather than good ones. Much of the time people have been dead many years before their hearts stop beating." Gye said to Marquis, in late response to his earlier statement. Marquis understood at once and smiled. Adventure was its own reward, they believed. But getting a shot at fortune wasn't bad on the side.

Gye looked out at the landscape and the easygoing grin slowly dripped off of his face. The larger chess game once again became forefront in his mind. With each dollar he swindled from the graves of the dead, he became one step closer to finding the man who killed his father. What a day of reckoning that would be… but not yet.

"Grandma, are you going to be alright by yourself for a minute?" The girl asked. The girl, a teenager about sixteen years old, was pushing her grandmother, about ninety six years old and blind as a bat, in a decrepit plastic wheelchair. She was pushing her through a new trail in the woods near their village, although the grandmother would've had no idea whether the trail was new or not. She didn't have very many ideas about much of anything, in fact, at her age.

"Grandma, did you hear me?" She asked again.

"Hmm? Who is that?" The old woman managed to ask. She was wearing glasses, the frames of which had fallen out decades ago; her cloudy once-blue eyes were visible through the frames. But she insisted on keeping the glasses on, as they were of some comfort to her.

The girl sighed and looked in a certain direction impatiently. Grandma wasn't keeping up all that well anymore.

She spoke with a fake, strained patience as the young so often do when dealing with the senile.

"Grandma, it's your granddaughter, Molly. I'm pushing you through the forest so you can get some fresh air, don't you remember?" She said.

"Oh of course, dearie. Of course I remember. Will Richard be along soon?" She asked confusedly.

The girl, Molly, sighed again. Richard, her grandmother's beloved, had been dead for close to two decades now. Molly stamped her foot impatiently before smiling slightly.

"Yes, if you wait just a moment, Richard will be along to talk to you. You'd like that, wouldn't you? You just gotta be patient for a minute, and he'll come to you." Molly said.

The old woman smiled contentedly at that answer and leaned back— as much as her frail bones would allow her to— in her wheelchair.

Molly smiled gratefully and practically skipped down the trail a ways before walking to join the boy waiting for her, sitting patiently at the base of a large oak tree. They smiled at each other. It was fall time; the leaves were vibrant shades of red, orange, and yellow; every time a gust of wind whispered through the woods, a group of them would jump from the protective arms of their trees and dance to the ground, joining the thousands of others that made up the forest floor.

The grandmother, unaware of the scene taking place behind her in the distance, looked upwards contentedly. She was waiting. For something. Or someone? What was it again? She frowned slightly, sending another crease to her face, one among the many wrinkles and creases that were each a testament to her many years of existence. Her graying hair was frayed and split, a strong contrast to the lovely auburn strands that had graced her head decades ago.

She heard a buzzing sound, but she was too lost in thought to pay attention to it.

It was a bee. Not too terrifying in of itself, to be sure, but this was no ordinary specimen. This creature was a foot long, with pure black eyes that resembled the fake eyes of a demented children's doll from a horror movie.

The old woman felt a pressure on her forearm, and she came back to the present. It was silent.

"Is that you, Richard? My dear, is that you?" She called out in her weak, frail voice.

No, she had not met Richard yet. Who had been with her earlier? Her mother? Perhaps that was it. But why couldn't she see? Her mother had had the most beautiful eyes, and everyone said she had her mother's eyes… what was happening?

There was a weight on her forearm. She shook her arm uncomfortably. It was cold, and she wanted to pull her blanket closer.

There was a sharp, painful sensation on the back of her hand, and she cried out. The weight left her arm, but the pain was growing stronger by the second. She tried to call for help, but no more sound could escape her lips. Her eyes stopped blinking, although they were just as cloudy as they had been before.

Some time later, the girl, Molly, came back.

"Ok Grandma, did you have a nice time with Richard? It's time to go home now." She said, extra sweetly and softly from behind into her grandmother's ear. She frowned when she received no reply, but that was not quite unusual. She shrugged and began pushing her back towards their village. She whistled a happy tune into the now-chilly fall time air, which was crisp as a new piece of paper demanding a new melody be written.

A day later, someone finally noticed that her cloudy eyes had nothing behind them, and closed her eyes for a final time. When the village doctor noticed the mark on the back of her wrist and began asking around for answers, a nice, tall man with an American accent and an expensive black suit told her that her services were no longer required and that it was nothing to be concerned about. The old woman's body went missing when he left, but the village doctor found some gold bars on her desk the very same day, and so was quite content to ask no questions and move on.

CHAPTER 3
SILVER LINING

Gye Storm was going to be late. He hated being late, which was why he was rarely seen without one of those old metal watches on his wrist- the strange kind that only told the date and time. He was old-fashioned in many ways like that, preferring the illusion of an idyllic past to the cold reality of the mediocre present. This would be only the second time he had been late to a date with his current flame, a lovely damsel by the name of Emily Addams.

Gye smiled as he thought of her. She was a creature of fiery passion, with flaming red hair and green eyes to match. She had a love for floral print dresses, picnics on grassy hills under cloudless skies, and flawed men. Her seemingly endless collection of shoes of every kind seemed to represent each of her various moods, which she was prone to change without warning. Gye found her odd predictable unpredictability enticing.

Their relationship had been going on for something like half a year now, although you couldn't tell that by listening to them. It was obvious that they were on intimate terms without truly knowing each other intimately. Gye preferred it that way, as someone with a lust to go adventuring in every direction but inwards. The same couldn't be said for Emily. She was always trying to change him- probably for the better, yes, but change just the same.

He pulled up to the restaurant and checked the time once again before sighing and hopping out of his car to rush in. It was eight fifteen at night. He was dressed hurriedly in a white dress shirt, the top two buttons left unbuttoned, with a distressed brown leather jacket on top. Burgundy pants and brown leather suede shoes completed the look.

Gye pushed through the double glass doors with one hand, clutching a hand-tied bouquet of flowers- streaked candy cane red and white tulips, red calla lilies, and red pansies- as he went in. Stamping his foot impatiently, he waited for the short line of people- which was not terribly long, but felt like an eternity as everything is bound to when one is late- to dissipate, and smiled hurriedly at the maitre d'.

"Reservation?"

"It should be under *Storm*."

"Ah, right this way sir." The man's face seemed to be suppressing a gentle smirk at the sight of the flowers and his lateness.

Gye could see Emily's unamused expression as he approached the table. The place was rather fancy, with plenty of natural light, velvety chairs, and elegant patterned table coverings. The baroque stylings of the place were to the taste of the old-fashioned but not dated.

"Sorry I'm late," he said. His sheepish grin elicited a small smile from her. "These are for you," he said as he placed the flowers in the center of the table. He didn't like apologizing— no, it wasn't quite that. More so, he didn't like having a *reason* to apologize.

Her delicate hands caressed the nearest pansy appreciatively.

"Oh my, they're lovely!"

"Not as lovely as you." He replied. Gye couldn't help but stop and stare as she admired the flowers. Their vibrant hues reflected in her eyes as if the goddess of beauty Aphrodite had decided to admire her own glamor in a mirror.

"Thank you," she said after a pause, "I hope you don't mind, but I started on the appetizers without you. The Parmesan Toasts are simply to die for."

He chuckled. A waiter poured from a bottle into two waiting glasses. He was off to the next table like a fleeting phantom. If not for the full glasses, it would have been as if he had never existed.

She clinked glasses with him and had a sip. Gye frowned at the taste.

"It's gluten free." She said, noticing his reaction. She was often following the latest quasi-scientific diet trends blindly, which resulted in frequently pointless diet changes that helped little in the way of health. This was one of those quirks Gye wouldn't have wanted to change.

"The band is playing so charmingly tonight, aren't they? Mmh. I can never get enough of smooth jazz." She said, looking intently into the corner where the band was playing.

"They never disappoint." He replied.

"I sure do hope jazz music makes a comeback. I'm so tired of this bland electronic stuff they make these days. It is *so* dull. Don't you agree?"

Gye had only been paying half attention to what he was about to agree with. He found that her lips were rather distracting him from the words they had been forming just then.

"Of course." He agreed.

She seemed to sense his distractedness, although she decided not to press the issue.

"Speaking of the arts, you remember my photograph of the lost tribe in the Andes that went on display recently?" She asked.

"Oh, of course! I love that one."

"Well, how did it look on display?"

He paused, unsure what she meant. He had just returned from his expedition last week (expedition was a polite word for the somewhat unpalatable reality), but he had, of course, not told her the truth about where he had gone. She thought he had gone to New York for a business trip. What kind of business he could not quite remember at the moment— what had he told her his profession was? Something about insurance, he was pretty sure. Probably. He did not want to tell her the truth, as decent pretty girls didn't seem to take a liking to dangerous adventurers who would probably find their way into a jail cell one day.

"What do you mean?" He finally replied.

"It was on display in the lobby of the High Line Hotel. That's where you told me you were staying on your business trip."

He cleared his throat self-consciously. This probably would not end well.

"Certainly, I had just momentarily forgotten. It looked lovely."

The music stopped. The band was taking a break, leaving the air devoid of any sound to distract from Gye's web of lies. It was an uncomfortable silence. Emily looked off into the distance with an expression of disappointment.

"Are you sure you saw it?" She asked.

"Yes, it looked-"

"Is that where you really went last week? Are you lying to me?" She interrupted.

His heart beat harder and he cleared his throat again. Did she know?

After moments of no response from him, she rolled her eyes.

"I gave you every opportunity to be honest with me! Your friend Rafael, by the way, is not very good at keeping secrets." She said.

That little weasel! He couldn't be trusted with anything. Gye gulped some grape juice, trying to delay the inevitable.

"So you know the truth."

"Not all of it, but enough to know you don't trust me enough to tell me the truth. What, you think I'm some kind of toy you can just pick up and play with when you want, then drop me? I trusted you. I thought what we had was real!"

"It was. Is. I just-"

"No. No, we're through. Goodbye, Gye Storm. Or is that even your real name? I don't know what to believe anymore."

She stood up and grabbed her glass as if to splash it on him, but then thought better of it.

"I want very badly to splash this all over your disgusting face, but I know how much you love that shirt."

"That's very considerate of you." He replied half-jokingly. She rolled her eyes and stormed out. Out of his life? He felt more sad than he wanted to. He felt that, even though he had barely an ounce of trust to squeeze out of himself, that he might have grown to actually trust her, and maybe even- but, no, it was useless to think of now. She was gone.

The waiter appeared again and began stacking the table items on a tray.

"I assume you will want to be leaving? I will bring the monsieur the check shortly." Behind that mask of civility there was a flicker of amusement. Gye nodded angrily.

He was, once again, only half listening. He held his head in both his hands and sighed. Just when he thought he had a chance to become something better than he was— he was always a better version of himself when he was around her— the flame was snuffed out. He was a candle, snuffed out by the wind of his own flaws. The music picked up again, playing some saccharine soulful love song. Gye hated every word of it.

"Ms. Jane Silver, are you ready?"

She snapped out of her reverie. Where was she again? She remembered her purpose as the world refocused from her daze. Oh yeah, about to interview for a research grant. The cold, marble floors of the office complex dampened her otherwise optimistic perspective. If this went well, it could be her big break into doing work that actually mattered, not interning for self-absorbed, greedy researchers more interested in making a buck than contributing to human knowledge.

Jane Silver was a biologist with a razor-sharp mind and a penchant for accidentally making men swoon for her. It was one of life's great annoyances, she reflected, that most men couldn't help but fall for her. It was understandable, though, as Jane was not hesitant to admit. She was a woman- yes, a woman now, of twenty two years of age- with an unnatural confidence and optimism. She had brunette hair streaked blonde, with blue eyes and prominent cheek bones. Her pale complexion made her full lips stand out like a cherry on top of a shortcake. Beauty, however, was something she did not value much in herself or in art. Contributing to human knowledge and the sciences was of far more interest to her than playing princess and going to cocktail parties. She even despised her own beauty, to some degree, because it made those around her view her as some lovely piece of art on a pedestal who couldn't possibly- no, certainly not- contribute to science. She rolled her eyes at the thought. The price of having the world's eyes was apparently not being able to control where they were pointed. She would change the world, she was sure of it, and getting this grant would make that a whole lot easier.

She glanced down at the manilla folder in her hands. It contained her ideas of the causes of some strange reports of biological anomalies lately.

One man, for instance, had claimed to have found a bee the size of his forearm. Perhaps these localized regressions to carboniferous-esque characteristics could aptly—

"Ahem, ah, Ms. Silver?" The attendant looked on with slight curiosity tempered by the boredom of a man who does so much in his job that he accomplishes nothing.

She looked up again, embarrassed to have gotten lost in thought again.

"Oh, do forgive me. Uh, yes. Lead the way, please."

The place was an example of the modern architect's obsession with glass and metal. The entire wall on one side of the hallway was an enormous, seamless glass pane, which blurred the scenery outside rather than simply providing a looking glass to the outside world. The result was large blotches of colorful, streaked light on the opposite metal wall. To Jane, this creation of beauty was of little consequence. A cement building would have been of equal meaning to her.

"Mrs. Entrave is ready to see you now." The attendant said, motioning Jane through the open door.

It was a quite ordinary, dull little office. Aside from the glass desk, the rest of the furniture in the room was rather gaudy. The walls were each painted different bright, tasteless colors which had no business going together. The carpet resembled a college dorm room's; a patchwork of olive drab and beige. The woman behind the desk was middle aged, with stark black hair and the complexion of someone who spends too much time tanning their skin artificially. Her round face was like a beachhead to the waves of fat rolls cascading down her neck. Every time she tilted her head, the movement rippled through her many chins like an echo in a canyon. Jane almost burst out laughing upon noticing the effect. The name plate at the edge of her desk was conspicuously large, as if she was trying to prove her own existence to herself.

Mrs. Entrave smiled a fake smile at Jane and extended her flabby left arm in greeting. Jane reluctantly shook her hand and sat down.

"Ms. Silver, I looked over your application in advance. It all looks very, very good." With every 'very' she nodded her head slightly, sending waves down her many chins. Jane was repulsed, but tried not to show it.

"Thank you, Mrs.—" at this point Jane glanced at the name plate quickly to ascertain her name. She had been too distracted by her unruly appearance earlier to take much note of the woman's name.

"—Entrave. I am glad you like it. I am tremendously excited about the opportunities this grant would afford me in this promising field, and with this compelling lead-"

"That's all very good, Ms. Silver. Unfortunately, we are rejecting your application." With this she shook her head 'no' slightly. Miniature ripples of fat streamed down her face, making the situation almost comical to Jane despite this devastating blow.

"But I haven't even made my presentation yet! Surely I can-"

"However," Mrs. Entrave continued, as if Jane had not interrupted, "we are prepared to double the grant if you are willing to do something for us of particular importance."

Jane paused. What could it be? And oh, what she could do with *double*…

"You see, Ms. Silver, an enormous opportunity has arisen which I think you will jump at the chance to take. A client company of ours, which does field work research for the United States military, sent a drone to surveil the forest area you indicated in your application— close to where that dreadful enormous bee was found- to see what kind of, um, *scientific* applications these creatures might have."

Scientific? Yeah, right. Jane was certain these creatures would be harvested for genes and used to make the next billion-dollar 'miracle' drug, or turned into military applications. But sometimes it was necessary to accept the help of deep-pocketed corporations— such as for this research grant— to help move the sciences along. Nobody would finance work just for the goodness of humanity, apparently.

Mrs. Entrave continued.

"Unfortunately, their drone equipment disappeared without a trace in the midst of that forest. They had promising reports of several creatures you would probably find interesting."

She said 'you' as if Jane was some kind of odd alien with strange motives. Jane was too distracted by the idea to be offended. The notion of the possibility of more *giant creatures* was astounding. So much could be gleaned...

"Our initial report confirmed your hypothesis about the elevated oxygen levels in that area. Why, we don't exactly know, and this drone was supposed to help us find out. Now we need to get it back."

"Why not just send another one?" Jane asked.

"You wouldn't want to see the price tag on this monster... let's just say there's an executive at this company in tears on the floor, terrified about what might happen to him if it isn't recovered. It's loaded with all kinds of next-generation sensors and equipment that the United States military would feel rather... *sensitive* about losing. Needless to say, we are too concerned about losing another air operation to take that route. We'll be sending you and a crew of other specialized people with a specific skill set to recover the drone via land. I know it's a lot to think about. You'll probably want to call your family and your boyfriend before you make a decision. I understand."

Jane nearly rolled her eyes.

"I'm single, actually, and I make my own decisions, thank you."

Mrs. Entrave looked startled.

"You? Really? My oh my, with looks like that you ought to be able to snag any boy you wanted."

"I don't need a man in my life, actually. I'm quite fine on my own, and without your advice if you don't mind my saying so." Jane retorted.

"But you don't want to end up alone, do you?"

"Mrs. Entrave, I-"

"You're not one of those crazy feminists, are you?"

Jane could feel her blood pressure rising. She took a deep breath and let it out again. This was exactly why she needed this grant so badly. Then she could accomplish what she knew she could accomplish without these annoying comments coming her way all the time. People would finally respect her for what she had accomplished and not take one glance at her pretty face and try to put her in a box.

"Mrs. Entrave, I need no time to consider. I will be taking part in the mission, and I will furthermore make certain that the results of this mission do not go on to support some fat cat while screwing over the rest of the human race. Thank you for your time."

With that she stood up and turned on her heel, leaving with the confident swagger of a woman who knows what she wants and how to get it.

CHAPTER 4
RECRUITMENT

"I can give you fifty thousand in cash now, forty thousand later."

Gye turned to Marquis. By this point in their 'career' they practically had a nonverbal language between the two of them— other crew members came and went— that made them a force to be reckoned with in negotiations. They worked well together, and had become quite an effective team.

"Trying to take advantage of us, ay? We've got a better offer already. You weren't the first buyer we went to, by the way. The last one offered us seventy thousand now, sixty thousand later." Gye said. Marquis' gesture reminded Gye that he was giving too round of a number- people seemed to go along with numbers that were more specific. Gye sometimes found lies hard to keep straight.

"Oh really? I don't believe you. How about you tell me who offered you that much and I'll just call them right up and make sure?" The buyer said.

"Certainly. We last went to Patton's." Marquis said. Again, a lie.

The buyer made as if to begin dialing the phone. Gye and Marquis called his bluff and remained stoic. He paused.

"Tell you what," He said, realizing his ploy had failed, "How is sixty five thousand now, fifty five thousand later?"

After a brief moment, Gye and Marquis agreed. Sweat was rolling down the brow of the buyer. He was obviously new to the trade.

"Pleasure doing business with you." Marquis said curtly as they left.

# # #

"Let's put 500 chips on black," Gye said. Gye and Marquis were gambling at Roulette, as men with newly acquired wealth and   no foresight are prone to do. The place was dingy and dark, with a smoky atmosphere like one taken straight out of a saloon in the wild west.

The wheel spun in its flurry of color that Gye was in no state to keep up with. It landed on black.

"It looks like you win, sir."

"Well, whoopty freakin' doo, that's better luck than I've had all this week," he mumbled, "let it ride again, on the first twelve."

It started spinning again.

"You really cared about her, didn't you?" Marquis interrupted. Gye only nodded forlornly in response.

"Looks like you win again sir." The dealer said.

"Bloody hell, what's a man gotta do to lose around here? Ugh." Gye said with a deep sigh.

The dealer was unfazed by Gye's reaction; he was already ushering the next customer to the table.

Marquis offered Gye a piece of a bagel, which he declined with a shake of his head.

"You've gotta eat something, my friend."

"Why? Isn't the point of eating that you go on living?"

"Wow. That bad, huh?"

"I guess… I just really wanted this one to work out. She seemed so… perfect." Gye replied.

Marquis rested a hand on his shoulder.

"Hey, why don't we throw another crazy party, like we did last time we sold something valuable? It'll get your mind off her." Marquis asked.

"That's where I met Emily, don't you remember?"

"Well, maybe you'll meet someone new."

"People aren't that replaceable, Marquis."

"That's true. But, I've been engaged for six months now, and if there's one thing I can tell you from that experience, it's that love is worth it, if you never give up on it. You aren't giving up on it, are you?"

"Oh please. Love is all nonsense, nothing but facades and trouble."

"Oh boy, you've turned into a drama queen. That's how you know you've gone too long without a party. I'll make the calls."

# # #

It was the kind of party where people wore the bright colors of youth and summer sunshine. It was a stark contrast to Gye's mood, but he could already feel it lifting in response. He didn't even know many of the one hundred and fifty or so people crowded around the large outdoor pool and surrounding barbecue and outdoor bar. Already the joyful sounds of fun were heard over the blaring loud music. It was electronic, the kind Emily would have hated. That afternoon, Gye danced to it.

Marquis cracked open a drink. He sipped some and sighed with contentment. Unexpectedly, his phone rang. It was from a blocked number. Marquis was curious, but decided to let it go to voicemail.

"You gonna get that?" Gye asked, holding his own beverage can in his hand. He was wearing a white tank top and khaki cargo shorts— typical party attire for him.

"Blocked number." Marquis replied.

Gye grabbed the phone from Marquis' hand without warning. He answered in a bad imitation of a french accent.

"Aloh, monsieur, you 'av reached Parcell's fine dining 'an restaurant. How may I help you?"

Marquis directed a faux glare at him and then laughed. The phone suddenly went on speakerphone unprompted.

"This is Inspector Mendes. Your voice has been recognized as Gye Storm, accomplice to Marquis Parcell in a recent theft of a certain national artifact of which I'm convinced you're aware," the voice said. There was a slight hispanic accent to the man's voice.

Marquis looked at Gye confusedly, not remembering which specific national artifact he was referring to. A look of recognition flashed across his face after a while.

"Oh yeah," he said with a grin, "that was a good time."

"I'm sure we have no idea what you're talking about. We're simply two tour guides who happened to have been in the area at the time!" Gye answered into the phone, dropping the fake French accent. There was a slight pause.

"Last time you said you were traveling salesmen." Inspector Mendes replied.

"Oh, ah, we change occupations often. We're more like renaissance men, really." Marquis said into the phone, barely repressing a laugh.

"You'll answer for what you're doing soon enough."

"Sorry, what was that? I think the signal is cutting out. Wha-... ave-... the-... click." Marquis hung up, pretending the communication had been disrupted. They shared a laugh.

"I'm feeling better already!" Gye said with a chuckle.

"Great! Now with that last haul, you should be able to pay me back for the Pizza you owe me." Marquis said.

"I thought I already did!"

"That's what you always say."

They chatted amiably for a while longer before Marquis noticed a pretty girl standing alone near the outdoor bar. She was holding a glass and a hotdog.

"Hey, you see her over there? She's cute. You should go talk to her." Marquis said.

"The brunette? I don't know."

"Well, she is a bit overdressed for the occasion." She was wearing a light peacoat over a black dress.

"Hardly. Anyways, in my opinion it is impossible to be either over-prepared or over-dressed." Gye replied.

"Whatever. Actually, I'm pretty sure you were overdressed when you went to Mardi Gras in New Orleans in a tuxedo," Marquis said.

"Hey, it was the first time I could afford a tuxedo in my life since I... went out on my own. Cut me some slack!"

"I wish you'd have taken notes from your former self then. Wearing a blazer over that flimsy excuse for a shirt wouldn't have freakin' killed ya, would it?" Marquis said. He was only half joking.

"Go pound sand. You know what, I will go talk to her." Gye said, taking a swill of his drink before walking away. Marquis laughed. Hopefully his friend would quit moping and get back to his ordinarily ornery self, and maybe this party would help.

Gye couldn't help but notice that she looked even more attractive up close. He smiled and leaned against the wooden bench about two feet from her. She looked at him curiously. He leaned in slightly before speaking.

"Excuse me, miss, but I'm afraid the sight of you has taken my breath away. I'd like you to put it back now," Gye said, leaning in as if to kiss her jokingly.

"Really? I hope you just came up with that. That was not at all creative and borderline offensive." She retorted.

"Hey, I've had a few of these," Gye said, gesturing towards the beverage in his hand, "so don't judge me." He winked. She laughed in response.

"And what might your name be?"

"Gye Storm. And yours?"

As he said his name, there was an odd flash in her eyes, but she quickly moved on.

"My name is Jane Silver. And you're early." She said.

"What?"

"Oh, nothing. I mean, It's a pleasure to meet you."

"It certainly could be." Gye said. Suddenly a passerby bumped into her, causing the hot dog she held in her hand to create a mess on her peacoat.

"Watch it!" She said angrily, trying to swipe the mustard off.

"Looks like that guy improved your outfit choice for this occasion some," Gye teased.

"Oh, bite me."

"If you're into that sort of thing, sure." Gye retorted with a grin.

"Oh, you're a daring one, aren't you?" She said, wiping the mess off with a bit of cloth.

"Who, me? Maybe I'm just optimistic." He said.

"Well, the way I see it, being an optimist kinda sucks. You see, as a pessimist, I'm either right about something or pleasantly surprised about how it turned out. You, on the other hand, as an optimist, can only ever be right about something or disappointed." She said. Her voice had a kind of musical, slightly raspy sound to it which Gye found oddly appealing. She was wearing a faint perfume— citrus of some kind, that was enticing in its intricate subtlety. She took a sip of her drink.

"That's a lot to think about. You seem like someone in possession of an interesting mind." He said.

"I overthink everything. It's an unpleasant side effect of being a scientist. I'm a biologist, actually." She said.

"Oh really? I only took one extra science class in college. Anatomy."

"Did you like it?" Jane implored.

"It was fun but I failed it. Although I have a feeling that if I'd have been studying yours instead, I would've aced it."

She rolled her eyes.

"You're just getting annoying at this point. And far less clever. Perhaps you should try something you're more likely to succeed at, like bowling against a double amputee."

"Ouch. Point taken."

At that moment Gye noticed Marquis frantically trying to signal him. He annoyedly looked to see what Marquis was pointing at.

Three feds in all-black uniforms with clearly visible handguns were sweeping the party. That couldn't possibly be good. Maybe they had actually been serious about whatever the phone call had been about? Gye couldn't quite remember at the moment. He turned to Jane apologetically.

"It's been lovely to make your acquaintance, Jane Silver. Unfortunately I have to leave right now, but let's meet up later."

"Oh, I'm quite certain we will." She said with a smile.

Gye made his way towards Marquis, trying to keep out of the field of view of the feds.

"What are they, cops? FBI?"

"Not sure. But it can't be good. How'd it go, by the way?" Marquis asked.

"Oh, she's remarkable. She has such a lovely voice, and I could listen to her talk about nothing forever." Gye replied.

"You seem smitten. Looks like this party idea worked." Marquis said. He was jovial despite the possible threat.

"I feel better, sure. This whole thing made me realize I was being a tad... dramatic about it all. I mean, why be sad about having your old Ford stolen when you can chase after a new Audi?"

"I thought you didn't like European cars." Marquis said.

"Just being patriotic. After all, America is all ten of my top ten favorite things." Gye said.

"Its government agencies, however, can be quite the pain in the neck." He said, gesturing towards the closest dark-clad fed.

"Let's split up. I'll lose them in the crowd out here, you go to your panic room." Marquis said.

"It's not a panic room! It's my *personal study*. It just happens to be thoroughly useful when I am panicking." Gye said. With that, he was off, dashing through dazed party-goers. He thought he vaguely recollected pickpocketing one of these guys at another party. What a small world, indeed.

He reached the inside of the house at last. There were a few people milling about here and there amid the expanse. The place was largely devoid of anything which might reveal the true aspects of Gye's actual taste and personality- all of the paintings and books were strategically placed and designed to give a certain impression to anyone gullible enough not to see through the facade. He was a man with a reputation for great taste, but who had never actually tasted.

Some repugnant old white man staggered into view and clasped Gye's shoulder with his sweaty, wrinkly hand. He had obviously had too much to drink.

"My boy, every year in America, two and a half white people are victims of racial discrimination. We need to band together and do something about this!"

"That's nice, buddy. Why don't you just sit down over here? I'm trying to avoid some people right now." Gye responded, exasperated.

"Listen here boy, our lives are nothing but hyphens between two dates. We've got to—"

Gye edged past him and ran away before he could finish his sentence.

He entered the bathroom and checked to see that no one was around. The inebriated old man was staggering towards him still, probably trying to impart some great life lesson to him. Gye had had enough life lessons for one life, yet had learned nothing from any of them. He looked at the full-body mirror on the opposite wall. Then, he pushed in a small camouflaged pane in the ornate mirror frame, and the whole thing swung off the wall like a door. It was, in fact, a door- the door to his secret room.

He closed the door behind him and turned on the lights. He hadn't been here in quite a while, actually, and was glad to finally have a respite from the business of life to finally take a moment and just relax. Surely he was safe from the Feds now.

The decor in this room was an honest reflection of Gye's true taste and personality. There was a wooden table and chair with several book cases near it. The yellowish light of the lone lamp cast a soft glow on the whole room. The walls were a simple stucco beige- unfortunately, quite the out of fashion hue- and the wooden furniture was honeycomb colored.

On the table and surrounding surfaces- quite haphazardly arranged, in the manner of a man who only loses things when everything is organized- were strewn about several artifacts and invaluable items which Gye had kept for himself. On the floor near his feet was the original edition of the book The Catcher in the Rye by J.D. Salinger. It was a book he had never actually read but fully intended to eventually. That was what he told himself, anyway.

Gye sat down at the desk and breathed in a quiet moment. He reflected on the many times he had sat here, in this simple wooden chair, to bask in the authenticity of the room and find his own center. This was the only place in the world where he was not playing a role or pretending about anything- it simply was, and was simply him. Even Marquis Parcell had only entered here when the house was first being constructed. Indeed, the place was more sacred to Gye than any cathedral or church. Its walls had heard more truth screamed from the soul than any confession room.

He reached into the drawer under the desk and pulled out an old sketchpad. Sketching was Gye's one attempt at art in his life. He had no talent for music, painting, photography, or singing, but he sure envied those who did. He was not a particularly talented sketcher, but it was the one thing Gye did where he didn't try to give an appearance of being better than he was. His sketches would never be hung in hallways and worshipped alongside Vincent Van Gogh, but it was enough to him that his sketches existed at all. Sometimes he even drew what he remembered from the lost or smeared pages of his memory- his father's face, for instance. The open page was a sketch of a couple holding hands on a roof, in Paris. The Eiffel tower and some stars were visible in the background. Truly, art is the way people create the beauty in life that they are afraid to life out.

The sound of movement outside the door caused Gye to freeze in fear. He flipped his sketchbook shut and spun around in his chair. The door cracked open and the three men from earlier stepped inside. They had their guns holstered, but Gye noticed how their hands never strayed far from the ready position.

"What is the meaning of this?!" Gye shouted, rising from the chair. He saw the old guy right outside the door. The old foggie had apparently tipped off the feds. The men gave no answer to Gye's question. One of them looked around in awe— Gye's paranoid mind envisioned that the man *knew* somehow about the farce that was the outside shell of the house. They were unwelcome intruders into the heart of his existence.

A fourth person entered, strutting in purposefully like a lion about to devour its prey.

"Hello again," she said with a pompous grin. It was Jane Silver.

"YOU? But what— why?"

"It's my job to convince you to join an expedition unlike anything you've ever done before."

"You know, I have a phone. You could have just called."

"I've been told that you don't respond entirely well to phone calls. Anyway, I wanted to evaluate you myself in person. We are prepared to offer you a substantial sum of money to lend your notorious talents to our quest." She said.

"Money? I have enough of that, at present. And besides that, this unwelcome intrusion has made me feel not very inclined to do what you want." Gye said.

She considered this for a moment and began pacing around the room. The lamp illuminated the highlights in her hair, and as she steeped her hands to appear thoughtful, Gye couldn't help but feel that he had vastly underestimated her.

"Do you want to end up in a jail cell?" She asked.

"If you're in it, maybe."

"You never miss a beat, do you? But let me make something as clear as I can to your apparently muddy mind. Your days of skirting the law are numbered. Eventually, you *will* blunder, and all of the people you screwed over to get this far will be waiting, will be *salivating*, like wolves, waiting for dead meat to be thrown into their cage," she said, touching some of the items on the shelves, "For your sake, don't be lunch for wolves. Also, it would be such a shame for these lovely artifacts to fall out of your hands. Why, this Jackson Pollock and this Rothko- you have terrible taste in paintings, by the way- are just begging to be returned to their rightful owners."

"Are you threatening me?" Gye asked, standing up out of his chair.

"Don't be foolish. This is an opportunity for you, not something you need to escape from. There are undiscovered creatures, things we've only dreamed about knowing fully about, just waiting to be understood. So join with me and the rest of the crew. It's time to do something for the world, not just for yourself."

"How dare you come into my home, uninvited, and speak to me like you know anything at all about who I am? You have no idea. Don't presume to know what I need in my life. I can take care of myself." Gye said.

"Be reasonable. You know as well as I do that you want something more than what you have right now. At least tell me you'll consider it." She said.

"I'll think about it." He said after a contemptuous pause.

Jane sighed and halfway rolled her eyes.

"Mr. Storm, don't give up this opportunity to be more than a glorified trash collector. I hope you'll make the right decision."

With that, she nodded at the three men and they exited together. Jane closed the door behind them.

"Well, at least that was considerate of her." Gye muttered. What had she meant about undiscovered creatures? He had seen something about an enormous bee on the news a few weeks ago. Perhaps that had something to do with it. The possibilities…

He sat back down in the chair and put his head in his hands. He had a lot to think about.

CHAPTER 5
THE OFFER

"You ever think about working for the Feds?" Gye asked. He was sitting with Marquis, both of them seated on bar stools at a counter.

"No way in hell. At least some of the shady folks we've done jobs for have had the honesty to call themselves criminals. The Feds have no such capacity for honesty." Marquis said. Gye felt his heart shrink. He was hoping to convince Marquis to—... to what? More than anything, to convince him to go on the mission.

"That's what they wanted— the Feds, I mean. They wanted me to join some sort of expedition."

Marquis spit on the counter in disgust.

"I trust the Feds about as much as I'd trust a shark with a bleeding kitten." Marquis replied.

"That's harsh."

"Listen, I know we've always worked together. But if you take that job with the Feds, you're gonna have to do this one alone."

37

Gye pondered that for a while.

"Look, I've got to go. I'll let you know if I get any new leads on a new project." Marquis said.

Gye sat at the counter for a while, alone. After some time had passed by, he walked out to the street to hail a cab.

Suddenly, an all-black, sleek, glossy sedan came rolling to a stop next to him.

A lanky indian man with frayed, graying hair and the facial expression of someone who is capable of murder before breakfast stood out of the driver's seat and motioned for Gye to get in the car. Gye was thoroughly uninterested until the man introduced a gun into the negotiations. Gye became significantly more cooperative after that.

"In the car. I will be taking you to a meeting you cannot miss. Don't try anything, I won't hesitate to end you." He said.

Gye nervously complied and got into the back seat. There was a gate separating him from the driver's and passenger's seat in the front row. It was solid black, opaque, and made it impossible to see where the car was going, as the windows were also blacked out. These people were not fooling around.

Gye felt every bump and jostle of the road as the car continued on- his inability to see anything in that pitch darkness heightened his other senses. He tried to imagine where the car was in the city based on the stops and turns he felt, but he was soon hopelessly lost, at the mercy of his strange and dangerous captor. He had the general feeling that they must be somewhere in the north sector of the city, probably heading downtown towards the bustling business center.

What if he was going to be murdered? Marquis' words about the possibility of sudden death came back to him. It was a frightening possibility that Gye had never actually thought through before. Now, it was as if his life was flashing before his eyes. He recollected mostly the mistakes and lost opportunities in life. If he made it out of this situation alive, he would have to make sure to add more to his life that made death worth fleeing from.

The car rolled to a stop at last. Oddly, there was the feeling of moving… upwards? Yes, the car was moving upwards even though it was stopped. It must be on some sort of elevator platform, then. How odd.

The platform came to a rest and there was silence for perhaps a full minute. Then the door was roughly jerked open by the driver. He stood aside coldly, waiting for Gye to step out. He did so and looked around.

The platform was a circle that was in the intersection of several hallways. Each one was metal on all sides- the floor, walls, and even the roofs were all made of shiny stainless steel. Not a soul was present except for Gye and his captor. The place was deathly silent. The hallways were shrouded in darkness- there were three behind him and two ahead of him- and none of them looked particularly inviting.

"Walk this way. Vaurien Kane wishes to see you."

Gye gulped. The name was of no recollection to him, yet it still struck a primeval fear into his heart. He felt strongly that this would not end well.

They reached the end of the windowless, creepy hallway and arrived at an enormous dull aluminum door. Gye's captor pressed a hidden button near the edge and it opened.

The inside of the large room caused Gye to do a double-take. It looked as if the unbreakable laws of physics had been casually rejected here. There were tables that looked like they were floating, and the lone window on the wall had many shards of glass frozen in place as if someone had captured the window shattering with a slow-motion camera.

There was a black desk in the middle of the room, which did indeed at first glance look normal. However, the legs of the desk looked as if they had been slashed through at an angle with a giant's sword- and yet, the desk remained standing.

The man behind the desk was the only normal thing in the room. He was wearing a white v-neck with a gray blazer. There was an odd scar visible on the left side of his chest. He had his hands steeped on the desk, and for some reason that gave the impression to Gye that this man was holding the room against the laws of physics with his mind. It was a terrifying sight- an extraordinary man in an ordinary shell.

He wore glasses with thick black frames that accented his graying hair- although he was not going bald- which he wore in a gentle, commanding swoop across his forehead. He had lines on his face which screamed of a life of control and power. There were only a few creases- not quite wrinkles- on his forehead. His face was slightly thin, with a large forehead and clearly defined jawline. He wore no beard, and his skin was somewhat more yellow than a normal person's.

"Thank you, Paaklan. You may leave us now." The man behind the desk said to Gye's captor. He pronounced every syllable and enunciated every word fully, which added to his German accent to create a voice that was a confusing mix of fake charm and chilly pragmatism. Paaklan nodded and left.

"I am Vaurien Kane. You may refer to me as God if you like," he said with a frosty grin. There was a span of silence for a few seconds before he spoke again.

"Aren't you going to introduce yourself?"

"Oh, um... Gye Storm." He said, offering his hand as if he was casually introducing himself to someone he had met on the street. Vaurien Kane ignored the gesture.

"Gye Storm? That name sounds oddly familiar. I cannot place it, though." Vaurien said.

Now that he was up close, Gye could see that the furniture was not actually defying the laws of physics— extremely thin pieces of carbon fiber were supporting each piece. A rather elaborate facade— but why?

Vaurien reached into a bowl next to him on the desk. It was full of grapes. He placed one on his lips and inhaled it into his mouth with a sucking plop. He reached for another one quickly and repeated the process continually, sucking a stream of grapes while never breaking eye contact with Gye. It was an unnerving experience.

He stopped after a while and sighed with refreshment.

"I discovered my love of this special kind of grape while hunting on the island of *El Matar* off the coast of Africa. That's an island where you can hunt people if you are very rich and so inclined, as I am." He enunciated every word as if he was savoring the evil-ness of each one's meaning. Gye felt a chill rip through his body.

"What, you don't have the money for that delightful sport?" Vaurien asked.

"Uh.. I think it's more that I'm not so inclined towards that sort of thing." Gye stammered.

"Oh. Pity. Well, you can always take another interest in food, as I did. I opened a restaurant chain with delightfully low prices and food which was advertised to look quite savory. I instructed the workers to allow the customers to wait in long lines for a long time, and then take their order and tell them to sit down. But the funny part," He said with a chuckle, "is that the food, it never arrives! Ah ha ha!" He grabbed another grape and inhaled it into his mouth, swallowing it with the gusto of a great white shark.

Gye was not sure what to feel, besides dread.

"I'm sorry, why did you bring me here?" Gye asked.

"Oh! I had almost forgotten. I have been informed that there will be a mission to explore this certain forest, which is said to be full of many exotic and previously thought-to-be-extinct creatures. I have further been informed that they have selected you to be part of the crew- why is that, by the way? I don't recall what your job is."

"Professional adventurer, I like to call myself. I take the jobs I'm interested in. Not all of them are legal, but all of them are better than rotting away in a cubicle." Gye said.

"I quite like you already, Mr. Storm. Which is why I want you to join my expedition instead. I will offer you much more money than they ever could."

"I have enough money right now, actually."

"I respect those that can see far enough beyond their own noses to choose power over money," Vaurien Kane said, "but why not have both?"

"Why do you want to do this? You don't seem like the kind of man who wants to use discoveries to benefit humankind." Gye said.

"Ah, quite perceptive, I see. The answer is quite simple. I am a member of a certain religion, whose name I will not waste on your ears. Some would call it a cult- those people usually end up dead." He said with a grin.

Vaurien Kane continued.

"These bloody scientists are always ridiculing us for our sacred beliefs. They blasphemously present their discoveries- which I'm certain are all made up- in order to attack us. They must be stopped."

Gye said nothing in response. This Vaurien Kane seemed rather delusional and certainly part of a dangerous cult- which made Gye afraid for his life.

"You don't seem particularly enthused by this offer of mine." Vaurien Kane said, looking Gye straight in the eye, speaking with a monotone, thick German accent. Gye was chilled to his core.

"It's rather exciting!" Gye said with as much enthusiasm as he could muster.

"I'm glad you think so, Gye Storm. I would be rather disappointed if you did not. I *will* stop this blasphemy, and I will destroy anyone in my path. For your sake, don't be in it."

"Of course not. I do need to check my schedule however. I'll see if I have an opening, can I get back to you?" Gye said. He thought acting as casual as possible was the only way to get out of there alive.

"Certainly, Mr. Storm. I expect to hear from you soon, or, if not, never again." He said with a stone cold smile.

CHAPTER 6
BON VOYAGE

Gye Storm looked at the phone in his hand, the number already typed in and ready to call. He was a tap of the finger away from accepting Jane's offer to join the expedition.

He had— briefly, of course— considered Vaurien Kane's proposal. Perhaps it would have been worth it to bend to the whims of a madman in order to secure enormous wealth. And each dollar was one step closer to finding the man who killed his family...

Impulsively, he tapped the button to call. Well, he was committed now. The phone rang a few times before it was answered. No voice spoke, however. After a few moments, Gye cleared his throat.

"Uh, hello. This is Gye Storm speaking."

"One moment, please." A mechanical voice answered. Gye could not tell whether it was male or female.

"I will connect you to Anthony Lafayette immediately."

Oh great, not him again. Anthony was perhaps the least competent person in charge of any agency whom Gye had ever met, even though he could not remember, at the moment, which agency that was. They all seemed to blend together in his mind— each one merely conjured up feelings of deep distrust. But Anthony was the son of some rich supporter of some political cause or other, and as such his position was locked in place tighter than anyone's who had gotten their position via their own merits. People who worked for the government were rarely the most competent.

"Mr. Storm, I'm so glad our people have got you to work on the right side of the law for once."

"I didn't call for a lecture, you incompetent buffoon. I choose my own path, thank you. It just so happen that this time, the dirty, lying scumbags I'm working for happen to wear nice suits and lapel pins of the American flag." Gye retorted.

"Now, now, Mr. Storm. I'm sure we can—"

"Where can I meet with your people to discuss the expedition?" Gye interrupted.

"Straight to the point, eh? Alright. Actually, I'll send someone to pick you up."

"Make sure they knock first. I often have… visitors… over."

"Oh really? I would've pegged you more for the type who enjoys their own company." Anthony said.

Gye hung up and stood to walk outside. He felt certain that he had made the right decision. He put on some music on his outdoor speaker system and took a moment to bask in the sunlight. There were clouds in the west, but there would be sunlight for at least a little while longer.

Gye opened his eyes as he heard a faint whirring sound. Curious, he looked around. Was it a car blazing past on the road? No, there was nothing there. Perhaps his speaker system was having issues again. The darn thing never seemed to work exactly right.

Gye turned off the music. Aside from feeling significantly less relaxed with the absence of his favorite tunes, Gye was further discomforted by the fact that the whirring continued. And it seemed to be getting louder.

He looked around in every direction— there was nothing. Fearfully, he looked upwards.

There were three incredibly quiet (for their kind) helicopters hovering near his abode. They were pitch black modified Blackhawk helicopters, each one sticking out sorely against the sky like raisins in pudding. Gye was too stunned by their sudden appearance to react in time. Within seconds, an airman in full combat gear descended from a rope ladder and rushed at Gye, with several others followed closely behind.

"Get on the ground! Hands above your head, move!" The man shouted in a booming bass voice. It held a note of commanding gruffness that Gye dared not disobey.

The airmen had Gye surrounded like he was on the top of their hit list. He had done some shady stuff before, sure, but what had he done to deserve this? Or perhaps Vaurien Kane had come to carry out his threat. With that thought an icy chill ran down Gye's spine.

The airmen dragged Gye to the ladder and held on until it was pulled back into the helicopter. Gye fell on his back and hit his head on the metal floor. There were shouts around him and the outside sky was a sickening blur, spinning and flying past them at a million miles per hour.

"Search him!"

An airman without a gun stepped forward and patted Gye down, looking for weapons.

"Getting frisky, are we? Won't you at least take me out to dinner first?" Gye joked.

The answer to his jest was a smack in the face with the butt of a rifle. In his reflection in a shiny piece of metal on the wall, he saw a thin red line of blood spill across his forehead.

"What'd you do that for?!" Gye demanded.

"Shut your mouth, scum. You speak again and I'll shove this grenade down your throat so hard you'll taste aluminum for a month."

That was enough to silence Gye. He didn't exactly fancy tasting aluminum for any length of time. Aluminum doesn't pair well with chicken, as any fine chef will tell you this side of the Pacific.

The ride in the helicopter was hell. The relentless whirring of the helicopter blade vibrated Gye's skull as if someone had decided to fire a machine gun pressed up against his head. The whole thing rattled; it felt like he was a rat in a cage, holding on for dear life against the inevitable torture as a giant took the cage in his hands and shook it.

Finally, the sight of a landing pad. As Gye was pushed out of the helicopter and half-fell, half-tumbled out of it, he stumbled to his feet. The sound of the helicopter blade finally quitting its encore act was nearly enough to bring Gye to tears with joy.

A voice came from behind him, striking a nerve Gye didn't know he had. It was one of annoyance; although it was an illogical annoyance, which was to say, the voice itself lent no obvious reason for immediate hatred.

"Wow, you fall out of a helicopter and somehow manage to make it look like you meant to do it. How do you do that?"
It was the voice of Anthony Lafayette.

Gye let out an audible groan and turned around. He saw Anthony's short, stocky frame, with the dark eyes of a teddy bear, and about as much intelligence.

"I specifically told you to knock!" Gye said.

"I'm so sorry, you see, I'm not so good at giving commands. I actually just wanted my men to go and get you in a car. Unfortunately I left out the 'car' part and.. well, they got you here didn't they?"

"Why does it always seem like you're barely keeping the agents who work for you from doing something sketchy? Well, you didn't keep them back this time. I ought to punch you." Gye said with anger.

"You mustn't speak with anger and words of violence, my good man. There is nothing in this world which cannot be solved with words."

"Ironic coming from the man in charge of the guns." Gye retorted.

"My friend, you hurt my feelings." Anthony said.

"We're not friends. And people of power cannot afford the expense of feelings, you pathetic worm."

Gye's angry (and likely to be later regretted) tirade was interrupted by an attendant official whispering something in Anthony's ear. He nodded as he heard the man's words. Gye looked around, seeing a plain, boring office building just beyond the landing pad. The surrounding area was a suburban myriad collection of various houses; some of which were painted appallingly cheerful shades of different abominable hues, which seemed to declare loudly to the world that the houses' occupants were happy. More likely, they were more trying to convince themselves, in their ordinary, boring lives, that they were, indeed, happy. Gye rolled his eyes at the thought.

"You know what, Gye, I have just received a report that a prisoner in our complex has been acting up. Come with me and see the power of words, which is mightier than any weapon."

"Whatever, hippy! I'll take a colt .45 any day over an adjective."

One of the surrounding soldiers snickered at this, and for this betrayal was silenced with a fearsome glare from the unamused Anthony.

"You three, come with me. The rest of you, return to your posts." Anthony ordered. It was obvious that the men under Anthony's command paid only lip service, and barely that, to his authority. It was not an unorthodox opinion to disrespect him— no, there was something about his mannerisms which made him seem like he'd make a better gardener than leader. Gye had previously heard it said that Anthony was the justice system equivalent of a college dean who is trying way too hard to be seen as cool and accepted by his students; this was an apt comparison, at least in Gye's eyes, as it always appeared that Anthony was perpetually being easily flustered by something or other. Gye relished the opportunity to see the inevitably catastrophic result of Anthony confronting a criminal— ironically, someone Anthony's men respected more than himself. At least the criminal had a backbone.

They descended down a glass staircase. It looked ridiculously expensive and totally unnecessary; exactly the kind of thing that made Gye see these people as a nest of ants hoarding anything they could get their hands on. Indeed, as the quartet of black-clad enforcers of arbitrary law escorted him down the stairs, Gye was struck by how they seemed remarkably like ants swarming down into a deeper, darker layer of a colony.

They waited momentarily as the 'interrogation' room (that was its purpose; although that was unlikely to be its use this time) was prepared.

"Sir, the prisoner is Zeke Kalghar. He was involved in an altercation with another prisoner in the line for food, where he shattered the glass and used a shard of it as a shank." A guard said.

Anthony nodded and sighed.

"Sometimes it's so painfully obvious to me that these people need more tender loving care." He said.

The guard snickered visibly, as openly disrespectful of Anthony as he probably deserved. He entered the room first and then motioned for Gye to follow.

"I hope you're not considering working here. This idiot is bloody delusional." The guard said to Gye before he entered. Gye laughed.

"No, this is just a pit stop on my road to taking my destiny into my own hands." Gye said.

"Good on you. Zeke is in here for murder, so try not to get too close."

Gye nodded and entered the room.

Anthony was seated across from the prisoner as Gye entered.

Zeke Kalghar- identified by an oversized name tag; with his name written, somewhat ironically, in a frilly font. The man's massive frame was stuffed into the largest orange uniform the place had available, and it was still not big enough. His enormous biceps seemed to laugh at the pathetic chains holding him in place. He was balding, or perhaps he chose to shave his hair bald, except for a ginger goatee. His face was pockmarked by a life story of hardships and hedonism, mostly made evident by a three inch scar that ran across his forehead.

"Good afternoon, Zeke! Thank you for coming to see me." Anthony said.

"I didn't have a choice, worm. Now go slither back into the dirt and let me be." Zeke Kalghar said. His voice was so deep that it was practically a growl. It reverberated against the walls and coalesced into the distilled essence of fear.

"Now, you've said a not very good thing just there, Mr. Kalghar! If we are to understand each other, we have to communicate well." Anthony said. His overly enthusiastic, naive voice sounded like a tin can in comparison to Kalghar's.

"You understand nothing, maggot." It was obvious that Zeke Kalghar had decided to play a physiological game with the incompetent Anthony. Gye leaned in, relishing the impending amusement. More than likely, Anthony would end up walking out in tears, having his feelings hurt.

"Let's get down to business. You committed some unsafe roughhousing earlier today that we aren't pleased about."

Zeke sat in silence; Anthony cleared his throat uncomfortably.

"I'm going to need you to communicate—"

"He got what was coming to him." Zeke interrupted.

"Mr. Zeke, you realize we will have to punish you for this vi- no, I cannot bring myself to say the v-word." Mendes said.

"You mean violence? I *breathe* violence."

"You know we don't tolerate use of those harmful words!"

"Do you think you're teaching preschool or something? Welcome to the big playground, you fool, where the slides are coated in blood and the monkey bars are constructed from the ribcages of the *weak.*" Zeke said. He spouted these words without any indication of discomfort or human feeling. Anthony was already beginning to falter.

"Let's take a step back here, and look at the big—"

"Why do you choose to meddle in the affairs of my domain, small one? You fail at every turn in the road." Zeke interrupted.

"I believe that everyone, regardless of their past mistakes, deserves a second chance! Everyone should have the dignity of being treated with trust and respect, even if they haven't quite earned it yet— it is my firm belief that if you show people kindness and love, they will eventually reflect those qualities back out to the world."

The guard rolled his eyes and sighed. Zeke Kalghar reared his meaty head back and emitted a laugh which was not unlike the sound of a volcano erupting. Anthony cringed and then continued.

"A great man once said that violence is the last refuge of the incompetent, and that's what I believe."

"Violence is the first tool of the realist."

"You think I'm not a realist?" Anthony inquired, looking genuinely hurt for some reason.

"You're a misguided, idealistic hippy. I used to grind the skulls of men like you to dust, and mix it with my clients' 'medicine'. You're nothing."

"I'm going to ask you to respect me as I respect you, Mr. Kalghar."

"You will never be anything more than an annoying, dripping faucet that everyone hates but is too lazy to shut off. You know what? I think I might do the world a favor right now and shut off the faucet."

The guard's trigger finger twitched in response.

"Threats are nothing to me, Mr. Kalghar. They are the smell of violence, and I don't believe in violence. I respect—"

"Respect this!" Zeke roared as he stood and pulled against the chains. He swung his fists at the impotent Anthony, but fell just short. The chains strained against the sheer force of his will. The guard rushed at him and held him back.

Anthony burst into tears.

"I just want you to respect me! Why can't I get you people to respect me?" He wailed.

Additional reinforcements had come in by this time. One of them escorted Gye to the hallway, barely refraining from snickering in bemusement along the way.

"I can't believe they pay me to watch this man make a fool of himself on a daily basis."

"Sounds like a sweet gig, my good sir. Anthony Lafayette apparently missed the part of school where they teach reality." Gye said.

"Right. Now, I will be escorting you to meet the person in charge of your expedition."

"Oh, it's not Anthony? Thank god. That would have been disastrous."

"Oh god no. Anthony is barely qualified to lead himself off a cliff."

# # #

Captain James Walker was a tall man, getting up there in age, with a lengthy salt and pepper beard and mustache. He had sharp cheekbones and a permanently furrowed brow, looking like a man who has the weight of the world on his shoulders constantly.

Gye could see all of this as he approached. He was not sure whether he liked this man yet; he looked as if he might turn out to be a man past his prime, trying to relive the glory days, like a shell of a bullet which has already been fired.

"Captain James Walker? I'm Gye Storm."

The captain appraised Gye with a steely look in his eye, as if he was inspecting a soldier's uniform. The extent of the flaws this man had immediately picked up was hidden to Gye; his facial expression revealed no emotion one way or another.

He extended his arm and shook hands. The captain was clad in a muted red uniform, with various medals and ribbons attached.

"Oh yes, the professional adventurer. Quite an occupation you have there." His voice was slightly hoarse, as it seems most people's voices become when they shout orders at others for years. As Gye stepped closer he couldn't help but notice the smell of cheese wafting off of the man.

"It's a living that makes life worth living."

"...Really? That sounds like some horse crap to me." The woman standing next to the captain said.

"You got me. I'm actually trying to avenge my family."

"Indeed. Allow me to introduce you to my esteemed colleague, Elicia Cantor," Captain Walker said, indicating the woman to his right. She was slightly shorter than Gye, about middle age, with thick-framed black glasses and short blonde hair. She had an angular, thin face that made every smile look as if it didn't belong. She wore a light blue dress shirt which accented her eyes, and a gold watch which indicated some degree of affluence.

"This is the immoral, hedonistic, yet extraordinarily capable Elicia Cantor. She is the world's leading expert on both geology and sin." The captain said. She smiled a fake half smile in response and extended her hand to Gye.

"Pleased to meet you. The good captain exaggerates, of course. I am no longer an innovator in the field of sin, although you should've seen me when I was younger. I made Hollywood look Amish." She said. She spoke with a soft, precise voice that seemed better suited for a lecture hall than an adventure.

"Gye Storm, professional miscreant."

"How refreshingly honest. I wasn't sure if Jane would be able to persuade you to join our little mission. I'm so glad she succeeded."

"She's very driven. For a woman, that is." Captain Walker interrupted.

"Sexism doesn't flatter you, James. It only shows your age." Elicia replied.

"I just miss the days when women were women and men were men." Walker replied.

"Pay no attention to this fossil, Gye. He's a perfectly palatable dinner companion when he's not reminiscing about the good old days." Elicia said.

"Take this backstabbing femme here, for instance. It's people like her that make me miss war. War was so simple— people shoot at you, you shoot back, you kill the bad guys. It's not fun but at least it's not complicated. Come back to civilian life and it's all about appearances and protecting people's feelings and other such drivel. No one says what they think anymore, except me." Captain James Walker said.

"Quite the soliloquy, James. But we must hurry if we are going to catch our flight. Come along, Gye."

# # #

"This is always my favorite part," Elicia said with a smile. They were in the passenger cabin of a small military plane, awaiting take off.

"Take off is the worst part! Of all of the people who die in plane crashes, most of them kick the bucket on take off or landing." Captain Walker said.

"Nonsense. It is only when we are closest to death that life becomes worth living." Elicia said.

"Where are we going?" Gye asked.

"We have an outpost deep in the heart of a certain mysterious rainforest."

"Thanks for being so specific. I was afraid you were going to be elusive about it." Gye retorted.

"You don't get to where I am today by giving away information unnecessarily." Elicia said.

They glared at each other from across the table, like two mountains refusing to be moved from their unassailable positions. Gye expected Elicia to falter under the weight of his stare, but she instead returned a withering barrage which caused his confidence to wilt like a plant in the sunlight. After a few seconds had passed by, Captain James Walker cleared his throat as if to declare a ceasefire.

With a rush of g-forces, they were up into the sky. The surrounding area blurred together; nothing more than watercolors spilled together.

"Such a pity," Elicia said with dismay, "these electric planes take all of the fun out of it. I miss the days of gas-powered flight. It wrecked hell on the environment, sure, but what a joy to ride."

"This is one of those rare moments where I must agree with you. You know how much it pains me to say the words 'you're right.'" Captain Walker said.

"A man more truthful than you would say those words more often." Elicia replied.

"You insult me. I am a man of the utmost integrity and honor."

"You see how easy it is to rile this man up about his legacy? I minored in psychology in college, and let me tell you, this man is a gold mine for psychological analysis." Elicia said.

"You'd see me as more of a mine field than a gold mine if you knew what was good for ya." Captain Walker mumbled.

"I excavated a mine field in '97. If you have the right tools its easier to deal with than you might expect." Elicia said.

"I snuck through one once. Lost a member of my crew, but it was the only way out." Gye interrupted. He felt a bit left out by the pre-existing dynamic between the two of them.

"That's it? Boy, with me, in the war against the chinks in their minefields, it wasn't our boys who were in danger. No, the mines hadn't a chance against us." Captain James Walker said.

He said it in such a wistful way that Gye imagined he should've been puffing a cigar as he reminisced, like a cold war veteran from a documentary.

"James! I'm surprised to see you reverting to racial slurs. Although now that I think about it, you seem to lose your head whenever you recollect that time in your life." Elicia said.

"I lead my men to glory and conquest. I did what was necessary. And the bloody commanders made me take the fall when the backbone-less suits got queasy about what was necessary for victory. It's always the same, to them. They want victory- they say so, at least, until they see what it takes to get it. Then they turn their noses up like a little girl seeing a cockroach." Captain Walker said.

"Oh, the strength of youth. I remember it well. Take note, Gye, of the value of youth. Intellect, for the most part, will stay with a man, and legacy follows you around like a stalker with an axe, but youth is swept away like dust in a river. Hold on dearly to your youth while you have it, for it is worth more than success." Elicia said.

"Funny, that's the exact opposite of what people have been telling me my whole life. Most people encourage me to squander my youth and sacrifice it to the alter of *possible* future success. How refreshing to meet someone who sees things *my* way." Gye said.

"It is better to be respected than to be young." Captain Walker said.

"But it is better to have your own respect than the respect of others." Elicia said.

"That's easy to say when your reputation is as bad as yours, my dear." Captain Walker replied.

"I have a reputation for doing what I want and living an enjoyable life. Anyone who has a problem with that needs to get their head out of their own rear end." Elicia said.

"Is there anything to drink on board?" Gye interrupted.

"If you're like me and can't even remember what water tastes like, then unfortunately, no. We're flying in Shia airspace." Elicia replied.

"Wow, you really are a hedonist. Water would be fine, actually."

"Well, you're in luck. They keep the water cooler somewhere near the front."

CHAPTER 7
DO NOT GO GENTLY

"I'm starving, where's the food?" Captain James Walker asked.

They had landed only minutes ago on a dingy landing strip in the middle of a forest with enormous trees.

Next to the landing strip was a building with a dome observatory, made of concrete, metal, and one side made entirely of glass. The whole building was the shape of an irregular polygon, as if it had been constructed with regards being only paid to the utilitarian aspect of fitting all of the building's functions compactly inside it, and very little attention being paid to the beauty or aesthetic value of the place. They were just inside the building's entrance, next to the large glass wall, with a delightful view of the outside world.

Gye remarked to himself that, if he had not long ago freed himself from having to hold a boring 'real job', he would have wanted to work in a place like this. It gave enough of the appearance of the untamed freedom of nature that the sad reality of being nothing more than a worker bee became palatable. He could see that the workers here were looking far more alive than at any other office he had yet seen-likely due to the feeling of working on a frontier. Gye was not the kind of man who was ok with being stuck in a cage.

When they arrived in the building's lobby, they were waved over to a couch near the window by two men; one, a cold, german-looking man with half-drooped eyelids and a disinterest in anything outside his head; and the other, a handsome Spanish man with flowing, wavy black hair and dark brown eyes. He had on a chef's apron and a contagious smile.

The man with the cold, disinterested disposition stood and bowed as they approached.

"Ray Kaymar, engineer." He said. He had no accent, which was surprising to Gye. He did not mince words.

The other man half-rose to extend his hand to Gye.

"My name is Royce Alavandréz. I was once ranked the second-best chef in the northern Madrid area by a respected magazine. I would have been the first best in all of Spain, but the whole thing is so political and cutthroat." He said. His accent made his words drip off his tongue like honey. Gye was immediately jealous of someone who could make words sound so good.

"Will you join us for lunch?" Elicia inquired.

"I suppose that would be a good start, as we will be spending a lot of time together soon on this glorious expedition." Ray said.

They left the lovely natural light as they moseyed towards the cafeteria. Ray and Royce were continuing some altogether uninteresting argument about whether the form or function of something or other was more important. Gye saw no meaning in that question. If he had to listen to this bickering during the downtime of the expedition, he would blow his brains out.

They turned down a hallway, which, in stark and unpleasant contrast to the lobby, was not well-illuminated.

In the middle of the dim hallway was a young feminine figure, stooped over a notepad she was holding in her hand, writing away. As Gye stepped closer he could make out her individual features. She looked up as he approached.

She smiled- and it was quite a lovely smile, showing off her full lips and the facial lines of someone who loves to laugh. She had a lovely light caramel complexion accented with chestnut brown hair and sparkling brown eyes. An immediately charming young woman if ever there was one, Gye thought. The dim hallway suddenly didn't seem quite so dismal with her in it. She was wearing dark blue jeans and a maroon jacket over a black t-shirt.

"I haven't seen you around here before." She said. She was soft-spoken and her voice was honeyed, rising in pitch as she spoke. She seemed to have a permanent smile that shone through the eyes and made her seem trustworthy.

"I'm just dropping by. I'm about to go on a dangerous adventure on the world's last frontier of the unknown. Unfortunately that's going to fill up my schedule for a while, or else I'd love to hang around and chat." He said.

"Really? They wouldn't let me join the expedition, so I had to settle with administration. You're so lucky. And it's too bad, too- if they'd have let me join, we could've gotten that coffee en route." She said. She ended the sentence with a puppy-dog frown, which made Gye chuckle.

"Gye, why are you talking to her? Let's get a move on." Elicia said. Gye noticed that Jane Silver had joined the others and was looking at him with a half-frown, half-smirk. There was another man with a curly mop of hair and sparkling blue eyes next to her.

"Looks like you've got to go. I'm Molly, by the way. Molly Hazelwood." She said.

"I'm Gye Storm. It's such a pleasure to meet you, Molly." He said. She gave a half-wave as the group walked away.

"She's looks so perfectly trustworthy. I hate her," Jane said, "Oh, and this is Anthony." She said, gesturing towards the other man.

"Anthony Lafayette, Ph.D., biological sciences." Anthony said, introducing himself as if for the first time, in a grandiose manner. He had a crisp, refined posh accent which sounded vaguely european, with an air of easy swagger. His clothes all bore conspicuous brand names and cultivated fabrics. Oh great, another self-absorbed upper-class poser whose parents had bought their darling child's success with stacks of green paper. Gye resisted the urge to spit on the man's expensive shoes.

"We've… met." He said with measured coolness while internally groaning.

They had been talking as they walked, arriving finally in the cafeteria. It was highly utilitarian, with no decoration of any kind; it was merely tables and a food counter in a room of medium largeness.

"I don't particularly care for adventure myself. It tends to get one dirty and thirsty and altogether improper." Anthony said.

Captain Walker rolled his eyes as he grabbed a tray and began filling it up with food. Gye could see from this process how Captain Walker had become fat.

"Most people who were raised by their rich parent's servants in disinfected, whitewashed rooms tend to say that." Gye said. The others looked on with interest to see how Anthony would take this insult.

"Wow, did someone tell you about my upbringing?" Anthony said quizzically. Gye smirked.

"Oh yes, definitely. It's not like I could tell your upbringing just by your aura. And by that, I mean your *perfume*." Gye said.

"It's British Sterling, actually. And just like all things, including this awful food, the British kind is better."

"You unpatriotic twat! I fought for this country. I bled red, white, and blue after getting shot in Asia. So don't come in here like being American is something to be looked down upon." Captain James Walker said.

"You bled red white and blue?"

"Metaphorically speaking."

"Perhaps you were actually bleeding for the French flag, *mon ami*. Or the Russian flag, or the British flag. There is nothing special about your colors or your country." Anthony said, waving the fingers of one hand in the Captain's face with haughty condescension.

Captain Walker fumed in exasperation. Anthony formed the words with such pedantic precision; it seemed to go perfectly along with the way he tilted his head and nodded whenever he was making a point, to give the impression of a human slimeball with slightly better hair.

"I have to say, there's nothing like european luxury cars. The American designs, it's function over form, it's just nothing. No human connection, no principles, just horrendously exaggerated fume stacks and masculine shapes that are obviously compensating for something." Ray said.

"Who cares about how something looks? If it's a car that works better, what does it matter what the shell looks like? Beauty is rather pointless." Jane said.

"Ironic for you to say, as someone who possesses it." Gye said.

"Perhaps one must possess beauty in order to see its futility."

"Perhaps one must appreciate the futility of beauty in order to see its value." Gye replied.

"But how can something be valuable which is evidently seen everywhere? As I saw on the way in, you seem to see beauty in a lot of people." Jane replied.

"Some more than others." Gye replied cooly.

Captain Walker chewed his food noisily and the others stopped their discussion long enough to look at him with disgust.

"What? Ever since I got out of the military, I can't get over the way real, fresh food tastes. When all you get to eat for days on end is dust upon dust, and spilled blood is in greater supply than drinkable water, you learn to appreciate a good meal." Captain Walker said. His tone was defensive, a far cry from his usual commander's voice. This was one of his insecurities.

"Eww, is that pastrami? I can't believe you would eat meat. People who eat meat are murderers. Just think about it for a second! How would you like it if, like, cows ripped out our muscles and put them on a fire and threw some ground up plants on them and ate their hearts out? Hmmm? You disgust me." Anthony said.

"Oh great, you're a vegetarian too? Hopefully you'll starve to death, and then the world can keep spinning without you complaining that it gives you vertigo." Gye interrupted.

"What are you, a cowboy? I bet that's real leather you're wearing." Anthony replied.

"As a matter of fact, it is. I skinned it myself. I, for one, can do things with my own two hands, which is something no one in your prep circle of friends or your pansy rich parents have ever done." Gye retorted.

"Do you feel manly for having insulted him? You men are all so alike. And predictable." Jane said. Gye felt his blood rising in his veins at her retort.

"If there's two things I learned in college, it's— well, the first thing is to not learn too much, because if you push too much learning into your mind, you'll squeeze out all of the beauty, and that's what makes life worth living. But the other thing, the one I learned much earlier than the first one, is that women are just as predictable as men. Men take a direct route from A to Z, and women like to take a detour past F and maybe revisit D a few times along the way. We're all just products of the chemicals in our brains, you see, and so our actions are equally predictable." Elicia opined.

"Utter hogwash! You prefer to say something that sounds good over something meaningful or something that makes any kind of sense." Captain Walker said with a note of disapproval in his voice.

"Words are just sounds, so they might as well be good ones."

"I hope you don't think you sound wise when you spout these epigrams! No one thinks of you as an intellectual."

"My dear, caring what other people think about you is the ultimate form of vanity." Elicia said.

"And so you must be the vainest of them all." Captain Walker replied.

"Unashamedly so."

"Hmmmph. This is all too much rubbish to take in over one lunch. You seem to be extra immoral with this newcomer around. Meanwhile I have run out of food— perhaps I can tip the station boy near the *meat* section to give me some extra." Captain Walker said, making sure to make eye contact with Anthony as he said *meat*.

Anthony didn't notice this jab, or at least pretended not to. He fidgeted with the fine cufflinks he had on for a moment before turning to Jane.

"Perhaps we should return to the topic of science on this expedition. Have you made any progress on the missing link in the oxygen-oriented hypothesis?"

"Nothing yet. The reason for this forest's existence remains a mystery to us."

Gye stopped paying attention to what they were saying as it became more nerdy and less intelligible. Were Jane and Anthony just coworkers, or...? The way he looked at her made Gye more than a little jealous. What the hell did she see in him anyways?

# # #

"We're calling it the *Venture* Rover. Six legs will propel the cabin structure through the forest like a giant beetle, crawling its way towards the advancement of science. Like Apollo 11, this craft will be one for the history books." Ray said. He spoke more quickly and more animatedly as he became more excited, making his words almost unintelligible.

"When will we get to see this thing?" Elicia interrupted.

"Momentarily. Behind these doors is the hangar where the *Venture* was created and now stands prepared for testing. Ten prototypes of various sizes were created in addition to the dozens of computer aided designs we began with. My design and engineering team- the finest in the world outside of Cupertino— has successfully overcome every challenge. These doors are better guarded than the Pentagon, which was my condition of joining this project. I am, I must admit, perpetually in fear that some rival designer will infiltrate my lab and steal my secrets." Ray said.

"Look, it's the Willy Wonka of engineering!" Gye said with a note of friendly jabbing in his voice.

"Wonka's chocolate is nowhere near as sweet as the taste of good design. Have you ever sat in a Bentley Continental, Gye?"

"No, but I've never sat on an Apatosaurus either, so I guess that's two dinosaurs I've never used as transportation."

Anthony took this moment to interrupt.

"You are an insult to design. Dieter Rams would roll in his grave to hear you speak like that." Anthony said.

"Dieter Rams was a german designer, you poser. Do not think that you can pretend to know about my area of expertise and expect to be taken seriously. Now, Gye, as I was saying, if you sit in a car like the Bentley Continental, you can feel through the goodness of the design that an actual human being truly cared about the design, and brought it down to the last detail from their mind into the world. Good design is consequent down to the last detail, is what I'm saying, and a lousy designer will shamelessly copy the results of this difficult process from a designer who took the arduous time to bring it to fruition. So laugh all you want at the fact that I take my craft seriously, but I won't apologize for wanting to protect my creation." Ray said.

"This is all too much, Ray. Perhaps you had better just show us the Rover. I haven't seen the full-sized version yet myself, and I am eager to see what you have come up with." Captain Walker said placatingly.

Ray Kaymar nodded appreciatively and turned to work at the door's many locks. When the last level of security had been satisfied (it was a fingerprint scanner), the double doors swung open and a massive room was revealed.

The hangar was mostly ordinary with the exception of the massive machine- or vehicle, rather- which occupied the majority of its space. The *Venture* was perhaps sixty feet long and twenty feet high, by Gye's estimate. The cockpit at the front had a double-paned reinforced window much like a jet airplane's, and the rest had the optimistic design and flow of sixties and seventies car designs in the United States. There were several observational windows on each side, providing an excellent view at the abnormal flora and fauna they were sure to seen see on this expedition. There were ornamental fins on the top near the rear much like a vintage Cadillac, and the off-colored aluminum exterior had a refreshingly textured appearance which defied the modern trend of glossy black everything. Perhaps Ray had been right about design. He was too smart for his own good, and so would probably either find himself promoted highly under the right people or, if he were put under someone with much power and little intelligence, he might find himself in an alleyway dumpster. That was the caveat of genius.

"I'll admit, I was skeptical about your theories, Mr. Kaymar, but I'll say you've done quite an exceptional job here." Jane said.

Ray only blushed slightly, an odd contrast to his usually stoic face. Oddly, for a man who rarely had any expression whatsoever on his face, he seemed to express the things ordinary people expressed through the face and other such ordinary things through his designs. Perhaps, Gye fancied, each curvature and change in the design along the way had been a product of Ray's feelings at the time.

"If it works as well as it looks, we've got ourselves a mission." Gye said appreciatively.

"I'm noticing some Walter De'Silva-esque influence on the underside curvature here." Anthony said.

"Would you stop talking about things you know nothing about already?" Gye snapped.

"Keep it frosty, boys. We haven't even set off yet." Elicia said. Her tone was jovial, which was a marked change from her usual monotone softness. Perhaps this was the first time she was actually feeling the excitement and adrenaline-inducing fervor of the mission. Would they discover things no one had yet seen, go to places no human had set foot upon, even in this crowded planet which had seen its fill of exploration? Gye hoped so.

Ray moved on and began showing off the interior.

"There are seven of us and only four rooms, so there will need to be some sharing." Ray said.

Gye turned to Jane.

"Shared living arrangements? If I land you as a roommate, this expedition will be way more fun than I thought." He said.

"Would you give it a rest already?" She replied.

"I prefer not to rest until a job is accomplished."

"Huh. You know, I had a neuroscientist friend who was doing a study on long-term sleep deprivation. This would make you a perfect candidate for it." Jane rolled her eyes as the joke apparently went over Gye's head.

"I knew I'd be losing sleep because of you, but not for that reason." He replied. She laughed in response.

"And here," Ray Kaymar continued— he had been remarking something or other about the quality of the leather seats in the common area- "next to the common area is a small kitchen, which will be the domain of our very own Royce Alavandréz, cook extraordinaire."

Royce smiled in response and looked around in the back. The counters were stainless steel, with oak trimming. Now that he looked at it, Gye realized, the entirety of the kitchen held the same aesthetic principle as the counter, with stainless steel being the majority element of choice and light-colored oak being the trim. There was even a stack of plates where the whole plate was evidently stainless steel, with an oaken ring about an inch thick forming a flattened torus around the outside of the plate. This attention to detail was maniacal, and Gye didn't know whether to be appreciative or scared.

"This styling must have cost a fortune! Will it even be worth it to recover the drone after your expense?" Elicia said.

"Three of these rovers would be a drop in the bucket compared to that flying monstrosity. It is surprisingly small, actually, but the technology inside could buy Peru." Ray said.

"I'm sure you're exaggerating!" Royce said.

"Maybe a bit, but you get the picture."

Jane ran her fingers along the oak trim, appreciating the evoked feeling of the universe being all in order. Perhaps all the chips were finally falling into place for her; with this capable crew, the drone would surely be recovered, she would get the research money, and certainly she could make many advances in her research while they were en route. There was, of course, the nagging question of how this forest was possible- the oxygen source and its complications were questions for another time.

Gye watched her as she was lost in thought. What was behind that facade of disinterest? What made her tick, what made life worth living for her? Why was she the way she was? She was a mystery he hoped to devour.

"Let me show you to the observation deck on top, where the cockpit is." Ray said.

"Ladies first." Gye said, gesturing for Jane to precede him up the ladder to the top deck.

"I didn't expect you to be the kind of guy to let a woman be first." She said as she went up.

"I'm a lot less selfish than I appear, as a matter of fact. I often let women be first... multiple times. That's how polite I am."

The ladder was aluminum with studded rungs to prevent someone from slipping. Jane watched as Gye came through the opening behind her. From the windows on this deck they could see far in every direction, and there were several machines of unknown function to her which loomed about in the room.

"Is that a Spectroscopic Sonar?" Gye asked, walking over to a complicated dashboard with a blinking monitor.

"Indeed it is! That will be your primary use to us on this voyage in our efforts to track down the drone. I've heard you're quite good with one of these." Captain Walker said.

"This one time, I tracked down a sunken ship that was a missing national treasure with one of these. I suppose I'm why its still listed as a *missing* national treasure." Gye said.

He looked up to see the rest of the group looking at him disapprovingly.

"*Allegedly*, I mean." He said with a sweet, faux innocent smile.

"What is a Spectro-whatever thing?" Jane asked.

"The Spectroscopic Sonar uses some complicated theories- it involves treating all matter as a fluid particle field, hence the *sonar*, if I remember correctly- but it basically allows us to track certain objects based on their radiative properties." Gye replied.

"We have a large array for detection on the hull of the storage deck, which is at the very bottom of the *Venture*." Ray said.

"How long did this take you to design? To my knowledge, the drone was lost only five months ago, and then they tried sending in the helicopter that never came back. Surely you couldn't have done all this in only that amount of time." Jane said.

"You are very keen, young lady. Yes, I must admit, I have been thinking about designing a vehicle like this one for the military for a few years now. I just never quite figured out how to pitch it to them, especially with illegal neutron weaponry being such a problem these days. One of the reasons I agreed to design this masterpiece, and convinced them to allow me to join this quest as an engineer, was so that I could see this baby in action." Ray said.

"You engineer types are très bizarre. But I can understand the drive to accomplish something. I guess it's like you have that same feeling I have about my work, only you feel it strongly about a lot more than I do." Jane said.

"That is an apt description. In my work, I often become infuriated when the mentally inept do not understand what I am telling them to do, or they do it wrong, or some other such nonsense. I have been referred to as 'that perpetually angry german engineer'-which, by the way, is ridiculous, because I am as American as freedom and good times under the stars. But they are accurate in saying that I am often angry, so I feel that I should warn you all not to say anything stupid lest you cause such an outburst from me." Ray said.

"I should hope that we can all get along." Anthony said, casting a disdainful glance in Gye's direction.

Gye merely smiled in return.

"In my line of work, you don't pretend to like the people you don't like, unless they've got a bigger gun than you. But Anthony, for example, has no guns at all." Gye said.

"Ah, a double entendre based on my pacifism and lack of biceps. If you used half of your wit for helping a cause instead of insults and robbery, perhaps you would find yourself in more hearts than jails." Anthony said.

"At least I can survive in a jail, pretty boy."

"That's enough. I won't have this kind of open disrespect between members of my crew." Captain James Walker fumed.

"So you're actually the captain of this voyage? I thought it was just a title." Gye said.

"Mark yourself well, son, I am indeed in control here. I should have you all refer to me as *Captain*, but I prefer to be lenient."

"That's all very well, James, but I believe we've got some equipment testing to get a move on with, so we can up and get started." Elicia Cantor said.

"This wench always knows how to rile me up. Who are you to call me James, as if you are talking down to me? Women always seem to have a sixth sense for how to rile a man up." Captain Walker said.

Anthony butted in.

"Actually, there are many more than the five Aristotelian senses, among them being acceleration, balance, and temperature. And besides that, your statement is sexist." Anthony said.

"You nitpicking twat, why are you here again?" Captain Walker asked flippantly.

"I have a Ph.D. in biological sciences, and you ask why *I'm* here?"

"Oh, did your parents buy you that too?" Gye butted in.

"I'm not ashamed to have been born to parents who worked hard to get ahead." Anthony replied.

"Didn't your dad inherit his eighty million dollar fortune from his father?" Elicia interrupted.

"Maybe that helped a bit, but my father worked hard his whole life to take the eighty million dollars he was given and turn it into an eighty two million dollar fortune! Now that's what happens when you work hard and apply yourself." Anthony said.

"You know, most of the time I can't tell if you're joking or not." Gye said.

Royce returned from the kitchen with miniature sandwiches on a platter.

"Behold, the first food made on this illustrious vessel! Like the first communion aboard the Apollo 11, this will be recounted as a moment of significance in history." He said.

"I think your hopes are a little high, but what the heck. Let me try one of those." Elicia said.

Everyone grabbed a miniature sandwich and began to eat. Royce scanned each person's face like a private investigator looking for clues. He obsessed over every twitch of the eye, looking for the slightest hint of affirmation or rejection. It was evident that a great deal of Royce's self-esteem was derived from other people's enjoyment of his culinary creations. Jane noticed this and thought of it as something that was likely unhealthy. Herself, she did not pay too much attention to the opinions of others except when they had something to offer her. As of now, Royce seemed satisfied with the appreciative reactions he had received from the room and took the empty tray- with a few crumbs- back to the kitchen. He walked with a new spark, which gave evidence to Jane's thoughts on the matter.

Jane looked over at Gye, who was looking out the window. He was tall, handsome, and confident, sure. She allowed herself a brief moment- just a small, teensy tiny one- to imagine herself with him. It was an enticing thought, to be sure. Just as quickly, she crashed that train of thought. She hadn't gotten this far in life by paying attention to silly, primal urges like attraction.

Captain Walker tested the announcement system from the cockpit. It screeched at first, giving those in the common area a frightful start.

"Everyone get up here, we are about to start off!" Captain Walker said through the speaker system.

As they all clambered back into the cockpit, Gye could not help but think that this was actually happening- really, *happening*. He was going to go adventuring without Marquis, and he would be working for the 'good guys' for once. Just a month ago he would not have seen this coming.

"All systems go, cargo loaded, requesting authorization to commence." Captain Walker said into the radio.

"You are go, *Venture*. Opening hangar door now." A voice replied.

With that, the enormous door that was holding the *Venture* Rover inside the hangar began to roll out of the way, freeing the rover like a crawling bug let out of a jar. Blinding daylight knifed into the cockpit windows and blinded those inside. The hangar had been darker than they had thought.

"Polarize the viewing glass, please, Mr. Kaymar." Captain James Walker said.

The world was viewable again, and they commenced. The rover lurched forward, leg by leg, with surprising agility.

CHAPTER 8
THE ROOMMATE

"And directly after the common area there are four rooms where each of us will be staying. Now, there are seven of us and only four rooms, and Captain Walker will have his room to himself, so that means each of us gets a roommate." Ray Kaymar said.

They were all standing in a tiny hallway which diverged into four small rooms. Ray had been giving them a tour of the *Venture*— its top deck, with the cockpit, laboratory, and engineering rooms, and the crew deck, which they were currently on, with the kitchen, bathroom, ladder, common area, and these rooms— and they had just now reached the far end of the rover.

"Now," Ray continued, "I'm sure you're excited to know who you're bunking with on this epic journey. This has been determined by careful consideration by Captain Walker— which, I guess, is why he gets a room to himself... but anyways, allow me to tell you."

"I'm crossing my fingers that I get you." Gye said to Jane.

She didn't acknowledge the comment, other than a quick glance in his direction. Her blue eyes took on an even deeper hue in this light, and as she looked on with lips parted ever so slightly, brow scrunched in concentration, Gye thought that she should have been a model rather than a scientist. Either way, she was certainly an interesting specimen to him.

Ray Kaymar continued.

"Captain Walker has his own room. Royce, you're with me. Jane, you and Elicia are together, and lastly, Anthony, you and Gye will be sharing a room."

Gye was disappointed; he did not relish the thought of spending perhaps months with this posh, hipster poser. Anthony, of course, was equally appalled.

"Excuse me, Mr. Kaymar, I believe there has been a mistake." Anthony said.

"There has been no mistake. Carry on." Captain Walker said, joining the group. He turned sharply in a quick right-face movement, a vestige from his time in the military. Gye had not noticed that the rover had not been moving for the last minute or so, as Captain Walker took a break from piloting to join them.

"Captain, I hate to say it, but I agree with Anthony. This wont work." Gye said.

"You'll make it work! That's an order." The Captain replied.

"I don't remember signing up to get yelled at by some old carcass in a suit." Gye said.

"I'm the Captain here, and you will respect me as such. I will not hesitate to throw you off of my ship."

"Your ship? Take it easy there, this isn't the Titanic. Although with your lack of leadership we're probably headed for the same fate." Gye replied carelessly.

Captain Walker grew red in the face. He was not any good at hiding his anger, and was evidently caught completely by surprise at not having absolute authority by default. Perhaps when he accepted the job he had thought it would be an instant return to the glory days- as he called them, anyway. The mind has an odd way of glazing over the darker shades of memory and choosing only to see the light. He saw this young man as a light breeze with, despite its weakness, threatened to blow over the house of cards that was his recollection of his past conquests. His anger was not so much directed at Gye as it was directed at the threat of having his rose-tinted view of himself put to question.

Captain Walker spoke deliberately, on the verge of losing his temper. He was not the kind of man to back down from a challenge to his authority.

"You may have gotten by this far in life without having to pay your dues or give respect to people. You may think you can continue to do so here. But you've never been on a crew under my command. I expect- and I *will* get- absolute obedience. Are we clear?" Captain Walker said.

"You know, as I have been saying the whole time, the Captain's decision should be respected." Anthony said in a weaselly fashion.

"Ever the sycophant, I see." Gye said derisively.

"James," Elicia called from further down the hall, "shouldn't we be getting a move on? I do believe we have a schedule to keep." She said, gesturing to her wristwatch.

"Of course. I was just making a small matter quite clear to these fine young gentlemen."

With that, the captain did an about-face and walked away. Anthony and Gye exchanged disparaging glances, looking at each other like two elementary school children who don't get along.

Gye opened the door to their room and gestured Anthony to enter before him in mock courtesy. As they entered the room, Gye was struck by the utilitarianism of its design. There was a bunkbed in one corner of the room, which nearly took up the whole width of the wall, and two desks on the opposite side. Between them, on the wall opposite the door, was a large window. The window was curved along with the hull of the rover, and slightly tinted green. It gave the already verdant vista a voracious view, like someone had used too much of one chemical in an old photography darkroom. There were various smaller items which Gye did not care to take note of in the room, one of which looked vaguely similar to a stereo system.

"So this is home, for god knows how long." Anthony said.

"I'm used to uncomfortable living conditions. I've spent more nights in city alleyways than I have in clean beds." Gye said.

Almost on cue, the rover was in motion again. The movement was surprisingly stabilized, likely owing to some invention or other by Ray or his team. Gye would have to remember to ask him about that later.

"Right then, I'll be taking the top bunk."Anthony said.

"Fine with me. Ever since I barely made it out of a collapsing tower, I've had no distaste for being close to the ground." Gye said.

"Actually," Anthony said, his tone rising in pitch, "I'll be taking the bottom one. Closer to Earth means closer to nature, and nature is above all else."

"Suit yourself."

Anthony dropped the large bag and suitcase he had been carrying with him on the floor and opened the suitcase. He had an unnecessary plethora of clothes— all of them in the latest fashions, even those which defied common sense— packed, along with what appeared to be facial cosmetics and various hair care products.

"I didn't think they'd let me bunk with a woman." Gye said jokingly upon noticing this.

"Don't be so old fashioned. Every self-respecting, fashionable man does what I do these days." Anthony replied, blinking a little faster than usual as he said it.

"Fashionable, maybe, but self-respecting, I don't think so."

"Self respect is merely a concept made up by the unfashionable to try and bring down the true rulers, like myself."

"You, a ruler? A drag queen is the closest you'll ever come to that." Gye replied.

"Clever, but completely misguided. I am only a man who takes more care of himself than cavemen like you who would be more than willing to wear animal skins if women didn't turn up their noses at that sort of thing." Anthony said condescendingly. Gye noticed that Anthony began using a fake British accent whenever he was being condescending. It only added to his view of Anthony as a pretentious fool.

"I need to get some fresh air," Gye said, "I can barely breathe in here with those reeking products of yours."

Anthony had no reply but to roll his eyes.

###

Elicia sipped a cup of coffee absentmindedly. She was sitting at the wooden table with Gye and Ray. It was early morning on the second day of their voyage.

"I'm not gullible enough to believe we're likely to run into these alien creatures they keep talking about. I didn't survive the way I did by taking people at their words." Gye said.

"Were you expecting to step straight into a fantasy world with dragons and aliens? I confess that'd be much more fun, but life is rarely fun, and always cruel. I've looked at their work and I'm pretty sure Jane and Anthony have got a solid biological basis for their ideas. Mind you, geology is the only rock-solid science, if you understand me. I'm none too keen on helixes and amino acids. They say they can explain life, but I've yet to meet a single biologist who can tell me what it's for." Elicia said. Her blond hair waved over her forehead like a flag on a pole as she dipped her head to drink the coffee.

"Heh, *single* biologist. That's all of them, there." Gye said.

"Watch yourself, boy. Those fools may wear their lab coats like armor and jump to conclusions faster than rabbits, but us scientists, we're all kin. And you're one to talk, aren't you? I can't picture you going steady with anyone." Elicia said.

Gye took a swaggering sip of his coffee. Ray sat there silently, listening to them talk back and forth.

"I had a bit of romance not too long ago. Didn't end too well." Gye said. Elicia chuckled gently.

"I see. Well, life's too short to make commitments. Better to live in the moment and be free." She said.

"Tell me… are you truly happy?" Ray asked.

"Happiness is the ability to avoid asking yourself that question." Elicia replied with a slight tone of discomfort.

"Ignorance is bliss." Ray intoned.

"Some might see it that way. I prefer to say that avoiding unanswerable questions is its own form of happiness." Elicia said.

"This is too much thinking for so early in the morning." Gye said, rubbing his temples tiredly.

"What, did you not get any sleep? That odd roommate of yours keep you up?" Ray asked.

"He snores like a weasel in a tin can. I'll need to get myself a pair of earplugs or perhaps just blast my brains out. Where is he, anyway? Haven't seen him today."

"He's up with Jane on the top deck. Said something or other about finding the epicenter of this forest and that the probability of running into our first anomaly today is nearly twenty percent. He also gave me advice on what spices to put in my tea- of course he assumed it was tea- but I'd prefer not to go down that path again if you don't mind." Elicia said.

"He's with Jane?" Gye sipped the last of his coffee and looked at the dregs contemplatively.

"And Captain Walker, naturally." Ray said.

Gye stood up abruptly.

"I think I'll get a better view of this lovely forest from the top deck." He said.

"A lovely view, sure. More of a bush than a forest, though." Elicia replied.

"I'm sure it'll get thicker as we go along. Probably a tighter squeeze for the rover too, but it's designed for this trek." Ray said.

As Gye climbed up the metal ladder rung by rung, with the *Venture* swaying gently in the background, he couldn't help but let his mind run through the possibilities. If these people were right, what kind of creatures might they run into? Hopefully rather small ones.

Captain Walker was chatting amiably with Anthony and Jane when Gye strode to join them.

"I was wondering when you would drag your carcass out of bed, Storm. I expect more discipline from you in the future." Captain Walker said.

"Are you being serious right now?"

"Captain Walker is always serious." Jane said with a smile.

"Perhaps too much so, truth be told. Ah well. We were just discussing our strategy. The readings from that machine of yours- if you can work it as well as you claim you can- should help us locate the epicenter of the forest, where the drone was programmed to head towards. We can hone in from there. Early reports indicate a very unusual, high mountain in the center of all of this. That, at least, should make navigation a bit easier." The Captain said.

"The feds will be pissed if they get their drone back and all it reveals is some pretty scenery." Gye said.

"Oh, we're confident it will be much more than that." Jane said. She dropped her voice to a whisper and continued "This whole thing goes much deeper than you know. Much, much deeper than any of us know."

"Intriguing, but we'll have to see." Gye replied.

"Always the skeptic. I'm not surprised." Anthony said.

"Always the killjoy. Also not surprised." Gye retorted.

"Enough. Gye, we are missing a radio component here that wasn't installed. Go and get it from the cargo bay. It should be in the box labelled A113." Captain Walker ordered.

"Aye aye, sir!" Gye said with a mock salute and dripping sarcasm. Captain Walker looked unamused and Anthony was a stoic as ever, but at least Jane cracked a grin.

Gye climbed down the ladder slowly, passing through the middle deck where Elicia and Ray were still chatting, with Royce now joining them. He had not yet been in the cargo bay, but the name felt pretty self-explanatory as to what to expect. as he passed down into it, his expectations were confirmed. There were many wooden crates and a few cardboard ones neatly stacked and organized in rows, like soldiers awaiting marching orders. It was mostly dark, with only one light turned permanently on casting some illumination upon the scene.

As his shoes touched down on the textured metal and rubber floor, Gye grappled blindly for the light switch. He had the odd sensation of fear that one has as a child, the feeling of turning off the lights and jumping into bed before the monsters have a chance to devour you. Finally he found the light switch- or, rather, the touch-sensitive button that turned on the lights- and the room became much brighter. There were no windows to the outside world in the cargo bay, and the whole scene had a look of dull, clinical utilitarianism, like a hospital or a prison, with none of the elegant design of the middle floor of the rover.

Where was the crate? A001— there was a start. He glanced through the crates until he got to the one labelled A113 and grabbed it. It was rather large, and heavy, as Gye was barely able to lift it. As he started back towards the ladder, there was the slightest shifting sound and movement in the shadows behind a row of crates, on the opposite side of the center aisle. Gye stopped suddenly. Slowly, he set down the crate and took a step in the direction of the sound.

"Is… is someone there?" He asked, feeling sheepish. Had he just imagined it? Was he sneaking up on a shadow? Yes, he must have imagined it.

Gye turned around to continue.

"Hi!" The girl said, standing three feet in front of him. Gye yelled and jumped backwards, banging his head on something metal. Through bleary eyes Gye recognized the girl from the hallway at the launch station. What was her name again? Why was she here?

"Gosh, are you ok? You seem to have hit your head pretty hard there." She said, taking a step towards him.

"It's, ah, not that bad. What… what are you doing here?"

"Remember me? Molly Hazelwood?"

"Oh, yes, of course. But, ah, what are you doing here?"

"Plotting world domination, what does it look like? You must've hit your head pretty hard there, I seem to remember you being a bit more quick-witted." She said, smiling.

Gye's head was beginning to clear. He heard steps on the ladder and turned to see Elicia Cantor coming down the steps.

"What was all that yelling about?—Oh, hello there, dear. How pleasant of you to join us. I was beginning to think this trip would get quite dull, what with all these men and their testosterone."

"Hello again, Elicia! I was hoping someone would discover me sooner rather than later. It might have been awkward if I jumped out in the middle of your voyage and surprised everyone. And I was starting to get hungry down here. Do you have food?"

"Why yes, we've got some, and a cook who looks quite delicious himself. Gye, are you quite alright? That cut looks nasty. It's a pity we thought to bring a cook but not a doctor. Whose idea was that?" Elicia said.

"I studied in the medical field for two years before I switched my major, actually. Although I have to admit I don't remember much of it. It was all so dull, which was one of the reasons I changed majors. Couldn't see myself doing a job I wasn't interested in. I want a job I don't need a vacation from, you know?" Molly said.

"So you've taken up being a stowaway, eh? Doesn't exactly pay well, but I suppose that could be fun." Gye said.

"Oh please, I came here because I wanted to pursue a life worth living- adventure, and being on the bleeding edge of discovery, that sort of thing! They just didn't take me seriously when I said I wanted to join the expedition. Why should they let the assistant go on something this important? The Captain said he wasn't going to have so many women on this trip to bother him. You know how dark-ages he can be sometimes. Anyways. They said it was a hard choice but they decided not to let me. So I decided not to give them a choice. So here I am! Let's make history." She said.

"I like the way you think, girl. You'll go far in life. We'd best take you to Captain Walker, though. Maybe you can convince him not to throw you overboard." Elicia said.

"Let me get this straight. You stow away on my ship, defy the orders not to come, and expect me to just be fine with that? Give me one good reason why I shouldn't throw your butt overboard?" Captain Walker said.

"You do realize we're not on a boat, right? And I'll tell you why. I'm sure I could tell you how this will be important and the adventure of a lifetime for me, and all that. But you're a sexist pig, so you would only balk at that. Let me instead ask you how your higher-ups would feel about the fact that a potentially dangerous stow-away managed to hide on your rover without you noticing for two days?" Molly said. She looked to Elicia as if to confirm whether she'd gotten it all right. She nodded. The entire group was present, looking on at the confrontation. Jane seemed indifferent and Anthony seemed interested.

"Are you in on this too, Elicia? And what, are you trying to blackmail me, young lady?" Captain Walker said.

"Yes, that's exactly what I'm doing." She replied.

They stared at each other in an iron contest of wills for perhaps half a minute before Captain Walker burst out laughing, guffawing loudly.

"Well, I can at least respect someone who good 'ol fashion strong-arms me instead of these kids," (he gestured to Gye and Anthony) "who snigger and complain behind each others' backs like schoolgirls. Welcome aboard, Hazelwood." He said, offering her a handshake. She accepted.

"Now make yourself useful. Everyone earns a place on my ship, no one gets a free ride to glory. You're dismissed." He said, turning back to the controls.

As they made their way down and reconvened in the middle floor, Molly pondered.

"I didn't expect him to give up so easily." She said.

Elicia chuckled.

"Likely he admires your tenacity, and your willingness to take what you want from the world instead of taking life's punches lying down. Besides, he's like an old guard dog. He pretends to be all tough and strong, but underneath he's soft and warm. Never tell him I told you that, though." Elicia said with a chuckle.

They were interrupted by Anthony yelling from the top deck.

"Stop the rover! I've spotted something."

CHAPTER 9
FIRST SIGHTING

They all rushed to the top floor to see.

"Where? I don't see anything!" Jane complained, jostling for a spot to look at out the window where Anthony was pointing.

"Look closer!" He replied. Gye found it harder to hate Anthony when his facades were down and his true passion evident.

"What, that tree stump?" Jane asked.

"No, there!"

"You can't just say 'there', you have to be more specific."

"Fine, approximately 2.5 meters to the left of the stump, latitude a forest in the middle of nowhere, longitude with this girl who apparently can't see what's right in front of her."

"Be more pedantic, why don't you? Here, give me the binoculars."

Gye did not see anything either, although he wasn't about to admit to it. To him it was just foliage and more foliage. It did nothing but conjure up memories of a certain assignment that one time in Guam...

"Oh, there it is! Oh my, what a magnificent butterfly! It must be a foot across at least in wingspan!" Jane said, barely able to contain her excitement.

Gye finally saw it as well. It was as if someone had taken a Tiger Swallowtail and stretched it out in all directions until it was so much larger than normal. It flapped its oversized wings in a light breeze to stay perched on a fallen log. What did this thing eat? Gye couldn't recollect what normal-sized butterflies ate. Were there larger versions of whatever normal butterflies ate for this thing to prey on? Were there also larger trees and flowers and... spiders? He shuddered at the spot. He remembered an Elementary School teacher telling him that ninety nine percent of all species that had ever lived and died out. If this forest had some of those still hanging around somewhere... oh, the possibilities. So these scientists weren't crazy after all.

"If I could get that thing to a restaurant in Mexico, I would be a rich man. The butterfly is a delicacy in many parts of that country." Royce commented.

"Ray, did you happen to put any oversized butterfly nets in the cargo bay?" Jane asked.

"No. Why would I have planned ahead for such nonsense as chasing after oversized worms with wings?" Ray replied.

"Caterpillars, not worms." Anthony muttered as an aside.

"A little bit of nonsense now and then is cherished by the wisest men. You're jaded before your time, Ray Kaymar. Engineering has killed your soul, it looks like. I know the cure for too much math- hard drinks and good times." Elicia said.

Captain Walker interrupted.

"Your immoral epigrams are inspiring as usual, Elicia. But we do have more pressing matters at hand. Ray, is there anything we could MacGyver into a net to capture the specimen for our analysis?" Captain Walker asked.

Ray Kaymar looked angered at that. Gye had heard about Ray's famous bouts of fierce anger from an underling back at the station. One time, they said, Ray had nearly gone insane and gone into a raging fit of destruction when the factory producing a part for one of his inventions produced half of the units in a shade of white only slightly different from what was intended. The difference was not even detectable by the human eye, but still Ray was infuriated by the factory's incompetence and the way they ruined his craftsmanship. Ray got the person responsible fired, and rumor had it even chopped off one of their fingers in his anger. Gye didn't know whether he believed half the stories told about him.

"Are we children chasing after every bright and shiny object that crosses our paths? We're here to recover the drone, not dillydally and loiter. Sure we can have a look at the pretty sights here and there, but our primary duty is to the people who paid for this mission." Ray said.

"Of course it is, Ray. But surely we can bring them back more than what they ask? I hardly think that they would have a problem with us taking ten minutes to have a look." Jane said.

"I'm sure Rockenhoffler incorporated will be more than satisfied just to get their massive investment back once we return the drone to them. What use is it to stroll through the garden of eden if you don't stop to smell the flowers along the way?" Molly said.

Ray paused for a moment. His face was hard and unreadable. Gye desperately wanted to have a closer look at the freakish creature, but he said nothing. In his experience, you never told anyone what you wanted so that they could never take it away from you.

"I suppose you're right," Ray finally said with a resigned sigh. His tone softened slightly. "There is an extra water purifier in the cargo bay. We can take the net out and use that, I suppose."

"Oh, thank you! This will be so exciting. I can't wait to have a look at this thing up close. It hasn't flown away yet, has it?" Molly said.

"No, it's still there. Let's capture it!" Anthony said.

"I used to do this as a kid with my friends all the time, catching butterflies." Gye said to Jane.

"You don't seem like the kind of person who had friends as a child." She replied.

"'Friends' is perhaps putting it kindly. I spent some time in a home for homeless kids. There were no butterflies there if you know what I mean, let me tell you."

"They were just other children, how bad could it have been?" She asked.

"You wouldn't have been able to tell by how they acted. I got in my first knife fight within a week. I learned how to lie to the people in charge very quickly after that."

They were talking while watching Anthony sneak up on the butterfly with a net. He was being very slow about it, but that was probably for the best. The butterfly appeared to be cleaning its massive wings with its proboscis.

"Do you still keep in touch with any of them?"

"I send a letter now and again, but those connections only mean anything on the inside. Everything good passes out of your life, because eventually it will die or you will die. There's no escaping it."

"I'm sorry to hear that."

"That's life, you've just gotta roll with the punches and fight back."

Anthony swung the net and missed the first time. The butterfly gave a mighty push with its massive wings and was up in the air. Anthony swung the net again and captured the butterfly. It struggled against the net, resisting this new threat to its freedom. Ray stepped in to help Anthony hold it down. They nearly lost control of it until Gye joined them. Eventually the insect stopped resisting.

"Surprisingly powerful little creature! Now what do we do with it?" Anthony asked.

"I assumed someone had a plan." Elicia said.

"I would offer my plan, but I do believe you all already know it. It involves the butterfly, a frying pan, and some imported spices." Royce said with a chuckle. He looked at least half serious.

"I hate that plan almost as much as I hate the southern half of California." Captain Walker said.

"What do ya have against California?" Elicia asked.

"Hippies."

"But at least-"

"Guys! We have more important matters at hand. Let's just close it off from the bottom and take specimen photos and then release it, eh?" Anthony said.

"Right! I'll go get the camera." Jane said, and ran off towards the rover.

"Who gets to pose with it in the photo?" Royce asked.

"No one poses with it, it's a specimen photo!" Anthony replied.

"Then how will the world know you didn't just fake the photo? It's gotta be convincing."

"He does have a point." Gye said, more to be against Anthony than for any other reason.

"No! We are SERIOUS SCIENTISTS!" He screamed.

"Calm down!"

"I'm already calm!" He screamed back. He was not already calm.

Just then Jane arrived with the camera. Royce snatched it threw it to Gye. Royce posed with a peace hand sign and Gye snapped the photo.

Anthony was furious.

"I don't know what game you preschoolers are trying to play here, but I'm trying to do science! Delete that picture now!" He said.

"I don't think so, pretty boy. We rather like doing what we want, and now what you scream at us to do." Gye said.

"Give it!" He said, walking towards Gye. Gye tossed the camera back to Royce, and Anthony jumped after it.

There was a sickening sloppy crunching sound and a squeal like a cat being stepped on.

No one dared look down.

"You know, I think I'm just going to walk back into the Rover now. No need to look down, there's nothing interesting down there. Oh god, what have I done? I mean, no, there's nothing. I might just leave my shoes out here— I have an extra pair— I'll just leave them for no particular reason, I just don't really like them anymore. What do y'all say?" Anthony said.

"Yep, sounds good!" Jane said. She looked like she was about to throw up. Everyone else chimed in as well.

"Let's all just pretend that never happened." Gye said softly.

"Pretend what happened? We just went out for a quick walk, that's all." Elicia said.

They moved on rather quickly from that point.

"So you, like, study plants and insects and such?" Molly asked Anthony. He smiled at her phrasing with his boyish grin, showing off his perfect, bleached teeth and his perfectly conditioned skin. Gye, sitting across from them at the table, hated the way he smiled at her— more because of his dislike of Anthony than anything else.

"That's one way to describe it, yes. I prefer to say that by looking into nature, we can look into the eyes of God."

Gye rolled his eyes. Anthony seemed to take on a thin Russian accent whenever he spoke unguardedly. Was that his real ethnicity? Gye couldn't tell what was real and what was fake with Anthony.

"That's poetic. What color do you think God's eyes are?" Molly asked, her own eyes widened with interest. Gye found himself repressing a snarl.

"God's eyes are like a rainbow of colors we've never seen and couldn't even dream of. Every poem that's ever been written, every picture taken or painted, every sparkle in the eyes of a couple in love, these things are the colors of God's eyes." Anthony said.

Gye nearly vomited.

"Oh, really? Perhaps you should throw in life's harsher reality in the mix with your butterflies and rainbows story." Gye said. Anthony winced at the mention of butterflies, but Gye pressed on anyways.

"Humans are evil beings, and you're trying to paint life like it's all fun and games." Gye said angrily.

"Gye, why must you ruin everything?" Anthony asked

Jane walked over to join them

"I don't ruin everything. If I see a train on the wrong tracks, perhaps it's best I derail it." He said.

"Did you know the first form of railway transport was invented by the ancient greeks in 600 b.c.?" Jane chimed in, completely unaware of the context of what was going on.

They looked at her frozenly until she caught on.

"Oh, am I interrupting something?" She asked.

"We were just discussing God's eyes. And then cake and blood and sin and trains... in all honesty, I'm a tad confused." Molly said with a nervous chuckle. She was trying to defuse the situation.

"People should just say what they mean more often." Jane said.

"She has a point. Hey, do you want to-" Gye started.

"—actually," Jane interrupted, "That's probably not so great of an idea. But please, do continue what you were all saying."

Anthony smirked and exchanged a look with Jane.

Molly spoke without making eye contact.

"I thought what you said was interesting, Anthony, but Gye's right. We can't have the good without the bad in life." She said.

Anthony looked crushed for a split second before slapping back on a facade of easygoing happiness. It seemed he could never stop pretending.

"I suppose that's true. There are interesting people, and there are people who are the human equivalent of nails on a chalkboard." Anthony said pointedly.

"I prefer to see the good in people." Molly replied.

"The world would be a better place if more people were like you, then." Anthony said.

Molly smiled slightly and looked out the window.

"Anthony, what do you think the-" Jane started.

"—I think I need to get back to work." He said with abrupt curtness, gathering his things and getting up to leave. Jane was left hanging awkwardly.

They sat in silence for a few moments.

"So... what do you do?" Molly asked Jane.

"I sure don't stow away on important missions I wasn't invited to. I fought hard to earn my place on this voyage. You snuck aboard.

You know, you were rejected for a reason." Jane said, grabbing her notebook and storming off.

Molly sat in stunned silence.

"I'll go talk to her." Gye said, and left as well.

She was left alone at the table. Her brown eyes glazed over slightly as she fought back tears. Was it really so bad, what she did? Was Jane right? She used her left hand to sweep her hair out of her vision. Molly was left alone at the table.

Vaurien Kane stood staring out the massive window of his office. The suburban scene sprawling before him looked more like a nest of rats than anything else to his eyes. All those people with their middle-class cars, mid-sized lawns, mid-sized houses, all so... *average.* None of them, not one in the perhaps six thousand homes in his view, were anything exceptional. They had too much luck to be born poor and too little aspiration to seize power and become rich. He adjusted his thick-framed black glasses and brushed back his graying hair. Vaurien's eyes flickered across the scene; as he did so, his easy, charming smile never wavered from his face. But there was nothing in that nest of rats to cause him happiness; no, he was expecting news.

As if on cue, there was a knock at the door. Vaurien turned around, sat at his desk, and pressed the hidden button under his desk to open the door. He reached into the recently-filled bowl of grapes and placed one on the edge of his lips, then sucked it into his mouth.

A lanky man with a tall, thin face and skinny arms strolled in. He was dressed in a cheap suit and tacky striped salmon and blue tie. His face seemed perpetually on the verge of bursting into a goofy smile. His ginger hair was receding— likely from the stress of his job— and there was something about his bearing that screamed his profession. He was an informant for the FBI. Or, more accurately, an informer for Vaurien Kane.

Vaurien bid the man to sit in the drastically smaller chair at the other end of the desk. He had been here many times before and so found nothing noteworthy about the strange furniture in the place. The desk lamp was new since his last visit, actually. Just like all the other furniture in the room, the lamp was an oddity. Its shaft was tapered to such thinness halfway up that it had the look of a very sharp knife indeed.

The man shifted uncomfortably, trying to become comfortable in a seat designed specifically to prevent visitors from becoming too comfortable.

Vaurien leaned forward, hands steepled under his chin.

"Speak." He growled.

The man cleared his throat nervously.

"I have further reports of the mission into the, um, blasphemous forest... which you requested. They commenced two days ago, sir, with a small crew. Their express mission was to recover the drone, which, as you feared—"

"I fear nothing." Vaurien interrupted in a half-whisper. It was quiet, but Vaurien was not a man who needed to yell in order to be threatening. It was said that his voice was like ice on the back of the neck, and it was impossible to feel safe around him... because no one was. Vaurien calmly reached into the bowl of grapes and grabbed one after another, sucking each one into his mouth with an eerie calmness.

The man's high, large forehead began to sweat. He quickly combed his fingers through his thinning hair, plastering it in the moisture. He was getting clammy.

"I'm sorry, sir. I mean, as you *suspected*, they are going to recover the drone and the recovered data and imagery will be published. The pubic will see it as irrefutable, I'm afraid, and so this forest of, ah, blasphemy will become another smear in the sight of, ah..." He stammered to a halt.

"You need not pander to me. I know you do not believe in what I believe; you are a blasphemer like all the others." His german accent was accented by the way he enunciated every word in almost lilting syllables. He ended the sentence by sucking in another grape.

The man wiped his sweaty brow with his cheap suit sleeve and nodded, continuing.

"Yes sir. Well, ah, I'm afraid to say that this would certainly be the death of your plan, sir. These amazing discoveries will be in the public eye for a decade or more. There's no way you can—"

Vaurien silenced him with a particularly loud slurping of a grape.

He allowed the informant to sit awkwardly in silence for a few moments.

"That will be all." Vaurien Kane said at last.

The man didn't move for a while. He was expecting something.

"Yes?" Vaurien said.

"Well, sir, there is, ah, the matter of my payment." He said hoarsely. He was exceedingly nervous.

"Oh yes." Vaurien said. He grabbed a suitcase from behind the desk and opened a drawer. He began placing bundles of cash in the suitcase as he spoke.

"Will you be continuing as my informant in this matter?" Vaurien asked.

"I think they're close to catching onto me, sir. I'm going to take this last payment and… well, I'll buy a beautiful ring and use it to propose to my girlfriend. If she says yes I'll use the rest of the money and travel the world with her." He said, his wavering voice taking on a wistful tone. He had that goofy smile on his face as he said so.

Vaurien smiled after a while and congratulated him. But his eyes were stone-cold and told a different story than his mouth.

Vaurien stood up and handed the suitcase to him. The man accepted it gratefully and stood to go.

"Just a moment. If you would come with me, I have a surprise for you. Come look out this window." Vaurien said.

The man did as he commanded, not sure what to expect, but very hopeful for the outcome.

As the man looked out the window, Vaurien grabbed the extraordinarily tapered sharp lamp and quietly snapped the head off of it. It was now just a very sharp, somewhat short spear. Vaurien came up beside the man and pointed with his free hand towards a certain building.

"You see that, right there? That is the secret seat of my religion's power. We meet in the utmost secrecy in a chamber there and plot the future of this planet. As of right now, you are the only non-member to know of its existence." Vaurien said with a proud tone.

"So… why are you telling me this?" The man asked, looking expectantly into Vaurien's eyes. He found nothing there but ice.

"You know what they say about this sort of thing. If I tell ya…" Vaurien shoved the razor-sharp lamp shaft up into the man's diaphragm and into his heart. His eyes fluttered weakly as his last breath left him.

"…I'll have to kill ya." Vaurien continued with a smile. When the man's soul had left and his eyes were nothing but glass, Vaurien Kane let the corpse slip out of his hands and hit the floor with a thud. Vaurien stared at his handiwork and smiled.

He reached for the last grape in the bowl and found it splattered in blood. He frowned, dropped it on the floor next to the corpse, and stomped on it until it's innards were splattered around like the man's were.

Vaurien Kane touched the intercom button and called his assistant.

"Lollia, it seems I've spilled my wine again. Please get someone to clean it up immediately, and bring bleach."

"Yes sir." Was the automatic reply.

He let go of the intercom button and surveyed the room. He looked at the lamp shaft in his hand— the end was a painter's brush covered in red paint— and dropped it as well.

He buzzed the intercom again.

"Oh, and Lollia… I'm going to need a new lamp."

CHAPTER 10
THE LAKE

"Why doesn't the light in the microwave work anymore?" Gye asked Ray Kaymar.

He looked at the microwave and then looked back at his sketchpad lazily.

"We're on one of the most advanced scientific missions in the history of humanity and you want to know why the microwave light doesn't work?" Ray asked incredulously. His eyebrows furrowed as they so often did, in anger.

Gye could only look on with mouth agape and cheeks flushing with crimson. He started to mumble something before Ray cut him off.

"Anyways," Ray continued, amused at Gye's embarrassment, "it's because the battery's nearly depleted. We'll need to stop for a solar recharge soon." Ray said casually.

"I thought you'd invent a way for this thing to run on air or something." Gye said.

Ray chuckled.

"Apparently, Gye Storm's promises don't make very good fuel." Ray said. His tone was kind.

"Touché… touché." Gye replied.

Jane and Anthony came down the ladder with an air of obvious excitement.

"We've spotted a deep lake up ahead, where we'll be recharging the rover. We'll also be taking some measurements, and if our ideas are correct, there should be some interesting specimens in the lake." She said.

"Let me be the first to suggest skinny dipping." Gye said.

"That makes you the *only* one to suggest that, Gye." Jane said, amused.

"We'll be swimming in biohazard suits, actually. We don't want to risk running into something dangerous." Anthony said.

Ray cleared his throat before speaking.

"What kind of… dangers?"

"One particularly fascinating— and quite dangerous— marine creature during the Carboniferous period was *Amphibiamus lyelli*, which is closest in phenotype to a modern crocodile. If this forest emulates the Carboniferous period as we expect, it is possible that we might run into one." Anthony said.

Gye stroked his beard as he was lost in thought. His blue eyes flickered at the windows of the Rover, imagining what might soon be seen.

Molly Hazelwood entered the room and looked around, looking lost. Suddenly the rover jolted and came to a stop.

"Bloody hell, I've spilled my tea!" Molly said sadly, looking into her half-spilled purple thermos.

"Bloody hell? I never would've pegged you to swear like a sailor." Gye said jokingly. Molly cleaned up the mess, while Jane looked at her with an air of disinterested contempt.

"Wow, look how much sugar is left at the bottom of the cup. It's practically a sludge!" Ray said, looking into the thermos. Molly blushed in response.

"I put way too much sugar in everything."

"That's disgusting." Jane muttered, looking out the window. Anthony frowned at Jane.

"Don't worry, I'm the same way." Anthony said kindly.

Captain Walker's gruff voice came over the intercom.

"Sorry about that, folks. Expect some turbulence as the stabilizers start shutting down to save power." Elicia's voice was heard in the background of the announcement, saying something indistinct to Captain Walker.

"The rover has a phase-based power conservation system," Ray explained, "that allows it to go much further than a conventional method."

"Maybe if you had spent less time on the pretty interior, you could've designed a longer-lasting battery." Anthony said derisively. Gye found the comment ironic, considering Anthony's adoration for aesthetics. Ray's eyebrows furrowed again. He didn't take criticisms to his decisions lightly.

"We only had so much time to design the thing. New technologies can't just be invented on the spot, it takes time even for the brightest. But what would you know, you've never created anything. You're just a leech piggybacking on others' success." Ray said. He spoke with an odd, dead calmness to his voice that was doubtless meant to intimidate Anthony.

If Anthony was intimidated, he didn't show it.

"Oh, I've done more for the world than make a pretty oversized tank that can't even go a few days without shutting down piece by piece. I'll have you know that my articles on the G zero phase of the cell cycle led indirectly to Dr. Drobnych's revised cell theory." Anthony replied.

"So you wrote something that contributed to someone else's great idea. That would be like Newton taking credit for Einstein's theories." Ray retorted.

"Humanity only climbs higher when we stand on the shoulders of giants. I might not have made the discovery myself, but I contributed."

Gye watched the confrontation with raised eyebrows. He was content to watch it play out without his interference.

Ray was getting angrier.

"You're so unbelievably dense! Do you even hear how ridiculous you sound?"

"You're resorting to name-calling. I think that's a good indicator that you know you're wrong." Anthony said with a smug smile. It was all Gye could do to stop himself from reaching over and punching Anthony's stupid face. Those green eyes and that mop of curly hair made Anthony that much more repugnant in his smugness.

"If you were right, I would agree with you." Ray said, his voice rising in loudness.

"If you were actually good at what you keep bragging about, I would respect you." Anthony retorted.

"Respect? What do you know about respect? You were born with a silver spoon in your mouth and I'm sure your diapers were Louis Vuitton or Gucci. You were brought up with servants telling you that you were something special, that the world revolves around you. Well, let me tell you something, Anthony Lafayette. You're not special. You're not even *good* until you prove to the world otherwise." Ray said. He had regained some of his composure.

"One thing is quite clear to me, Ray Kaymar. Insults and properly working machines are both things you can't make."

Ray's face reddened.

"You're an insolent fool." He said. The glass cup he was clutching shattered in his hand, sending water and blood spilling across the table. Molly rushed to Ray's side.

"We've got to clean the glass out of this wound right away. Come with me to the bathroom sink." She said, guiding him. Anthony looked on without doing anything, apparently in a bit of shock from having caused such anger in someone. He was used to people just putting up with him. Gye surprised himself by feeling bad for him. As much as he hated Anthony, he was far from the worst human being he had yet encountered.

Molly bandaged Ray's hand and he offered a weak nod of thanks.

"I'm going to rest until we arrive at the lake. I find myself tired." Ray said, heading to his room.

###

"Which one is mine?" Gye asked. He was standing with Jane, Molly, Anthony, Royce, Ray, Elicia, and Captain Walker. There were six biohazard suits on the wall, each one black with one bright color on the sides. Their respective colors were white, red, yellow, green, pink, and blue.

"Each suit is unisex and one size fits all. We brought six suits in case the drone was found underwater, and one person was going to have to stay behind at all times. Now that Molly has unexpectedly joined us, we now have two people staying behind at any given time." Ray said. His voice lacked the pride and passion that usually accompanied him when he spoke of his creations. Gye noticed that he kept his bandaged left hand close to his torso.

"I'll take the white one." Captain Walker said.

"No surprise." Anthony muttered. Captain Walker turned to him expressionlessly.

"Are you insinuating that I'm a racist?" He asked.

Anthony, not expecting the direct response, only mumbled indistinctly.

"For the record," Captain Walker said, "my wife is African American. I may be old-fashioned, but I'm not some old man on a porch yelling obscenities."

"Oh." Was all Anthony could muster in response.

"I'll take the yellow one." Gye said to break the silence.

"I won't be needing a suit. I can't stand being underwater." Royce said with a shudder.

"I won't be much of a swimmer with this hand, so I'm out." Ray said with a hint of despondence in his voice. Elicia took the red suit, Anthony took the green, Molly took the pink, and Jane took the blue.

They opened the hatch to the outside world. A ladder automatically descended from outside the hatch to the ground to aid their descent. Gye was last in line. Even though they weren't diving, Ray and Royce both came outside, likely just to enjoy the feeling of freedom that was being outside. The sun was shining brightly on the scene— there was only one cloud in the entire sky— and the view was beautiful.

There was a mountain range directly in front of them as they walked out, with one extraordinarily tall mountain in the center of it. It was snow-capped despite the relentless sun. That was where they were headed later on.

They had stopped the rover at the edge of the beach next to the lake. There were a few washed-up logs and pieces of driftwood on the beach, but other than that it was relatively clear for a place no human being had set foot in, possibly ever.

The lake itself was sapphire blue, and was fed on the opposite side by a waterfall perhaps fifty feet up. Behind the waterfall was a rocky hill. It was a picturesque scene, with lush green forest surrounding the lake. One particularly enormous tree dominated the left side of the view. It was most similar perhaps to a birch tree, only at its size, its leaves were probably the size of a car. Gye thought that he could have taken one down— if he could climb that high— and used it as a blanket with plenty of room to spare.

Gye noticed that Royce Alavandréz had already scurried off to investigate a patch of oversized mushrooms— very dull things with thin dark-brown caps and lanky off-white, tall stems. He lost sight of whatever Ray was doing as they waded into the shallow end of the lake. Anthony, Gye had noticed, was toting a camera protected in a waterproof case. The group was in a haphazard arrowhead formation, with Captain Walker in his white suit at the tip of it. He turned around, saluted them, and dove into the water. Gye, Jane, Molly, Anthony, and Elicia followed suit.

"Intercom test. Everyone check in." Captain Walker said. They each did so.

"Each of your oxygen tanks contains one hour of oxygen. I will remind you of the time elapsed every fifteen minutes until the last fifteen minutes, where I will remind you every five minutes. Are we all clear on that?" Captain Walker asked. They replied affirmatively.

"Stay with someone at all times. All right, let's do some exploring!" Captain Walker said.

Gye looked at the intercom controls on his wrist. It was a simple white band with eight buttons- the six colors corresponding to each team member's suit color, as well as a black button. The black turned off the intercom completely. He could select one or multiple colors, depending on who he needed to talk to. It was a very simple system, but it took a little getting used to.

It was strangely peaceful under the water. The intercom was silent, and all Gye could hear was the sound of his own heavy breathing — drawing from his oxygen supply— and the faint sound of his flippers hitting the water. As he went deeper and the water became less clear, he put his hand on the side of his goggles and flipped the switch there. It used a microcomputer in the goggles to process the images he saw and increase their visibility. With that, he could see much further.

There was a flurry of movement amidst the bubbles some twenty feet down and to the left.

"Captain," Gye said, selecting the white button on his wrist, "movement detected over here. Over."

"Received, Mr. Storm. Jane, come check this out. Over."

They floated closer on opposite sides of what they had spotted and closed in. What was it? Hopefully not that thing Anthony had been talking about earlier. Gye didn't exactly feel like being fish food just then.

"I don't see anything." Jane said at last through the intercom.

"Huh. It must've moved." Gye said sheepishly.

"Or maybe you got excited and pointed out something that wasn't there, no?" Anthony said, swimming closer.

"I'm sure he saw something." Molly said defensively.

"Well, in any case, let's keep moving."

Suddenly a large creature the size of a semi truck blazed past them. Molly grabbed Jane and pulled her out of the way just in time. It had fins and a stunted nose. It stopped suddenly and brayed at the group almost exactly like a dolphin, except in a deeper tone.

Elicia swore into the intercom and swam away as quickly as she could. Gye heard Jane breathing heavily. Anthony fumbled with the camera before snapping a shot just as it swam away.

"It seems to be a predecessor of the dolphin." Anthony said.

"Aren't dolphins only in the ocean, though? We're in a lake." Captain Walker said.

"There are several variants of dolphins that reside in freshwater, Captain. Everyone, it wont harm you as long as you don't get too close." Anthony said.

Jane turned to Molly.

"Thank you for pulling me out of the way. You could've been hurt!"

"Oh… I wasn't thinking. I'm sure you'd do the same for anyone else." Molly replied meekly.

"I'm not sure that I would have. Regardless… thank you. I'm not saying I agree with what you did, mind you." Jane said.

Elicia had made her way back.

"What was that thing, James?"

"It was… I'd have to describe it as a dolphin, but far less friendly and more likely to chop your head off." He said with a chuckle. It was odd hearing his gruff voice laugh. Gye could just see his white beard through his visor.

"Everyone be more careful. Move on. Fifteen minutes have elapsed." The Captain said.

Gye swam towards where the waterfall was feeding the lake. Elicia wheezed into his intercom.

"You see those… rock formations… under the entry point?" She said between wheezes.

"Yeah. They look like tree rings."

"Around… twelve million… years old!" She said. She caught up to him and finally caught her breath.

"That fish directly ahead looks like a spear with flippers!" Molly said.

"Now that's an interesting one. There's a few of them swimming together! Perhaps we should watch to see if they turn on each other like human beings do. Here's a life tip, young ones: the way to win is to be the first one to turn on the others." Elicia said. Gye was too enamored with the sights to pay attention to what she was saying.

The creature in question did, indeed, look like a spear with flippers. It looked like a ridiculously elongated salmon.

"Want to dive deeper?" Molly asked.

"I'll make my way gradually." He said, distracted by the beauty of the sight. Molly shrugged— a difficult gesture to communicate through a biohazard swimsuit— and swam off.

Gye stopped for a moment to admire the view. Light filtered through the lake's surface and danced down into the darkness below. The calm inpouring of water from the waterfall soothed his soul. It was all so gentle... or so it seemed. Gye knew that the lake was filled to the brim with creatures whose only pleasure was in surviving those above them in the food chain and preying on those below them. Not unlike himself, Gye reflected.

"Twenty five minutes remaining. Yes, I know I'm late." The Captain said.

The Captain swam close to Gye and pointed down at an odd colony of creatures floating just below them.

"See those dome-looking floaters? Reminds me of a strawberry bomb in the war." Captain Walker said.

"Strawberry bomb?" Gye asked quizzically.

"So called because they looked like strawberries. We military types are a creative bunch, I know. But they would drop a few of these some miles apart over an area, and each strawberry bomb would slowly descend and fire out smaller bombs through many tilted exits, like the seeds on a real strawberry. The strawberry bomb would whirl in circles as it descended, so the bombs would fly out over a wide area in a massive circle of destruction. Quite the sight, really. Struck fear and shrapnel into the heart of many an enemy in my day." He said, reminiscing. Gye had a closer look at the creature— much less pretty and slimier than a strawberry, really— and then drifted away.

Jane swam close to him and pointed below.

"I saw something moving down there. Want to go after it?" She asked.

"Alright. But you're leading me to my death and you survive, I'm definitely going to haunt you from beyond the grave." He said jokingly.

"Mutually so." She said with a laugh. They descended together.

The goggles switched to night vision as it became progressively darker.

"Look!" Jane exclaimed, pointing at a spot on the lake floor. Gye had to scan for several seconds before seeing the movement she was referring to.

There were several frog-like creatures jumping on the lake floor. One of them was the size of Gye's helmet, and it was chasing down an elusive fish. It gobbled it up with one flick of the tongue. It was plump, with milky-white skin (or so it appeared through the goggles) and eyes that looked like those of a doll with googly eyes. Gye laughed at the sight of it.

"Careful, those are probably poisonous to the touch." Jane said through the intercom.

"I wasn't planning on touching them!" Gye said.

"Well, you are the mischievous type."

"I just can't stop myself sometimes. I was meeting with a... client... once, and one of his lackeys said something about being late to a coincidence. I thought that was ridiculous, so we argued about whether it was possible to be late to a coincidence or not for about ten minutes before it came to blows. I'm not exactly proud of that one. Cost me a good payment too." Gye said.

"My life has been so much more... tame, than yours. I must say I'm jealous."

"This kind of life aint for everyone. It's only ten percent looking cool and ninety percent pain." He said.

The Captain's voice interrupted over the intercom.

"Fifteen minutes remaining."

"We'd better head back." Jane said. Her voice sounded disappointed.

"Hang on, there's some flower-looking thingies on the lake floor. Here, let me get a bouquet for you." Gye said.

"Oh, please don't disturb the flora! That would be barbaric." She said. But she swam closer to have a look anyways.

"They're blue, just like your suit color." Gye noticed. He reached out and plucked one from the group.

"It wouldn't be a crime to take just one." He said. She stayed motionless and silent for a few seconds.

"I just specifically asked you not to do that. Do you ever listen?" She said, obviously annoyed.

"What's wrong with taking an underwater flower?"

"Everything! You're ripping it out of its habitat for no reason! Well, a rather stupid one. I thought maybe you could chill out and stop hitting on me for like five seconds, but apparently not."

"Well,—"

"We'd best be getting back." She interrupted abruptly, taking the flower out of his hand and placing it back where they had found it. She darted upwards and he followed behind. They went the whole way back in silence. Gye broke off from her and sped up to the surface alone.

He broke the surface just as the captain was ordering everyone to return. He took off his helmet and noticed Ray standing, propped up agains the rover. He made his way towards him and realized he was smoking a cigar.

"Oh, you're back early." Ray said apologetically.

"Where did you even get that?" Gye asked.

"I had these cigars smuggled in from South America. I hid them behind a panel in a compartment I designed specifically for this purpose."

"Of course you did. That smells disgusting." Gye replied.

"Yeah, yeah, but a man's gotta have his vices to stay sane. I had hoped to smoke this in peace. Perhaps you can keep it a secret for me?" Ray asked. He coughed violently just then into his sleeve.

"If you don't succumb to lung cancer along the way, sure. But if you do, be advised that the cat would be very much out of the bag."

Ray laughed and put away his cigar, fanning the air around him to clear away the smoke. The others surfaced and made their way towards the rover.

Royce Alavandréz appeared from the other side of the rover with a chef's hat on.

"You're all just in time! We'll be eating outside. I thought a picnic might be just the thing for us." He said.

"That sounds splendid! I can smell the onions from here." Captain Walker said.

"Those are mushrooms, actually." Royce said with an offhand air of mischievousness. Gye chalked it up to the man's eccentricities.

Gye hadn't noticed how hungry he was until the mention of food. He made his way to the prepared table along with the others and sat between Elicia and Royce.

Royce Alavandréz turned to the grill beside him and grabbed a spatula, which he used to transfer the seared mushrooms into the soup. He added a few more spices and then dished out a bowl of the soup for each person at the table. While they had been gone Royce had also prepared a few other items for their feast. There were brown, soft rolls which softly reflected the world around them— like those in a bakery window— as well as lemon cakes and one white mushy substance Gye couldn't identify.

Gye turned to Elicia.

"Can I help you get something?" He asked.

"Yes," she chuckled, "I'll have the Spanish. The cook, I mean."

Gye laughed at the joke and handed her a roll. In truth, he could not tell whether or not Elicia was being serious. She always spoke of pursuing life's pleasures above all else, but was it all a charade? Gye was genuinely curious. Was it possible to lead a life devoted to succumbing to every primal desire that flashed across the mind?

"Why all the food?" Jane asked.

"It is… a celebration. In my own way, and on the wrong day according to tradition, I celebrate *Dia de los Muertos*, or day of the dead. I do not observe it closely, as I have been an American citizen for a decade now, but I like to… spice things up, I believe is the expression, yes? I like to spice things up." He said, his Spanish accent coming through stronger than usual.

"What is this, um, day of the dead?" Gye asked.

"To put it quickly, we celebrate the lives of those who have passed. Although I have seen it celebrated much differently in America, where it seems to be another excuse for sorority sisters to wear revealing skeleton costumes and attract men at parties." Royce said.

"You shouldn't talk so much, Royce," Elicia chimed in, "it makes you less attractive when you get a bit sexist."

Captain Walker uttered a quick prayer for the food and they dug in. Jane was seated on the opposite side of the elongated table from Gye. He sighed to himself. More than likely, he thought, he had damaged his chances with her irreversibly.

He slurped up the soup with astonishing gusto. It was creamy and spicy at the same time, a combination Gye had not previously thought possible. Although he was no chef, Gye could identify the onion, garlic, rosemary, squash, and butternut which permeated this elixir of flavor. It seemed to melt into oblivion on his tongue, teasing each taste bud and leaving them wanting more.

"Wow, this soup is spectacular!" Molly said, dipping a roll into the delightful concoction. Steam rose from the soup and reminded Gye oddly of campfires he had had as a boy, surviving in the woods. He remembered teaming up with a pack of other boys to increase their chances of survival, but it had all fallen apart over the affections of some girl. He remembered how their uneasy alliance had been so easily shattered, and he had been left alone again. The girl just stole their supplies in the night and ran off anyways, so the whole conflict was moot. People are so easily driven to do stupid things, Gye reflected. None more so than himself.

"Are you quite enjoying this delectable meal, Gye Storm?" Elicia asked.

"It's so good that I would trade half of the make-out sessions I've had in the last year for another bowl of it. Basically I can't get enough of the stuff." Gye said. Elicia chuckled.

"Really? I would've thought of you as the kind of man who put food on the second rung of the ladder of natural urges." She said.

"Ordinarily yes, but have you *tasted* this?"

"It's simply to die for. A strange expression, that. *To die for.* There's very little in this world that I would die for, truly. Once your heart beats its last beat, you're done. You only get this one shot at life. That's why I've never understood people who do things like dying for a cause. It seems so perfectly ridiculous, if you think about it, to give up your life for anything at all. Is there anything you're willing to end your existence for, Gye?" She asked. Her voice was taking on a very slight slurring quality. Gye took little note of it, instead noticing a particularly wavy cloud floating across the sky on the whispered breeze of a word from God.

"Hmm? Oh. To die for something… I can't remember who said it, but that reminds me of a saying from an army general. He said, 'the point of war is not to die for your country. The point of war is to make some other poor bastard die for *his* country'. I see things like that." Gye replied.

"How do you mean?"

"Well, if you think of it as *dying*, that is an insane thought, like, who would do that? It's *insane*. But if you flip it around," Gye said, gesturing with his fingers in a flipping around motion (which he found surprisingly difficult to concentrate on and had to repeat a few times to get it right) "it makes sense. My sister, I would've made some other poor bastard die for her." Gye said. He heard the others buzzing around in conversation like a hive of bees. Buzz buzz buzz buzz buzz. How odd they sounded.

"I let my second husband die, actually," Elicia mused, "well, it's not as bad as it sounds. More like I just wasn't paying attention when he had a heart attack. I didn't love him, though. My first marriage was the only one I did for romance. All the others were… strategic." She said.

She might have continued talking after that, she might not have. Gye didn't know. The world glued itself together and was so close together, so far apart at the same time; it didn't make any sense, but then again, perhaps the point was that it didn't need to make sense.

Gye stretched his arms, leaning back in the white plastic fold-up chair as he did so. The tablecloth over the matching plastic table was also white. The texture was square upon square upon square upon square… and… moving? Gye blinked the illusion away. He glanced at the others. He noticed that Royce had not actually eaten any of his soup, and was casually watching the others as he bit into a roll. What was going on?

"Look at the pictures I took!" Anthony shouted, showing off several horribly composed and framed photos on his camera. No one replied to his exclamations. That poser never learned when to shut up…

Suddenly everything was in black and white. No, that wasn't right. Everything was in such sharp color, all so suddenly, the contrast dilating beyond control… the colors moved in waves, expanding outward and contracting endlessly inward. The universe split, and it tasted of raspberries. Of course! Gye had the mental image of someone swinging a string with something tied to the end, swinging it around and around faster and faster until it seemed to be a solid object.

Perhaps that was the true nature of solid matter. It was not truly solid, no, it was merely a wave, oscillating so quickly that it seemed to be solid…

Gye noticed Molly painting an invisible picture with invisible brushes and paint. Suddenly he saw that she was conversing with DaVinci, and he was showing her the finer aspects of painting. Good for her!

Elicia was mumbling something to herself, Jane was giggling uncontrollably, Ray was trying to build a mini tower out of everyone's spoons, Captain Walker was sleeping, but Anthony… Anthony was screaming, running back and forth, screaming about the giant human finger and how it was trying to poke his soul until it bled. As if Anthony had any soul to begin with.

And Gye… Gye was not there. He looked down at his own body and was sad to find it nonexistent. He could see the ground below his perspective where his feet should have been. He tried to pass his hands in front of his face, but there was nothing there, nothing there… it was so freeing, to not exist. Gye sighed comfortably. There was no more pressure anymore, no body to tack him onto the earth like a tack into a map…

Suddenly, Molly grabbed his hand, and he was real again. His body came back, and he could feel her hands enclosing his. Reality was such a drag.

"Do you hear that? The music? Or is it music? You know, that… *sound*. The way everything *is*. Ah, oh, it's so beautiful! That's Bach, isn't it? The trees are vibrating. I feel them pulsing, it's a symphony, look! The trees are the woodwinds, the rocks near the beach are the percussion, the rover is the brass section… and we are the choir! Oh, sing with me Gye, sing with me!" She said.

He never got the chance to sing with her, however. A cloud of darkness swept over the place and faded him to black. A painful flash overtook it all, and the blurry faces of his father, his mother, and his sister, all dead, swept across the vision. A tear fell forcefully from his cheek as he was, for the thousandth time, caught back up in the emotion and despair of the moment.

Thankfully this vision of loss was soon eclipsed by an enormous drowsiness. Oh, the bliss of sleep. He dreamed of white plastic, white plastic chairs.

CHAPTER 11
THE AFTERMATH

There were clouds, white clouds. Gye was falling through them. No, wait, he was being sucked up through them.

With a plopping sound, Gye was yanked back to consciousness. He felt a sharp pang of pain in his temple— the onset of a vicious headache. Why did he have a headache? What happened? Oh yeah, Royce had served them soup with psychedelic mushrooms in it. Uggggh.

Captain Walker was snoring loudly. Gye rubbed his eyes and sat up. Oh, too quickly. Much too quickly. His headache intensified as the blood rushed from his head. He was sitting in the field of grass some twenty feet from the rover and the white plastic picnic table. His eyes wandered over the lake, over the waterfall, over the mountain range in the background, and found themselves resting on his companions.

There was Molly, sitting up with a dazed expression on her face. Captain Walker was snoring, Ray was rubbing his temples, Elicia was lying face-down on the picnic table… then there was Anthony.

Anthony was sitting up against a leg of the rover, sobbing into his hands. Jane was sitting next to him, trying to comfort him, but he was in agony.

"I saw… terrible things." Anthony said.

Gye stood up slowly and made his way in their direction.

"Darkness… so much darkness. A man, a laughing man, with half a clown face and the other half a skeleton, laughing, screeching at me to die, to die… oh god."

Jane noticed Gye's approach.

"He seemed to have had what they call a 'bad trip'. Different people's bodies respond differently to psychedelic substances." Jane said.

"I watched a documentary about that once," Gye said, "what this stuff does. If you do it repeatedly it can really mess up your brain. Someone needs to keep an eye on that shifty Spanish cook." He said, plopping back down on the grass near them.

Anthony started shivering.

"Why do I feel so cold? My heart has lost the will to survive. Ah." He dissolved into a sea of trembling fear.

"Help me get him inside." Jane said. Gye nodded and they propped him up and brought him in. They laid him down on his bed gently, wrapping him in blankets as he shivered. He mumbled something indistinct before nodding off into an uneasy slumber.

They found Royce sitting comfortably in a swivel chair in the room across the hall from the one Gye shared with Anthony. He was looking out the window, calmly, with a mug of hot cocoa in his hand. He had a cheeky grin on his face, looking on with those dark brown eyes of his. He nodded and bobbed his sweeping black locks of hair as he did so.

"Quite a lovely view, isn't it?" Royce said, glancing outside.

"You have a lot of explaining to do." Jane said furiously.

"What is there to explain? I found some delightful mushrooms that happened to have some… psychedelic properties." He said.

"My friend had to live out a horrific nightmare so you could get your laughs at our expense? What in seven hells is wrong with you?" She demanded.

"Take it easy, will you? It was just his imagination. He'll be fine when he wakes up."

Jane put her hands on her hips and stormed out of the room.

"How was your experience, Gye?" Royce said, sipping from his mug of hot cocoa.

"Luckily Anthony was the only one forced to experience a hellish nightmare. For me it wasn't so bad. But I'm not sure I'll be able to eat your food anymore." Gye said.

"Oh? Fine, I will only do this the one time, I swear."

"You'd better believe it. You try to screw with my brain again, I will break you. If we weren't locked in this moving tin can together I would have thrown you out already. But it just so happens I'm trying to clear up my name with the feds because I rather like living in America, and I'd like to legally stay here." Gye said.

"I love it when people spill information when they're angry. It makes them so much more predictable." Royce responded.

"People like you are why I have trust issues." Gye said.

"You wouldn't have issues at all if you just stopped trusting people altogether. Consider this a life lesson, Gye Storm." Royce said.

Gye rolled his eyes and walked out.

Elicia met him in the common area near the entrance to the rover.

"Wasn't that a fun trip? I haven't done anything that extreme in over a year!" She said excitedly.

"You often get poisoned by crazy Spanish cooks with psychedelic mushrooms?"

"Believe it or not, this is at least the second time."

"At least?"

"My memory gets hazy in places." She said with a wink.

Someone had woken Captain Walker, and he waltzed into the room lazily.

"I don't know about the rest of you but that was the best sleep I've had in decades. Melatonin's got nothing on that stuff, I'll tell you one thing." He said. His gruff voice was cheerier than usual and he stroked his beard as he spoke.

"I've never done anything like that before, it was very... odd." Molly said shyly.

"Never?" Elicia asked incredulously. Molly nodded and Elicia laughed in response.

"I could teach you a thing or two about livin', girlie. I haven't felt so alive in a very long time!" Elicia said.

"I don't know about the rest of you, but I'm not exactly okay with having been poisoned with something I didn't consent to. That's probably illegal, at least it should be." Ray said, stepping in.

"Ah, speak of the devil." Captain Walker said as Royce Alavandréz entered.

"You know, I raced horses in Spain when I was at university. My nickname was 'The Spanish Devil'. What a strange coincidence that you should mention it now." Royce mused.

"Well, Spanish Devil, I owe you thanks for the best nap of my life. As a military man I am strictly opposed to recreational usage of… things like that. It is improper and immature. I reprimand you for imposing this on us without our consent, and when we trusted you as our cook, no less." Captain Walker said.

"The only thing I imposed on you was a good time, Captain." Royce said with a devilish grin.

"Not on Anthony, or so I hear."

"Ah, most regrettable, that. But he needed to be shaken up a little. He was one cocky son of a gun. Hopefully that problem will be a little tempered now."

"You can't just manipulate people like that!" Molly said.

"Oh, the trespasser has something to say, eh?" Royce said derisively.

"Oh please. I saw an opportunity to chase my dreams and I took it. Can you fault me for that?" Molly retorted.

"Please, we are straying from the matter at hand. Royce, henceforth, I order you as your captain not to put any mind-altering substances in anything you serve to me or the crew for the duration of this voyage. Are we quite clear?"

Royce sighed.

"You Americans with your puritanical ways never cease to kill my buzz. But ay, I understand. You'll have no more good times from me."

The conversation then turned to the rest of the voyage. Anthony eventually rejoined them sheepishly, refusing to look at Royce directly but saying very little.

Vaurien Kane was dressed in a British peacoat, dull green vest, black dress pants, and black top hat. He walked with a cane in his hand and a monocle on his left eye, although he needed neither of them. They were more for appearances, really. And appearances were everything in the Order of Fire and Blood.

He strolled casually down the street, watching the plebeian people and cars pass by, knowing and suspecting nothing of the god among men that he was. Ozymandias strolled in their midsts, and the people wept not, though they looked upon his works without knowledge. Soon, they would. Soon they would look upon his works and despair.

But first he had to get into the meeting. Due to the necessity of secrecy, they could not hide their headquarters in plain sight.

Vaurien Kane casually strolled into the darkened alleyway, the buzzing sound of the nest of rats that was the city fading in his perception. He made his way to an old dumpster that was pressed against the brick wall that lined the alleyway. He looked all around him to check that he was alone before reaching into the neck of his vest to retrieve a special necklace. It was a triangle ruby with gold extrusions in a particular pattern on the opposite side. He pulled it from the gold chain around his neck and placed it just so on a bumper sticker that had been placed seemingly haphazardly on the side of the dumpster. The bumper sticker was an icon of a flame, with the words "Isaiah 24:4-6" on it. There was a clicking sound and the dumpster sprung away from the wall, tilting outwards like a heavy door from the bricks. Behind it was revealed a humble, thick wooden door with a brass, keyless handle. Vaurien opened the door, stepped inside, and heard the distinct rumble as the dumpster closed off the entrance behind him.

It was dark in the hallway before the old fluorescent lights flickered to life. The walls were peeling, old wood with chipped paint. The paint had fallen off over many, many years, revealing the many layers of paint that had over time covered the halls. Now it was decrepit.

Tap, tap, tap was the sound of Vaurien's cane as he walked down the hallway. The old wood floor creaked under his weight, and the lights flickered ominously as he walked.

As he walked he could hear the sound of the ambient din from around the next corner. Doubtless many members of this secret order had already arrived. He reached the end of the hallway and turned the corner.

Ahead was the amphitheater of the order. It was three quarters of a circle, with three rows of seats around, the ones in the back a level higher than the middle, and the middle row a level higher than the inside ring. These rings sat perhaps fifty people. The stage in the very middle was empty except for the dais at the noncircular part of the amphitheater. On the dais was a long stone block that served as a desk for the eight Lords of the Order who sat in the places of honor there. In the center, with four of the Lords on each side, sat the High Lord of the order. The High Lord was the priest of the order, the bridge between the members of the sacred order and the supernatural.

There was a dull roar among those present. There as a noticeable drop in conversation as Vaurien entered. He was a rising star in the order, and people were sure to notice his presence in here.

The place was dimly lit and smelled mildly of rot. There were no windows; the only light source were eight large candles placed equidistant from each other in the inner circle. Past the outer circle each of the eight directions branched off into locked doors. The oldness of the place was an illusion for the benefit of the more gullible members of the order. In fact, the building itself was state-of-the art. It was said that the Order of Fire and Blood would rise from the ashes like a Phoenix when its champion had been revealed. That was, in fact, why the headquarters of the order had been dubbed *The Phoenix*. And

Vaurien Kane intended to be their champion. He took his seat in the second ring, near the middle.

The High Lord- a fat, bearded old black man by the name of Ashara Kimeno— rose to bring the meeting to order. The room instantly grew silent. Each of the Lords at the table wore black chain mail and a large pin— which was either a flame or a drop of blood depending on how you looked at it— but the High Lord was the only one who wore a crimson cloak announcing his position. Ashara Kimeno began the incantation.

"Ancient spirits, we rise as one this day to further your will for this planet. Guide us, give us strength. Teach us your ways and give wisdom to our spirits. Give us the power to bathe the earth in a sea of fire and blood as justice for their sins, as you have commanded. Your servants do your bidding." He said. Ashara Kimeno then took a blue dagger to his palm and sliced. When there was enough blood on his palm he placed it on the book in front of him— which only the High Lord was permitted to read— and shouted that the meeting had begun.

Each of the Lords then, in turn, spoke of matters of importance to the order and its aims. Vaurien aspired to be a Lord of the Order. These men in charge were shadows of the men who had come before them. They knew nothing of real power, no, they merely repeated the words they had learned from the greats who had come before. Vaurien Kane knew that he could return the order to greatness, if he could just get the chance. But as of yet he could not become a Lord, for it was difficult to do so. To become a Lord of the Order, one had to choose a weapon from times of old— spear, sword, mace, axe— and fight and kill the fire lizard in the spike pit. The fire lizard was said to be a descendant of the dragons from China, but no one had ever actually seen one spit fire.

But that wasn't the hardest part, truth be told. In order to take the challenge in the spike pit, one had to first be found worthy by the High Lord. This was a rather political process, and no one had been allowed to fight the fire lizard in the spike pit in over a decade. Vaurien knew that he had to get some sort of leverage over the High Lord in order to achieve his goal.

One of the lords, who seemed as ancient as time itself, was speaking when Vaurien tuned back in.

"The most pressing threat," he said, somehow still able to speak even though he looked about two and a half eternities old, "to the Order these days is the media. The *Daily* newspaper has got one of their journalists sniffing around us." He said.

You fool, Vaurien wanted to say, you're wrong. So wrong about it all, so weak, so unable to see the magnitude of the threat that would soon be upon the Order. If the drone were to be recovered, the mockers and scoffers of the world would use it to proclaim vicious lies unto the nations. The Order would shrivel and die under the weight of that 'discovery', and the Ancients would be mocked. Vaurien would not let the drone be recovered.

He listened through an hour and a half more of tedious discussion before the meeting as near a close. When there was finally a lull in the business of the Order, Vaurien raised his hand to speak. If he couldn't be a Lord and rouse the Order to new glory himself, perhaps he could raise the issue here.

Instead, the High Lord ignored him and pressed on with another twenty minutes of tediousness and irrelevancy. Vaurien rolled his eyes and sat back in the oaken chair. Perhaps the Order had already doomed itself into laxness.

When the High Lord finally ordered the meeting adjourned, Vaurien waited for most of the other members to gradually file out before making his way towards the High Lord.

There was a gaggle of two or three sycophants at the heels of the High Lord, as there always was whenever the opportunity presented itself. Vaurien waited patiently before he could speak to the leader alone.

"High Lord Ashara Kimeno." Vaurien greeted. It was customary to greet the High Lord only by his title and last name, but Vaurien used the man's first name as the slightest form of disrespect towards him. It was noticeable enough to be interpreted as intended, but subtle enough not to result in trouble for Vaurien.

"Vaurien." The High Lord responded in kind. His crimson cloak shifted with the man's enormous weight.

"As I have said before, we are drastically underestimating the threat of the effort to recover the drone I mentioned-"

"-And as *I* mentioned," The High Lord interrupted, "you are wrong on that count. Now unless you have some pressing new business, I must be on my way."

Vaurien collected himself before responding.

"Well, there is the matter of the fire lizard challenge-"

"-I said *new* business, Vaurien. We've been over this. I have not been led to allow you to take the sacred challenge as of this time. Goodbye." Ashara Kimeno interrupted again.

Vaurien Kane could only watch, flustered, as the man walked out, his massive black chain mail clinking as he hefted his weight out of the room. He just wouldn't see.

Vaurien was left alone in the room. It was eerily quiet with all the members having left. He eyed the stone table and the place of the High Lord in the middle. He double-checked to make sure everyone had left before slowly sitting himself down in the sacred seat. It might have been sacrilege, but he didn't care. This seat would soon be his, he vowed.

As he sat there, hands on the table, he grabbed the book of the High Lord and held it until the blood had dripped from the cover and onto the floor. He took the ice-blue dagger— from its ornamentational place on the table— and cut his own palm. Blood seeped out of the cut, a crimson wave drawing the sandy beach that was his palm. He stared at his life's blood for a moment.

He placed his blood on the cover of the book, watching it smear where the High Lord's and been, and Vaurien Kane laughed. He would rise, he would conquer, he would prevail.

CHAPTER 12
GIANT DRAGONFLIES

"Perhaps here I see the crime scene
Where someone was given a toxin
Or suffocated until all they had
To breathe with was oxygen." Anthony recited.

"What's that?" Ray asked.

"A little something called culture. Poetry." Anthony snarked.

"Didn't take him long to get back to his usual ornery self, now did it?" Elicia said as an aside to Gye.

"Unfortunately not." Gye sighed.

Captain Walker came down the ladder in slow, methodical steps and wheezed as he plopped down on the deck. He was a vestige of his former fit self after years of being out of the military.

He sat down at the large table next to Elicia. Jane was in a single couch chair near the heater in the corner— it was a cold morning—

reading a book, and the rest of them, with the new inclusion of Captain Walker at the table, were having a chat.

Royce bursted through the kitchen door with arms full of plates.

"I have made.. an apology, here," he said, passing out a plate to each person at the table, "to make up for what I did to you all at the lake. I am truly sorry, you see. It was just that those mushrooms looked to be such a delicacy, and I couldn't resist trying them out... so here I am, please accept this treat as a token of my apology to you." Royce Alavandréz said. He brought out a dish filled with steaming apple fritters. He placed it in the middle of the table and passed one out to everyone.

"Please enjoy," he said, taking a bite out of one himself.

"Gye, I'm designating you as our taster. If nothing terrible happens to him, I'll have a bite." Captain Walker said. He seemed a bit more chipper than usual this morning.

"Please, you insult me!" Royce said.

Molly bit into hers immediately.

"Mmm, this is really good!" She said. It was a pointed action of forgiveness on her part of Royce. He took it as such.

"You made them in the french style, *au mode!*" He exclaimed happily. It seemed he had quite forgotten the events that had happened to him with the mushrooms, or at least willed it out of his mind. Nevertheless he waited almost a full minute to see if any ill effects beset his companions before digging in himself. He closed his eyes as he savored the rich flavor.

The others, including Gye, dug into their fritters with gusto. They tasted of nutmeg and cinnamon in particular, balancing out the tartness of the preserved apples.

Gye noticed that Jane, sitting alone in the corner, had not had one, nor even noticed what had gone on at the table. Gye grabbed a plate, placed a fritter on it, and made his way over towards her.

She shut the book hurriedly and tried to casually hide it from his view.

"Here, I thought you might want one." He said, handing the plate to her.

"Oh, thank you." She said distractedly, her voice a pitch higher than usual.

"What're you reading there?" Gye asked.

"A book." She replied coyly. Gye feigned disinterest, waited a few seconds, and suddenly grabbed the book and quickly walked away.

"Hey!" Jane Silver exclaimed, indignant.

Gye started reading the title and description out loud.

"*Away On a Breath*, the romantic story of a couple who fell in love as children but were separated when she moved away, and so they spent the rest of their lives searching for each other, the ones they knew to be their perfect soul mates. They have several near-miss meetings; once they would have been blissfully reunited if he had stayed in a coffee shop just ten minutes longer. Find out what happens next." Gye read.

"Ugh, are you done? Give it back." She said, trying to play it cool.

"Surprisingly interesting premise, thought I didn't think you were into this sort of thing." He said.

Elicia was the only one who noticed what was going on (the others were engrossed in food and conversation) and she looked on with a mischievous grin.

Jane rolled her eyes.

"Real life romance is just a distraction that lasts for months or years. Reading about romance is a distraction that lasts for just a few days if you're a fast reader. And it gets the idea out of my head, to tell you the truth. Better to waste a few hours than a few years." She said.

"Years? How dull!" Elicia said.

"Dull? Hardly!" Jane replied.

"I assume you have experience to the contrary then, eh?" Elicia asked.

"I had a romance of years, as a matter of fact. Or at least I thought it was a romance at the time. We broke up when I walked in on him with my best friend. Turned out he had started cheating on me just six weeks after we started. Since then I've seen the truth much more clearly, that it's a waste of time to chase after people because people are invariably liars." Jane said.

"Not all people-" Gye began.

"-That's what everyone says, yet that is what a liar would say, isn't it?" Jane said. She kept the passion from creeping into her voice.

"But you said it wasn't dull, dear." Elicia said.

"Oh, it wasn't dull, from my petty little perspective of naive trust. You can have a good time at many things even if they're self-destructive." Jane said.

"Amen to that." Gye said, looking to the side casually as he took another bite of the delicious apple fritter. He was trying to keep this conversation from ballooning into an argument.

"Quite true, my dear. It just reinforces the fact that life must be pursued in the moment. Let people take you places you want to go and drop them when they stop moving in the right direction. Seek the pleasures of life and you will find happiness." Elicia said with a nod.

"I hear you over there, Elicia. Are you filling those kids heads with them fool notions of yours? Don't listen to a word she says. She's a hedonist through and through, let me tell you." He said.

Elicia raised an eyebrow but said nothing to disagree.

"Thank you Royce, for this lovely treat. I'm sure its pushed your grievance out of our minds." Captain Walker said before standing.

"Gye, with me. We need to confirm our destination."

Gye nodded, placed the plate on the small table next to the couch, and followed Captain Walker up to the second floor.

They climbed the ladder in silence— if you could call it silence, with all of Captain Walker's wheezing.

"The Sonic Spectroscopic Intervalometer, or SSI for short. I need you to work your magic on it and make sure the drone's last signals were coming from where we think they were coming from." Captain Walker aid, looking out the window at the mountain in question.

As Gye set to work, Captain Walker paced back and forth.

"You see that monstrosity of a mountain right there? With all the ice at the top? Jane and Anthony tell me that's probably got a great deal to do with this freakish forest. I didn't understand much of what they said, obviously, but I bet we're in for some surprises." Captain Walker said.

Gye listened distractedly as he manipulated the controls beside the screen.

"You see all these green markings here? They're definitely concentrated on that mountain… they're concentrated vertically. That means the drone must have stayed in place pretty near the top and remained transmitting for at least a day before going down."

"What does that mean?"

"Aren't you familiar with the Kessler effect? No? Imagine the Doppler effect but mapped to a three dimensional object, which is… Oh, never mind. I'm guessing it means the drone… crashed into the mountain, I'm assuming, and for some reason wasn't able to get back up into the air. That's good news if you want to recover data from it. If it was transmitting, it's likely fairly intact."

"So it's towards that dreaded mountain, then?" Captain Walker asked.

"It looks that way." Gye said.

Darkness swept over the scene. The edges flashed white, and the dream melted into Gye's consciousness.

It was the same familiar scene he always dreamed. His family, on that one fateful day. Lost to him forever. Their blurry faces shattered into mere feelings of loss and despair. Why did life love its cruel quirks so much? He didn't know. With a shudder he awoke, sweat pouring down his brow. Revenge was not yet his.

"The forest is thinning out, it looks like." Anthony observed, looking out the window.

"Hopefully that means we can go a little faster, without having to dodge trees all the time." Elicia said.

"Captain Walker's been getting lazy lately anyway and just plowing them down. Good thing I reinforced the frontal plates." Ray said.

"Yes, good. You know what else is good? I can probably count this expedition as community service, now that I think about it. I'll be finally free." Elicia said.

"Why do you have to do community service? Did you do something?" Gye asked.

"Ah, yes. Misunderstanding with the cops involving financial fraud. I got off really easy, actually." Elicia said.

"I think community service is lovely. You get to help people and protect the environment if you go recycling." Molly said.

"Oh yes," Elicia said, "they're desperate, hurting people who need our help. So in other words, screw 'em." She said.

"I would be disgusted if I remembered how to be surprised with you." Jane said to her.

"What? It's only community service. Community service is the art of spreading as many pauses as possible over as little work as possible while still fulfilling the minimum requirement for a tax write off. Or a lighter sentence, in my case." Elicia said.

"Maybe to you. But-" Molly started.

Suddenly there was a great whirring sound, like a small helicopter had whizzed past the rover.

"What was that?" Jane asked.

They all rushed to the windows to look out. The rover lulled to a halt.

"There! Look ahead, on that flower- that thing's the size of a grand piano!- oh my god, it's a giant dragonfly!" Anthony exclaimed.

"Look, there's more on the other flowers! We're waltzing through a field of them! My goodness, what an amazing sight." Jane said.

The rover slowly creeped to the center of the field.

There was one blue one which buzzed furiously above a flower, sending dust and particles streaming through the air. It's eyes looked almost orange with the sunlight hitting them directly. They looked rather terrifying if one were to look at them directly in the eye. The black detailing on the creature's long tail made it look almost like an

Italian sports car with armor. Its wings looked like stained glass windows, with black honeycombs encompassing each window to the environment.

"The oxygen level in the atmosphere must be at least thirty percent here for these *Meganeura* to exist." Jane observed.

"Those two are fighting!" Gye exclaimed, pointing towards what he saw.

There was another blue one and a green one at half-tree height in the air, buzzing around each other and nipping whenever they found an opportunity. The object of their battle seemed to be a duller blue dragonfly, presumably a mate they were competing for.

Green swerved under the left of blue, coming up to bite at blue's abdomen. But Blue flipped itself mid-air to land behind Green and bit onto Green's tail. There was an audible shriek as Green struggled to dislodge Blue, but to no avail. Green began to bleed out from the wound at its tail. Finally the part of the tail Blue was holding on to tore off altogether. Green fell to the ground and twitched until it died.

"I think I might be sick." Molly said.

"This is fascinating!" Jane said.

An hour or so later, they were munching on subway sandwiches and watching the view.

"Time to move along now," Captain Walker said, raising his bulk with effort from the single couch in the corner.

"But I'm almost finished with my painting!" Molly exclaimed. She was sitting by the window with a paintbrush in hand, painting onto a paper-sized canvas the scene of a giant dragonfly perching on an oversized flower, looking out onto a scene filled with other amazing creatures— Gye specifically noticed a line of lady bugs that looked oddly like a line of red cars in traffic.

"My, that's lovely!" Elicia said, coming for a closer look.

"Jovanović would be proud." Anthony said.

"This is amazing art." Gye chimed in, looming over her shoulder.

Molly continued, adding some detail to the wings and the clouds.

"To create art is an admirable pursuit. It is remarkable that art exists, I think, in an evolutionary standpoint." Elicia said.

"How do you mean?" Ray asked her.

"Art does not provide food like hunting, does not gather water, does not store food for winter, and does not keep predators away. And yet the appreciation of art is as programmed into our brains as walking." Elicia said.

"Social utility. As highly social mammals, art can be looked at as a social contribution, which is an ability that provides a leg up over competitors. Survival of the fittest isn't always about the strongest, but the most adaptable to change. If the fittest members of the population are the ones who cohere well in their society, then the ability to create and appreciate art becomes a social boon, and ergo an aid to reproductive chances." Anthony said as if reciting from a sociology textbook.

"Pictures can be pretty, sure, but I don't sympathize with the desire to spend time creating things that have no inherent use." Jane said.

Molly bit her lip and frowned slightly. Gye mused.

"If something contributes to people's happiness, doesn't that make it useful enough?" Gye said.

"Unusually, I agree with Gye," Anthony said, "even from a rather dull, unartistic standpoint such as the one Jane has suggested, altruistic behavior such as creating things for the enjoyment of others is to be admired." He said.

Jane seemed taken aback slightly that Anthony had not sided with her. Gye smiled vaguely, pleased to see a rift in their friendship. He knew that that was a selfish thought, but he accepted it nonetheless.

"From my, as you said, *dull* standpoint," Jane said condescendingly, "the creation of art would not be interpreted as altruistic behavior that is done for the benefit of the individual's society. No, no. It would be rightly interpreted as done for the benefit of the individual to gain social standing against the others in her— ahem, in *the individual's*— society." Jane said pointedly.

"I'll tell you what I think," Gye said, interrupting the catty conflict with a bit of honesty, "some things don't need to be explained by science. It's important to leave some frontiers unconquered, because they're worth more to us as human beings when they're things we can aspire to understand than as things which are quantified scientifically. Honestly, who cares about the evolutionary advantages or societal whatever of art? It's not important to me or to most people. What's important is that art inspires us and gives us beauty in our lives that otherwise wouldn't have been there." Gye said.

Jane shrugged and looked out the window. The group lapsed into silence after that. Gye thought about Jane's reaction and concluded that art must have been something Jane had desired to find in herself, but never developed a skill for, and so she attempted to malign it out of her life. How sad.

Gye had no artistic talent, although he was musical to some extent, being able to play the acoustic guitar rather ably. As someone with a hard past, he found art to be a respite from the dullness and the harshness of existence. Art represented the good side of humanity that he had so often been unable to see in his life.

By then they had slowly creeped out of the field and onto drying dirt ground. Ahead the incline of the mountain loomed, but between them and the sloping base was a snaking canyon. It was full of dirt and warmth— not nearly as scorched looking as the Grand Canyon, but with a recognizable similarity.

"Through the canyon and up the mountain." Ray said, looking ahead.

The field slowly gave way to reddish-brown, cracked dirt. The *Venture* rover slowly made its way down one of the few sloping inclines that led into the canyon— it was mostly a sheer drop on every side with few exceptions— and made slow progress. The slope was still rather steep, at perhaps a forty five degree angle. Gye occasionally found himself suddenly surprised by the incline and panicking to stay upright

— despite the fact that he was perfectly fine— much like the sensation of waking up in the middle of the night feeling like you're falling.

Gye thought the valley in the middle of the canyon to be about three hundred feet down from where they were. There were massive slabs of granite sticking up like prehistoric statues, slanting on the gentle incline of the rolling hills. The base of the valley, with a river running swiftly through the center of it, was flush with luscious green growth. Gye could make out the sight of some large beetle-like creatures climbing the looming mountainous faces.

Anthony was standing with Jane near an observational window. Gye overheard them discussing something.

"I've been observing half a dozen creatures resembling the *Trigonotarbida* over the last few days. They appear to be following the rover from a distance." Anthony said with a tone of concern.

"Following in a group? Odd behavior for an Arachnid. Do you think they could be dangerous?" Jane asked.

"I can't tell exactly how large they are, but they appear to be the size of a kitchen table. I doubt they would target us, but anything goes when everything's extant." Anthony said.

"Don't want to squish a spider that big." Jane mused.

"Did someone say something about spiders?" Molly asked.

"Not spiders, precisely. Taxonomically speaking—" Anthony started.

"—I don't really care whether the spider takes a taxi or not. If its creepy and crawly and gross, I want to lock myself in a room until its well out of the way." Molly said.

Elicia peered up from what she was reading.

"Funny thing about spiders— oh wait, there's absolutely nothing funny about spiders. Only vicious, disgusting little creatures who need to be stamped out as quickly as is physically possible. I'm being one hundred percent serious right now. Did anyone think to bring a giant gun or anything to smite these creatures with?" She ranted.

"We can't just go around killing things!" Jane objected, "we have to leave them undisturbed so they can be studied and we can learn from them. There's bound to be invaluable information to be gleaned from even a small deoxyribonucleic acid sample of one of them." Jane said. Anthony nodded his agreement.

"You science-y people can have all the fun you want playing games with satan incarnate, but I'll be staying in the kitchen, thank you very much." Royce chimed in.

There was a general air of agreement. Captain Walker stepped down the ladder to join the rest of the group.

"We will be making camp at the river down in the middle of the canyon just before sunset." He said.

"You're pushing the engines too hard, Captain. The last thing you want to do is let the *Venture* break down in the middle of the most dangerous forest on the planet." Ray said.

"Nature isn't dangerous, actually. There are just some evil people who provoke perfectly innocent creatures." Anthony said.

"That's some amazingly naive b—" Gye started.

"—That's not exactly scientific, I think is what he means." Jane interrupted. They exchanged a glance.

"What do you mean, dangerous? We're sealed in this moving tin can, aren't we? We should be pretty well protected." Molly Hazelwood said.

"The truth is, we have no idea what lies between us and the drone. There could be things we couldn't hypothesize or imagine, and contrary to mister sunshine and rainbows over here, they wont be pretty little butterflies for us to gawk at. No, those freaky spider things are bound to be just the beginning. Watch your back." Ray said ominously.

"Anyways, I came down here because I need some snacks. Royce, get on that pronto please." Captain Walker said.

"A man with your figure would be better off with fewer snacks, I think." Royce grumbled.

"I'll pretend I didn't hear that. And if there's any caffeinated drinks left, bring me one of those." Captain Walker said.

CHAPTER 13
CAMPFIRE

The rover stood like a metal beetle next to the bank of the river. Its metal feet sunk slightly into the faintly mushy ground, but it stayed firmly in place. The sun was just beginning to crest the looming rocky facade of the canyon walls, sending a cascade of golden light flittering through the calm yet swift river, making the whole scene come alive with golden hues. This coronation of the day with a crown of golden spectacle marked the end of the sun's slow waltz across the darkening sky.   But the moon had not come out yet. The sun was still making its last steps across the sky and would soon be gone, but not yet.

"I feel jet-lagged from being cooped up in this tin can for the past week. I need some fresh air." Royce Alavandréz said.

"What about the arachnids? I don't want to be outside while they're around." Molly said.

"We actually haven't seen them in the last few hours. They seem to have stopped following us, which is good news, I think." Anthony said.

"Thank god for that." Captain Walker said.

"What do y'all say we have a campfire tonight? We can even play games and roast marshmallows." Molly said. Her eyes were bright with the happiness that idea brought her.

"Do we have marshmallows?" Elicia asked.

"I saw some when I was, um, hanging out in the cargo bay." Molly replied.

"Sounds like a great idea!" Anthony said.

"It's dangerous." Jane said pointedly.

"No more so than diving in that lake was." Gye said.

"Well, I for one am needing to stretch these pudgy legs of mine, so I'm definitely going out. Ms. Hazelwood and I will be doing this lovely campfire idea even if we have to do it alone." Elicia said.

"I am in agreement, which means we're doing it. Everyone out!" Captain Walker ordered.

They gathered wood for the fire and Captain Walker carved some sticks to be pointy enough to cook on the fire with.

"I was hoping we wouldn't have to open these packaged meat atrocities." Royce said, referring to the package of hot dogs.

"Shut up, I'm an American and the hot dog may as well be our official national food, so I ordered some brought aboard." Captain Walker said.

Gye dragged three logs around the fire pit for them to sit on. He sat down with Molly on his left and Elicia on his right. To Molly's left was Anthony, followed by Jane, Royce, Ray, and Captain Walker.

"I can't eat those nasty hot dogs. Eating meat is murder." Anthony said.

"That's ludicrous. Also, I literally saw you eating a mini corndog yesterday, you lying—" Gye started.

"—I guess his adherence to his values varies based on how hungry he is." Ray jibed.

Anthony said nothing, but his face had melted into a crimson complexion not unlike that of a tomato.

Gye chomped into his hot dog and grinned as the grease and flavor melted into his mouth.

"America. Land of the free. Home of the brave. Creator of the Hot Dog." Gye said.

"Yes, I suppose the hot dog is equally as important as liberty." Jane joked.

"America may be a shadow of its former self, but at least it can still produce a good hot dog." Ray said.

"Nothing like the good ol' days," Captain Walker mused, "where women were women and men were men. You could say the word gay without being scrutinized, and the bible was still taught in schools."

"There's no way you were alive way back then, James. Don't be such a geezer, it doesn't bode well for your future." Elicia said.

"I've been an old man since I became a teenager. No sense in stopping now." He replied.

"I've never understood why people point backwards in time at an era just as flawed— or more so— than the current era and say it was the epitome of greatness. If nothing was wrong back then, it would still be that way. No, change is a good thing." Anthony said.

"I remember when change was something you carried around in your pocket, not a mantra shouted by unhygienic college students who haven't showered in weeks but want to put a stop to some sort of repression invented by someone on the internet twenty minutes ago. You're a bunch of hippies, the lot of 'ya." Captain Walker said.

"That's offensive—" Anthony started.

Captain Walker waved him off, interrupting.

"—Your generation just wants to say those words to make them feel like they're having their own Rosa Parks moment. You're not standing up to an unjust system, you're standing up to your own feeling of not measuring up to those who came before you."

"This has gone on too long," Jane interrupted, "with the two of you clashing. Yes, progress is a good thing, but we also need to make sure we're not marching in the wrong direction over a cliff somewhere."

"Anyone want a marshmallow?" Molly Hazelwood interjected.

"I'd love one, actually." Anthony said graciously.

"The key to the perfect marshmallow," Gye said, "is to continuously rotate it so you get a nice even spread."

"My diet plan did not account for marshmallows today." Royce fretted.

"Man up and have a ball of stuck-together, rather questionable sugar clumps." Captain Walker said.

"The irony is not lost on me. I know I'll regret this." Royce said.

"Life wasn't meant to be regretted, it was meant to be lived." Elicia said.

Gye glanced to his left a ways. Jane Silver was having a hard time getting her marshmallow onto the spiked branch. Gye leaned over Molly and Anthony and did it for her.

"Thanks." She said, blushing slightly. Or maybe it was just the heat of the campfire. Either way, her cheeks bloomed like a rose into full crimson color. Her blue eyes had a sparkle like a princess in a Disney movie, and the sparkle danced in her eyes with the fire's light. She was quite the attractive creature, Gye had to admit. While everyone else continued talking Gye stole a few glances across the fire at her. Once, she caught his gaze and casually looked away. But Gye thought he noticed a smile playing with the edges of her lips.

"Who wants to play Two Truths and a Lie?" Molly asked. She clearly wanted everyone to say yes. After they had all somewhat begrudgingly agreed, she smiled.

"I guess I'll go first then. Hmmm." She thought for a moment, looking skywards in concentration.

"Here goes. Ok. I'm deathly afraid of earthquakes, I've been painting for a decade now, and…. I once stole from my school's lost and found." She said. Gye thought it was obviously the last one by the way she trailed off.

Everyone else seemed to agree and said so. She blushed at how easily they guessed hers.

"Alrighty then! Gye, you go."

He brushed his hair back and thought for a moment.

"Ok. I was expelled from middle school for getting into a fight, I had a labrador named Charlie, and I'm obsessed with avenging my family." Gye said.

"The first one!" Elicia said.

"I think it's the third one." Anthony said.

Everyone else decided on the second answer.

"Elicia, your turn." Gye said after nodding an affirmation.

"Oh, a Cantor never spills personal details. But oh, just the once I suppose. I had my second husband poisoned, I had a fling with

President Oakley a decade ago, and, oh, I suppose… I'm planning to betray you all." She said with a flippant laugh.

"The last one, at least I hope. What was President Oakley like?" Jane asked.

"A strong man, with a good taste in wine. I'd say the last name fits him." She said.

"How scandalous. And he was elected because of his family values, too. Oh, the irony." Gye said.

"Did the media ever find out?" Jane asked.

"Of course not, darling. I never kiss and tell, and President Oakley was quite the discreet man." Elicia said.

"My turn, I suppose," Captain Walker said, "alright. I taught elementary school mathematics for two years, I was discharged from the United States Army for my rash actions while in command in battle, and I competed in the Olympics once."

"That's a tie between the first and the last one in my opinion." Royce Alavandréz said.

Captain Walker's face turned an angry shade of red.

"What, it seems obvious to you that I was a bad commander?"

"No, that's not it," Royce replied hastily, "I just, uhh,…" He stammered.

"I'm just messing with you, Spaniard. It's the first one, by the way. I never taught elementary school, but I did compete in the olympics for wrestling once." Captain Walker said.

"Ray, your turn." Molly said. But when she looked at him, he was fast asleep.

"Looks like its lights out for him after a hard day's work." Captain Walker said.

"What does he actually do?" Jane Silver asked.

"He engineers, and such." Captain Walker said vaguely.

"I mean on a day to day basis, what does he contribute to our team?" Jane asked.

"He, like, maintains stuff, I think."

"I think he's just sort of along for the ride." Anthony said.

"Anyways," Molly said, obviously eager to change the subject, "Royce, I guess you go."

"I have bad hearing, I lost ten thousand dollars in a bet once, and I was born in Spain." Royce said.

"Obviously you were born in Spain... I'm going to go with 'you lost ten thousand dollars in a bet." Captain Walker said.

"Wrong. I don't have bad hearing, but I did lose ten thousand dollars on a bet." Royce said.

"That sounds like an interesting story. Do tell." Molly implored.

"Not much to tell, really. I became very... inebriated... one night, and one thing led to another and I ended up betting on the losing fighter in a massive spectacle boxing match." Royce said.

"Toquille versus Enger?" Captain Walker asked.

Royce nodded.

"I didn't know you were also a boxing fan." Royce said.

"Not so much of a boxing fan as a riot fan, to be honest. That's also why I watch international soccer." Captain Walker said.

"As far as I'm concerned, rioting is the only thing that makes the existence of the country of Brazil noteworthy." Gye said.

"No offense, Royce." Gye added quickly.

"None taken. Brazil speaks Portuguese, actually, so I have no particular empathy for them." Royce said.

"Glad to hear that." Gye said.

"Jane, I believe it's your turn." Molly said. Her tone was suspiciously casual, as if she thought Jane might ruin the atmosphere of fun she had created, so she tried to make it sound like such a turn of events would not effect her.

"Let me think. Hmmm. I haven't listened to music since my favorite artist passed away— I love electronic music, none of that awful Jazz stuff—, I suck at mathematics, and I've never gone hunting." Jane said.

"You're quite the gentle soul, so I think the lie isn't the third one." Elicia said.

"Not as gentle as you might think." Gye said.

"I would answer, but I think it would be cheating for me to answer because I know Jane so well." Anthony said.

"I'm going to say the lie is you're bad at math. I've never heard of a scientist who was rubbish at math." Gye said.

"Wasn't Einstein bad at math?" Royce asked.

"That's a popular misconception. He was actually a mathematical prodigy from an early age. If I'm not mistaken, he mastered calculus before his sixteenth birthday." Anthony said.

"Which one was the lie, dear?" Elicia asked.

"Gye was right. I'm a better mathematician than Stephan Hawking was at my age." Jane said.

"Who's that?" Captain Walker asked.

"You don't know who Stephen Hawking was?" Jane gawked.

"Even I know that, and I didn't even finish High School." Gye said.

"My turn!" Anthony interrupted.

"This should be unintentionally hilarious." Gye said as an aside to Elicia. She chuckled.

"Ok. I can recite fifty digits of Pi, I'm subscribed to twenty five different fashion magazines, and I once went backpacking in India for two weeks." He said.

"Based on the items I've seen spread about the floor of our room when I've been away for a while, I can personally vouch for the fact that the second one is no lie." Gye said.

"You're like, science-y and stuff, so I'm going to say the Pi thing is probably not a lie." Captain Walker said.

"Correct. Yeah, I've never been to India, but I'd really love to. I hear its got beautiful landscapes. I could post them to my social media profiles." Anthony said.

They conversed until they had each, slowly, one by one, fallen asleep.

CHAPTER 14
A RUDE AWAKENING

There was a faint sound like the wind rustling through grass. Gye's eyes slowly drifted open. It was just before dawn, judging by the general darkness with a soft bit of light creeping over the mountains. Gye rolled over and tried to go back to sleep.

He heard the sound again. The faint, faint crackling. There it was again, like a ticking on the edge of his consciousness. Groaning, he rubbed his eyes and rolled to sit up.

The sound stopped. Through the darkness he could see the vague outlines of the river running through the canyon and the looming sides of the canyon itself. Around the still-smoking remains of the campfire there were the outlines of his companions. They all appeared to be asleep.

The indistinct sound faded back into Gye's hearing, only with an odd metallic flavor this time. Squinting, he tried to find the source of the noise. Perhaps it was only some anomaly of the river, some chunk of prehistoric metal slowly shifting down the river from millions of years ago.

But no, the sound was coming from behind him. He could have sworn it was getting louder. Slowly, growing more and more apprehensive, Gye turned to look. His breath caught in his throat and his heart skipped a beat.

Even in the dimness, Gye could tell what was happening. The outlines made it clear enough. They were all over the *Venture.*

The spider-like creatures, the arachnids Anthony had mentioned, were crawling all over the rover like it was some larger creature they had all worked together to bring down in a great hunting escapade. Gye could not tell how many there were, but there were too many.

Gye shuddered deeply and felt the goosebumps rise all over his skin. His mouth was suddenly dry and he couldn't move.

A minute must have passed before he regained enough composure to realize the danger his companions were in.

He tried clearing his throat quietly, but it did no good. They heard nothing in their deep slumber. They were too lulled in by the seductive powers of sleep to be bothered with the immense, crushing problem at hand.

Gye whistled lowly in Captain Walker's direction. He stirred, but so did one of the arachnids on the rover. Gye saw it turn its eight gleaming, dark eyes in his direction. He shuddered again involuntarily. This was the stuff of nightmares, from the deepest, most repressed part of his darkest dreams.

The arachnid plopped off of the rover with surprising agility and sprang in his direction. Its eight legs were a nightmarish blur as it crept towards the campfire.

Gye decided to risk it and shook Elicia's body— adjacent to his around the campfire— until she reluctantly woke up. He silently motioned her to awaken Captain Walker. She squinted without understanding at first, but then shrugged and moved to comply. She had not yet seen the peril facing them.

The noise of this caused Molly to stir. She sat up and smiled, stretching her arms wide. She must have been a morning person, Gye reckoned.

Molly and Elicia finally saw the creature at the same time.

Elicia froze in fear. Molly screamed.

What happened next was a blur of seconds. The rest of their group all awakened in various stages of confusion. Captain Walker instantly jumped to his feet, arms out like a boxer in defensive position. The arachnids on the rover simultaneously freaked out and thrashed about on the *Venture*. The sound was as if someone had put something metal in a rusty blending machine. Pieces of metal were flying off as the arachnids attacked the rover.

Ray bellowed a horrified battle cry when he saw what they were doing to his creation.

The arachnid that had been slowly creeping towards them earlier sprang at Captain Walker. Limbs flailed, there was an awful screeching sound, and the captain landed a savage blow the one of the creature's two biggest eyes. The empty pool of blackness that was the eye collapsed into a gelatinous liquid under the weight of his blow.

Elicia, Anthony, Molly, and Jane got behind Gye for protection. He was wearing the same white t-shirt with a brown leather vest over it from the night before, but by now the t-shirt was stained with dirt. His disheveled hair could not have helped add any sort of confidence to their perception of his ability to protect them. He was fully awake, however. The massive adrenaline rush had seen to that.

He spread out his arms protectively and faced the confrontation. By now a few other arachnids had peeled off from the group on the *Venture* and were rushing towards the group.

Captain Walker did not seem to be doing too well against the arachnid. He was holding his own defensively, swerving and dodging with an agility one would not expect given his out of shape form, but he was making no progress in actually defeating the creature, and he was running out of time.

Gye waited until the captain had fended off a particularly harsh jab from the creature before lunging at the back of its head. He yelled with everything he had in him as he decimated the creature's head between his two well-toned arms. All those extra nights spent at the gym finally paid off.

His hands were sticky with fluid, although Gye could not tell its color because of the darkness. The arachnid's body withered and screeched until it lay motionless at his feet. He felt sick to his stomach, looking down at the carcass. Fluids oozed out of its hairy gray body, some of which immediately stained his brown combat boots.

The other arachnids slowed their advance nearly to a halt at the sight of what Gye had done to their compatriot.

Gye resumed the protective gesture with his arms spread out and looked spoke over his shoulder.

"Run! Now! Get out of here!"

Gye turned to see Anthony, face to face with one of the arachnids. It was advancing methodically, step by step, until it was toe to toe with him.

"Nature is never harmful," Anthony said, convincing himself. He put out his hands in a gesture of surrender and smiled. The arachnid, confused, only hissed at him.

"See, nature is never evil!" Anthony said. His innate fear soon overcame his bravado, however, and he slowly backpedaled back to the others.

"You're only lucky, Anthony. Run, go!" He yelled.

The others were quick to oblige. Except for Ray, who stood, awestruck at the horror that had become of his baby. The rover made a deep metallic groaning sound as it slowly crumbled under the assault of the arachnids.

"You savages destroyed my prized creation!" Ray seethed. Not that they could understand him, of course.

Ray's face turned so bright red Gye thought it would burst.

"Ray... Ray, you need to leave. Run, run now, before its too late."

"They killed... they..." His words were lost as intellectual mind turned to savage animal lust for revenge.

With a wordless, throaty scream Ray charged at the arachnids with all his might, flailing his fists with a holy wrath.

This ill-advised attack was enough to give the creatures pause, however. Ray's unexpected bravado triggered the ancient, primal question of fight or flight in their primitive brains.

At least one of them chose to fight. Ray punched into the creature's underbelly with all his might. Two screams resulted; one from the creature, and one from Ray.

"It bit me! Son of a gun, it bit me!" He screeched, running back towards Gye.

The group of arachnids found its courage again at the sight of Ray fleeing and they pursued.

Gye turned to run in the direction he had last seen his companions running. It did not take long to almost catch up with them. They had ran through the river where it was appreciably shallow and were kicking up a storm of dust as they ran for their lives away from the arachnids. Gye heard the splash of many legs in the water following closely, not far behind him.

"Run run run run run!" He heard Jane yell repeatedly.

Captain Walker was having trouble keeping pace and was holding his arm to his chest protectively.

"I've been bit!" Ray screeched as he caught up.

Captain Walker grunted.

"That makes two of us." He panted between ragged breaths.

"They're on our heels!" Elicia shouted.

Gye didn't dare look back for fear of stumbling and falling. He knew that if he fell, it would be the end of him.

They were nearing the base of the incline up the hill in one of the few areas where the canyon walls were not insurmountable.

"Can't... run... any... more!" Anthony panted, wheezing like an out of shape old person who had been smoking for decades.

"Keep going!" Gye shouted.

The incline was beginning to cause a burning sensation in his legs. They didn't have much time left.

He spotted an area up ahead where a chunk of the canyon wall face had fallen off— perhaps a meter and a half tall— with smaller rocks around it. That was their only hope.

"Fend them off from the rock!" Gye bellowed, surging forward to lead them. In the darkness of the hour it was difficult not to trip and fall, but thankfully, no one did.

He slowed down to bring up the rear of the group. Molly sprung to the top of the rock like an olympic jumper. Jane clambered up the other side and Captain Walker helped push Elicia to the top. Gye bounded up the side just in time to watch Royce fall from his attempt to climb up.

"Grab my hand!" Gye shouted. The arachnids were closing in with a horrifying amplified screeching sound, like a pack of wolves who have picked up a scent and refuse to let it go.

Royce muttered curses in Spanish. The creatures were seconds away.

Gye saw the fear in Royce's eyes, the knowledge that death was inevitable. He let out an earth shattering scream, his whole body shaking, as the reality of his situation dawned on him. There was no escape, there was only pain, there was only unescapable, inevitable pain. Gye felt Royce's pulse racing in his hand like an automatic machine gun, his body trying to put up one last bit of resistance to death. But it was no use. Just like every struggle against death, this one ended with death being paid its due.

"No!" Gye yelled as the arachnids tore Royce's body from his grasp. With an awful sloshing sound, Royce's legs were yanked clear off his body. Like a candle in the wind, Royce's life was snuffed out. All that remained was a body to be ripped apart by the disgusting creatures making a feast of his body.

Gye backed up, horrified.

"Don't look down there." He said quietly.

They understood, by the look in their eyes. They huddled together, crouched on the center of the rock. The arachnids either weren't capable of climbing the rock or did not possess the reasoning to figure out how to do so.

After what felt like hours, the arachnids began to fight among themselves over the remaining scraps of the body. They soon dispersed, leaving half a dozen splotchy corpses on the ground where the weaker and less fortunate of the short-lived band of creatures had met their ends.

"Are they gone?" Molly asked, her eyes welling up with tears.

"Yes. And so is Royce." Ray Kaymar said angrily.

"How very like life, to end like this. Ironic, if you think about it. He turned nature into food all his life, it was his passion. And at the end he became food for nature." Elicia said.

"That's enough, Elicia. Let us respect the dead, although I can see that a proper burial is out of the question. I am the captain, I will say the traditional rites," He said, "let me recall…"

"Father, we commend to you
The spirit of our fallen man
Let him find his way through heaven's gates
To leave footprints in heaven's sands

Let Saint Peter make no objection
For he lived a life most true
Let him pass well into your arms
Let him find solace with you

Lord above, grant your mercy
Let your son's blood cover him
Let Satan's claim pass over him
And forgive him well his sins."

The captain grimaced and held his arm to his chest.
"Ray, how's your bite?"
"It looks like none of the creature's poison actually broke the skin. Thank God for that." Ray said.
"I wasn't so lucky." The captain said.
"What do we do now?" Anthony said after a pause.
"Get to the rover and see if we can't get it running." Captain Walker said doubtfully.
"I saw what they did to my baby," Ray said, "and it wasn't pretty. At best, it might be able to crawl along on mostly even ground. But there's no way we can continue the mission in it. If we are to continue, it'll have to be on foot."
"I'm not sure we should continue at all." Jane said.
"Curse this. Molly, were there any first aid materials in the cargo bay?" Captain Walker asked.
"I do remember some, yes. Next to the Nitrogen detector units, yes." She said.
"Good. I'm going to need to use it if I don't plan on dying in the next few minutes, and I don't plan on dying any time in the near future. Or ever, really. The point being, let's get a move on, please." The captain said.

"This should stop the venom from killing you for now, but it will only neutralize it for a while. If you don't get medical help and get it soon, you will die. We're talking a week, tops, before you collapse." Molly said. She was trying to deliver the information with the tone of a doctor who was merely stating facts unemotionally, but it was obvious by the way her voice quivered that she was scared for his life.

"Thank you, Molly. Without you I'm sure I wouldn't have even made it this long." The captain said.

The rover's hull was decimated, with long gashes running along the sides from the cargo bay to the observation deck. The beautifully crafted design of Ray's had been rendered unrecognizable. Shreds of the chassis and hull were barely attached to the vehicle's fundamental structure. Ray's initial estimate had been correct; the *Venture* was almost completely non-functional.

"Gather around everyone, please. I have come to a decision. This is not easy for me, but this is what must happen. We have to turn back." He said.

"We cannot. We can't turn back." Anthony said.

Gye was surprised by Anthony's bravery. Was this the same guy who had been stymied by fashion trends a week ago? He had changed. Probably for the better.

"I know none of us want to give up. But you've seen what these creatures can do. We can't risk going on." The captain said.

"Anthony's right," Jane said, "we can't just abandon this mission. If we don't recover the drone and go packing home like wimps, no one will set foot in this forest again. They'll say it's 'too dangerous'. You know how people are these days, no one takes risks or does anything dangerous anymore. But enough about that. We have to make sure the world knows about this and the secrets of this forest are made known, for the good of mankind." Jane said.

"Quite a speech, Ms. Silver, but how will you locate the drone? You can't exactly carry the instruments with you. They're too large and heavy." Captain Walker said.

"We know approximately where it is, do we not? We can go by my memory and look around for it. People used to find things that way all the time, back before radar turned everyone into couch potato—" Gye started.

"—yes, that should work," Jane interrupted, "I'm sure we can pull it off. Well, I'm not sure. But that's the beauty of it." She said.

"You're willing to climb up that mountain— do you see how icy it is? —for science? You're crazy." Molly said, pointing at the mountain in question. To call it a mountain was probably an overstatement, but it did cut an imposing figure on the horizon.

"It's only about three miles up, actually. It's like climbing Mt. Naavki back home." Gye said.

"You're going to have to use the rover to get back on your own. Get some medical attention. And then search for us, I'm sure we'll need it!" Elicia said.

"Of all my years of commanding, in the Army and elsewhere, I've never been more proud of the people under me than I am right now. Right then, carry on without me. Gye, you're the captain now. Gather what supplies you can carry from the rover, and may God be with you." He said.

CHAPTER 15
LURKING

Vaurien Kane sat in his swivel chair behind his unusual desk and propped his feet up. He reached for the phone and dialed a number. A smile tugged at the corner of his lip as he thought about his plan.

"Who's speaking?" The voice on the other end said.

"God." Vaurien Kane answered.

There was a silence on the other end for a while.

"I told you not to call me on this line." The voice said.

"God works in mysterious ways. Why, you do not even know what will happen tomorrow. What is your life? You are a mist that appears for a while and then vanishes."

"Hans Ulbricht speaking. I have the information you requested. It's not much, but I think it should help." Hans said.

"Well, get on with it." Vaurien said.

"As you command. This Ashara Kimeno, which we called by the codename Easthaven, was contacted by our federal agency. We were hoping he would provide information on the cult- pardon, the group of which you are a member, which we deemed to be potentially dangerous at the time. All I know is that he accepted some items worth a moderate sum of money, but I have no information on whether or not he was an informant, or still is." Hans Ulbricht said.

"It is enough. Corruption is corruption. One must be willing to cut off an infected limb to save the whole body. I am a qualified doctor, as you may have heard. The world's first rib surgeon, actually." Vaurien Kane said.

Silence answered him.

"Because of the Genesis story—" Vaurien started to explain.

"Will that be all, sir?" Hans Ulbricht interrupted.

"Yes, yes I believe that will suffice. Expect your reward within a week." Vaurien said.

There was silence for a few seconds before the man spoke.

"Is my little angel safe? Tell me, is she alright?" He asked.

Vaurien laughed.

"What, you have become anxious, yes? You are such a good father to care so much. My own parents faked their own deaths when I was only six to get out of having to deal with me. They couldn't handle my greatness, I assume, as with any mortal being. So I killed them." He said with a laugh.

"Let that be a warning to you, Hans," Vaurien Kane continued, instantly changing his tone to one of icy clarity, "let that be a warning to you of how I treat those who think they can turn their backs on me. I do not tolerate weakness."

"Yes, sir." Hans Ulbricht said, trembling.

Vaurien Kane hung up the phone and laughed again.

"Paaklan, get in here." He said into a microphone at the edge of his desk.

The old Indian man entered without speaking a word. His spectacles and wild gray hair made him look a proper mad scientist.

"Paaklan, let Mr. Ulbricht be reunited with his daughter for a day or so. Then kill them both in their sleep."

Paaklan merely nodded.

"Aren't you going to ask me why I would do such a thing?" Vaurien asked.

"It is not my place to question you." Paaklan said.

"Very good, Paaklan. But in case you were wondering, it was because he interrupted me." Vaurien said.

"Quite reasonable, sir." Paaklan replied.

Vaurien turned to look out the window.

"Send a message to Ashara Kimeno. Tell him I know about Easthaven. Tell him he wont be standing in the way of me taking the trial this time. And tell him, in no uncertain terms, that I own him now. He will be the puppet I control with the strings in my hands, and I will make my puppet dance until I am bored of him."

CHAPTER 16
UPWARDS

"This bag is too heavy." Anthony complained.

"Then maybe you shouldn't have packed your twenty million cosmetics, genius." Gye snapped.

They had started off the previous day, walking laboriously through thick underbrush towards the mountain, which they had come to affectionately nickname 'Mt. Impossible'. The temperature was unbearably high in the heat of the high noon sun, sweat was dripping from their brows, and Gye's temper was running thin.

"I have to look my best at all times." Anthony said.

"For WHO, Anthony? For WHO?" Gye nearly yelled.

"For *whom*." Anthony replied pedantically.

"It's taking every bit of my self control not to hit you right now." Gye said.

"Guys!" Molly interrupted, "we're going to need to keep it civil if we're going to make it anywhere without killing each other first."

"She does have a point." Anthony said.

Gye spit into the oversized shrubbery to his left. He hefted the pack on his back and continued on wordlessly.

"Is that an agreement?" Molly called out.

"Just keep walking." Jane said derisively.

"So do we know for sure where the drone is, or are we searching for a dead canary in a coal mine?" Elicia said.

"What's that supposed to mean?" Ray asked. He was the least perturbed by the heat.

"I realize that doesn't make sense. Don't judge me, I'm extremely dehydrated." Elicia said, panting. Her golden hair was a frizzy mess sitting on top of her head like a bird's nest.

"We could sing marching songs!" Molly suggested enthusiastically.

"Captain Walker was the only one of us who was in the military. I don't think the rest of us know any marching songs." Gye said.

"We could make one up!" She said.

"How are you possibly in such good spirits? More than likely, we are going to die before this is over." Jane said.

"I don't think you'll die, Jane. You have a survival instinct in you. I'm not so sure about myself, though." Molly joked.

"We're all going to make it out alive, I promise you." Gye said loudly.

"You don't know that." Jane replied.

"I do. We're going to be fine." He said.

"I think he's right," Molly said, "good people always make it through the hardest of times if they just keep their heads up."

"Good people don't survive, people who are willing to do whatever it takes to survive are the ones who survive." Elicia said.

"Being good is its own reward." Ray said.

Elicia laughed it off. Anthony stumbled and his bag fell and split open on the forest floor.

"Oh no!" He said, frantically trying to contain the spilled materials before their contents were lost to the earth.

"It'll only make you lighter." Gye said, holding back a chuckle.

"Here, let me help you." Molly said. She set down her own bags and knelt down to help him in his futile task.

"Careful with that! That cost me two hundred dollars a bottle. It's a special French blend." Anthony said.

"It's not getting harder to breathe as we go up. That's a good sign that this mountain is the source for the unusual amount of oxygen in the air." Jane said, not paying any attention to Anthony.

"Ray! Stop eating all of our food. Jeez, you can't carry the food bag anymore." Gye said, noticing Ray sneaking a hunk of bread.

"How much is left?" Jane asked.

"We *had* a weeks worth of rations for each of us if we only ate twice per day. Ray, how long have you been snacking?" Gye asked.

"I thought this food was just my ration! I thought we each had our own." Ray said timidly.

"You must have the metabolism of an athlete." Jane said.

"Don't worry, I'm sure we'll find something edible." Anthony said.

"I'm sure Adam & Eve thought the same thing about the fruit in the garden of eden. And I'm sure whatever we find will be just as poisonous." Ray said.

"Look at that greenish-yellow spherical fruit thing over there hanging from the tree. That looks edible." Elicia said.

"Eating anything out here would be like playing Russian roulette with nature. We should wait to do anything like that until we're desperately out of food." Gye said.

"Think about it strategically. If we eat without using our rations now, we will have enough food for when we're at the top of the mountain, which almost certainly wont have any easily available food." Elicia said.

"She's right. We'll have to risk it eventually anyways, so we may as well take the risk now." Jane said.

"Alright. How do we tell if a fruit is likely to kill us?" Gye asked.

"I assume we could just look for things that look similar to fruits we're familiar with, like an apple or a banana or something." Anthony said, standing up.

"That makes sense. How do we decide who'll be the first to try it?" Molly asked.

"Rock paper scissors?" Gye suggested.

"I say we all try it at the same time. No use having just one of us get poisoned, right?" Ray said.

They eventually agreed on that and tried the piece of fruit together. Several hours later they were still alive, and so concluded that the experiment had been a success. Slowly the seemingly endless foliage passed by and they could feel the incline of the mountain becoming slowly steeper. They were making steady progress. They stopped to refill their water and rest for a few hours when they happened upon a small waterfall.

The waterfall cascaded from a hill protruding from the mountain. They made their temporary camp at the base of the hill, in the shadow of the mountain's embrace. The sun had moved quite far across the sky; they would have to make camp for the night soon. The waterfall seemed as good a place as any.

Gye opened his eyes when he heard someone humming. It was Molly. She was sticking her tongue out subconsciously as she sketched something with pencil and scrap paper.

"You should really rest instead of doing that." Gye said.

She seemed startled by his interruption.

"Oh, I've only been drawing for half an hour or so." She replied.

"What are you drawing?" Anthony asked, his interest piqued.

"Just all of us by this waterfall, together." She said, blushing slightly.

"Neat. I actually minored in art theory in college. I particularly enjoyed the works of Rothko. He was such a brilliant painter, willing to go against the grain of society and do something with his own ideas." Anthony said.

Gye just rolled his eyes. It was all too easy to get into an argument with Anthony about the dumbest of things, because Anthony made everything dumb by association, it seemed.

"What are you talking about over here?" Elicia asked, sitting down next to them.

"Molly drew a picture of us." Gye said.

"How adorable. Let me see." She said.

Molly showed her the picture shyly.

"You have such a lovely artistic eye, dear. I used to say that art was the window to the soul. Then someone said the eyes were the window to the soul and I realized that made much more sense." Elicia said.

There was a crackling sound made in the top of a tree behind them. They instantly stopped talking and turned around to try to locate the source of the sound.

"What was that?" Jane whispered.

"If that's a spider up there, I'm just done. I can't deal with that again. No way." Molly said.

The trees closest to the small waterfall were not as large as the others on the mountainside. The gentle cascading sound of the waterfall masked the sounds of the fauna which occasionally flittered by, but it was not enough to disguise the sound they had just heard. The air seemed to take on a somber silence and their ears strained to listen out for any new threatening sounds.

"I don't see anything." Gye said.

"Maybe it was just the wind cracking a branch or something." Ray said unconvincingly.

They heard the sound again, once again behind them. They whirled around as one to see what was making the noise.

In front of them, perched on a fallen tree, was a fat reptile creature that looked like a bloated frog mixed with an oversized gecko.

"What on earth is that?" Gye asked.

"It looks like a fat version of the Geico mascot!" Molly said.

"It's an Eryops! It's a carnivore, but unlikely to see us as a meal. We're too big." Jane said.

"Don't get too close. It could be dangerous." Anthony said.

"This one's an adolescent or younger. They could grow up to five feet long, this one's only like two feet long." Jane mused.

An oversized mosquito buzzed past and landed on the other end of the log. In a split second the Eryops' long tongue flicked and caught the unfortunate creature. It threw its head back and gulped. Then it flicked its tongue out again lazily.

"I wish we had these around the backyard when I was younger. Would've taken care of the horrible mosquito problem, at least." Gye said.

There was a breezy whisking sound from the direction they'd heard the sound in the tree earlier. Another Eryops snatched Anthony's pack with its tail and, with a series of chattering clicking sounds, called the other Eryops. They jumped off together, bounding up the nearest tree.

"No!" Anthony screeched. It was the screech of a man in immeasurable pain. It was the sort of sound Gye would have expected from a man who had just been castrated, not a man who had just lost a seemingly inconsequential pack of cosmetics and esoteric skin products.

"Geez, calm down!" Ray yelled.

"That's pretty funny. You just got robbed by the Geico mascot." Molly said, giggling. It was strangely satisfying for Gye to see Molly laughing at Anthony. Even Jane couldn't help but crack a smile. Elicia was too fascinated by the two Eryops scampering up into the treetop to notice or enjoy Anthony's pain as the others had.

"How could they do this to me? I thought I was one with nature! Nature can't hurt me. I am a friend of nature. I recycle. I protested global warming on the White House lawn for every night for a week. I burned down a coal plant in High School! What more could I have done to prove my worth?" Anthony cried out.

"You burned down a coal plant?" Jane asked incredulously.

"My dad bribed the chief of police to find it an accident. He told me to keep my mouth shut about it. Oops." Anthony said, wiping a tear out of his eye.

He staggered to his feet and seethed angrily, clenching his fists hard against his sides. He tried to jump up the tree gracefully like the two Eryops had done, but he only crashed into the heavy trunk and fell with the grace of a drunk Australian ballet dancer.

"You'll have the climb the other side," Gye tried to explain, "because it's on an inclined plane, you can't get up on that side."

Anthony stumbled to the other side in his odd mix of rage and bottomless sadness and took hold on a jutting out nub that was low enough on the tree trunk for him to get a footing on. Gye watched in bemusement as Anthony's tiny muscles trembled under the effort of the simple climb.

"You should help him." Jane whispered to Gye.

"Why would I do that?"

"You might earn his respect." She replied.

Gye didn't care too much about earning anyone's respect— he was of the view that if someone didn't respect him, it was their loss— but wanting to impress her nonetheless, he shrugged and easily hauled himself up alongside Anthony on the tree. Elicia whistled at him, but he couldn't tell if she was doing it ironically or not.

"C'mon, grab right here. There you go. Come on, let's get your purse back." Gye joked.

"It's not a purse, it's a satchel." Anthony replied weakly, but he did as Gye commanded.

They ascended perhaps twenty feet before they came upon a large branch. Anthony plopped down hard at the base of the bench, sitting against the trunk of the tree like a sloth which has no intention of moving for the next few hours, if at all. Gye had to jump and grab onto a point further along the branch (because Anthony was taking up all the space closest to the tree) and haul himself up. Even he was panting by the time he sat up on top of the branch. He waved down at the others before looking up.

The two Eryops sat side by side, stone-faced and motionless, at the edge of a nest which sat comfortably on the next branch higher than theirs, about four feet up and a third of the ways around the tree. The strap of Anthony's leather satchel was hanging out of the nest visibly. Gye could just make out the curve of an egg behind the protection of the Eryops.

"They're in their nest! They're protecting their young." Gye whispered loudly to Anthony.

He looked up, dazed, and then looked off into the forest.

"Reptiles usually don't make nests in trees, they must have found it and commandeered it. Besides, they must be siblings protecting their mother's newest eggs, because these two are too young to be breeding. Unless the Eryops was much smaller than we first thought." Anthony said hazily.

"Whatever. They've got your 'satchel', as you are so adamant in calling it. And I'm one hundred percent certain they're going to freak out if we go anywhere nearer to that nest, so what exactly is the game plan here? How badly do you want your satchel?" Gye asked.

"If they try to eat any of the products in it, they'll probably be poisoned. I'm quite certain that at least one of those chemicals would cause   scale loss in reptiles. Makes a great hair un-dyer though." Anthony replied.

"So? Are we going to let them lap it up and die then? Or dye, as the case may be. Excuse the pun." Gye said.

"That's not funny." Anthony said without any conviction. His ordinary orneriness was ousted in the face of the situation at hand.

"Fine. What are we going to do then?" Gye asked.

"Why are you letting me decide? You usually take charge." Anthony said.

"Well for one, it's your satchel we're talking about, and two, I'm only helping you because Jane asked me to." Gye said.

"You do realize you have no chance with her, right?"

"I wouldn't be so sure, my pessimistic companion. Now, what are we going to do here? Be aware that I'm only willing to go so far in this endeavor. I won't risk my skin to save your bag." Gye said.

"What's going on up there?" Ray shouted up. The lizards whipped their heads in unison at the new sound instantly, obviously on high alert.

"Come on, we both know you'd do anything to impress Jane. Especially if it's dangerous." Anthony jibed.

"I'm getting tired of this. Choose an action already." Gye demanded.

Anthony just shrugged and looked back into the distance again. "I don't know." He said.

Gye rolled his eyes, grunted, and stood up. He inched along the branch until he reached near the end, where several thinner branches deviated from the main branch. He snapped one off and returned to Anthony.

"You should probably start climbing down now." He advised. Anthony looked up at him expressionlessly and then complied.

"Here goes nothing." He said. He glanced down at the group below. Maybe Anthony was right. Wait, what was he saying? Of course Anthony wasn't right. That was an oxymoron.

He bent his knees and then jumped off the branch. Mid-jump, he put the branch through the leather handle of the bag as it was dangling below the nest, and then rejoined his other hand to the other end of the stick like he was zip lining without safety equipment. When he had completed that (in less than two seconds), he aimed for the closest branch below and hooked his crooked elbow around it, stunting his fall. He heard hissing above from the Eryops but didn't waste a second acknowledging it.

Gye slung the satchel over his shoulder and then clambered down the trunk of the tree quickly, burning his hands in the process. When he was just above Anthony he jumped off the trunk, bent his knees mid flight, and tucked and rolled once he hit the ground. He rolled into a standing position and walked to the group nonchalantly.

The Eryops were bounding down the trunk now, just behind Anthony.

"That's the coolest I think anyone's ever looked while wearing a satchel." Elicia quipped.

"Thank you, but I think we'd better run now!" He yelled, grabbing the other supply bag he had left on the ground earlier and taking off. The others, Anthony among them, followed suit. The Eryops were much slower on the ground, and they were soon left behind. Gye heard one of the Eryops, and then the other seconds later, squeal loudly in what he assumed was frustration. The group slowly jogged to a halt.

"Whoo! Now that was exhilarating." Jane said, panting out every word. Her cheeks had turned rosy red with the effort and she had a fresh tear in the left knee of her light blue jeans. Gye smiled at her.

"Life's always an adventure when you're with me." He said.

"Um, where's Ray?" Elicia asked.

They looked around in horror to find that he was nowhere in sight.

"Ray!" Gye shouted.

"The problem with adventures is that in reality, there's always a price to be paid." Anthony said.

There was an indistinct yell from the direction they had just come from in answer.

"We have to go back for him. They might be chewing him up alive!" Gye said, breaking into a jog. The others followed, Elicia panting hard, barely holding up the rear of the pack.

They were suddenly upon him. Ray was on his knees, the two lizards at his feet. A knife flashed, and he continued skinning the dead creatures.

"I got tired of running." Ray said in a low, husky voice. He grinned and went back to work.

"We should've thought of that. Nice work, Ray." Gye said, somewhat awkwardly.

"You killed them? But you didn't need to!" Anthony said.

"Of course we needed to. They were dangerous and also food. This ancient part of the world doesn't know a human being's place in the food chain, and I'm about ready to teach it." Ray said.

Anthony was at a loss for words. Gye expected him to come up with some savvy retort, but he just sat down, his back against a tree trunk, and held his hands around his knees and rocked back in forth slightly.

Gye found the image slightly disturbing, so instead of processing it, he tuned into what Elicia was saying.

"He's right, you know. Ray is, I mean. I know scientists are supposed to 'look, don't touch' and all that as much as possible, but this is a matter of survival. We're not in some museum, we've stepped back three hundred million years into a land where survival of the fittest is being refined and so is the pecking order. We're the fittest, and it should be our top priority to survive." Elicia said.

"I agree," Jane said reluctantly. "leaving things exactly the way we found them is great and all, but I rather like my own skin a bit better than an Eryops." She said.

"Gye, help me start a fire." Ray interrupted. While they were talking, he had already finished skinning the Eryopses and driven a carved stick through each of them. They were ready to be spit-roasted. All that was missing was a fire.

"Wow, you're very efficient. The stereotype about German seriousness isn't entirely wrong." He joked.

"I take great pride in my German heritage. The stereotype doesn't bother me, as a matter of fact it is a relief that my people are known for something so admirable as good work." He said.

Gye muttered some noncommittal agreement and placed some rocks in a circle to contain the fire. He had a blaze going in moments, and Ray placed the first spit roast over the flame.

"Aren't you scared of burning down the forest?" Anthony asked.

"If it gets even a little bit out of hand, we can just smother it. Or if you want to be extra careful about it, we can use your drinking water to put it out like the firemen you see on TV." Gye said.

"I'm good with just smothering, actually. And I'm too hungry to care that this is meat. Are there any plants around here that look like spices?" Anthony mused.

"This one over here looks vaguely like a garlic." Elicia said.

"How do you know what a real garlic plant looks like?" Gye asked.

"I used to be quite the... *gardener* when I was younger. These days I have turned my efforts into more fruitful pursuits." Elicia said.

"Of course you were." Ray said derisively.

"Don't knock it 'till you try it." Elicia said.

"I'm adding it." Jane interrupted. She ripped up the plant and used a rock to crush the budding bulbous white plant. She then threw it indiscriminately onto the spit. There was a new spark in the flames as some of the particles drifted into the larger flame and caught fire. The reptile was dripping some blood where Ray's knife had pierced the muscle, which wasn't exactly appetizing.

The sun had fully set upon their corner of the earth. The forest at the base of the mountainside was dim; with the light of the fire shining brightly in their eyes, the rest of the forest disappeared into a sea of darkness.

"Creepy-crawly creatures are afraid of fire, right?" Molly asked.

"It's dangerous to them, so yes, we should be safest right next to the fire." Anthony said.

"I'm just anxious because last time we slept next to a fire, we woke up with creepy crawly spiders tearing our rover apart." Molly said.

"We'll take turns posting a watch. We used to do this all the time right after we bagged something valuable." Gye said.

"Who's 'we'?" Molly asked.

"Marquis Parcell, my partner in crime so to speak, and some hired guns if we thought we could pay them more than they would get if they betrayed us. That's how humans work. Every single person is for sale to the highest bidder." Gye said.

"That's how it should be. People who aren't tied down to petty ideas are the ones who end up with an advantage in life." Elicia said.

"Do you have any moral spine? At all?" Ray asked. He pushed a hand through his wavy hair and shook his head, obviously not approving of Elicia's ideas.

"What's the alternative? Being a slave to dogma." Elicia quipped.

"Can you just stop it? The lizard is burning." Anthony pointed out.

Ray quickly took care of the situation.

When they had divided the lizard meat among themselves and devoured it (for they were extraordinarily hungry by this time) they prepared to make it through the night.

Elicia's pack had only two blankets in it, so the had to share each blanket among three people. At Jane's insistence, it was decided that the blankets should be gender segregated. Elicia, Molly, and Jane (with Elicia in the middle to separate the two who did not quite get along) shared a blanket, as did Gye, Ray, and Anthony, in that order, although Gye had the first watch of that night, so he did not get to sleep right away. He put out the fire and stood up against a nearby tree.

He could feel his unshaved beard beginning to tickle his skin. That was the trouble with adventuring, he always forgot to bring a razor. He stared into the darkness, hoping against hope that worst was behind them.

CHAPTER 17
ONE WITH NATURE

Gye woke to a faint high buzzing sound. He had ended his watch hours ago and had just been enjoying the deepest sleep he had experienced in years. Unfortunately, the sound had pulled him from the land of blissful sleep back into the land of the living. The shame of sleep is that it brings even the most powerful of men to the position of death. Gye's back ached in the middle from the awkward position he had been sleeping in. Ray was still sleeping like a rock directly next to him.

The others were slowly stumbling into consciousness as humans are prone to do; rarely does one snap into a state of awakening, rather, it is a gradient one must travel from sleep to awakening and back again.

There was a dim light filtering and flittering through the trees; it was as dim as Gye's state of consciousness, and was growing more lively at about the same rate.

Gye gave the surrounding area a cursory glance. He was surprised to see Anthony still standing against a tree, on watch, like a stone statue over an ancient courtyard.

Gye stood up slowly, rubbing the sleep out of his eyes. It was a mostly cloudy day, but it looked like they would have a good deal of sunlight for at least the next hour, judging by the sky.

He made his way to stand directly behind Anthony and cleared his throat gently. Anthony did not move.

"Anthony?" Gye said inquisitively.

"It makes sense now. All of it." Anthony said. He spoke as if he had discovered the answer to life's oldest riddle. Or perhaps he had discovered the question for which the answer was already known.

"You were supposed to tell Elicia to relieve you hours ago!" Gye said.

Anthony turned to face him. His eyes looked sunken into his face, his skin had taken on an unhealthy yellow appearance, and he had blemishes on his skin that had obviously been covered up before.

"I've discovered things more important than sleep. I looked into the darkness surrounding us and I found the light within myself. I'm free now. I got rid of all my cosmetics and all of my products, the things I thought I needed to be the person I thought I was. But I looked upon the darkness and saw that it was beautiful; and it was beautiful not because it masqueraded as light, but because it was unashamed to be exactly what it was... darkness. So now I have seized that same freedom for myself. That's the reason I only thought I was one with nature before, when actually the purity of nature could see right through my facade and into my soul, which was completely lost under the enormity of my fakeness. Oh, I have discovered a new freedom." Anthony said, looking out into the distance, not making eye contact.

"No one's more glad to hear that than me, let me assure you, but you're sleep-deprived now. You wont last long." Gye said pragmatically.

"That doesn't matter now. You'll see. You'll all see, soon." Anthony said.

"What's that supposed to mean?" Gye asked. Anthony had all the mystical aphoristic air of a fortune cookie, but without the breath of fresh air that was the whimsicality.

"Look over there. Do you see them? I'm sure you heard the buzzing. It is their magnum opus, their symphony, their music. And they're calling to me. Do you see? Tell me, Gye Storm, do you see?" Anthony asked.

Gye looked with an expression of vague concern at Anthony before following his line of sight.

There, where he was pointing, was a group of translucent, colorful creatures with half-circle wings on each side. They were almost spherical, looking suspiciously like someone had blown up bubble gum and left it in its shape.

They weren't just vibrant hues of color; near the fringes of each shape the colors blended into the environment behind them like a shimmering chameleon-esque camouflage. They were also slightly reflective, as Gye could make out the surrounding forest in their skins. If they did, in fact, have skins. It looked to Gye like nature had taken the top of a Jellyfish, thrown it up on land, given it wings, some weird colors, and thrown in a dash of LSD to boot.

"Guys! Everyone, wake up! You've got to see this." Gye said over his shoulder. They stirred awake at his urging and made their ways over to where he and Anthony were standing.

"Are the spiders back?" Molly asked, a tone of dread creeping into her voice.

"They were Arachnids, not spiders, technically speaking... oh, who cares." Anthony said vaguely.

"What's with him?" Jane asked.

"He's discovered how not to be a douche, apparently." Gye replied.

"Oh, you should take notes from him then." Jane said irritably.

"Touché. But he's discovered some interesting creatures over there." Gye said, pointing in the direction he was referring to.

Jane gasped when she saw them.

"They're so beautiful!" Molly exclaimed.

"And probably dangerous." Ray cautioned.

"No." Anthony whispered.

"What?" Ray asked.

"No, I know they're not. They're calling me, they're telling me, they're showing me how to be free. To be one with nature, I must give up all pretensions and all lies. That includes the lie that I am just like everyone else, comfortable to live at the pinnacle of human society and experience life that way. No, I belong out here. I belong *here*. That's the first time I've ever felt that feeling in my entire life. I didn't feel it when

I was growing up, I didn't feel it when my parents told me they loved me— no, I'm sorry, that's another lie, they never told me they loved me. I don't think they did. But I've finally found where I belong, and its right here. Right here." Anthony said.

He began walking towards the creatures (they were probably half a football field away) with his hand out like a blind man trying to avoid being hurt.

"Wait! What are you doing?" Jane asked.

"I told you. I've finally found where I belong. Please don't try to take this from me." Anthony said over his shoulder, not stopping his slow advance.

"But—"

"Please. Just, please. This is what I want." Anthony said.

"But... are you sure?" Jane called out.

"I've never known anything so deeply in my life. I have found my destiny, and it is here. Continue on without me. If ever nature is done with me, I will find my way back to you, friends. But please don't try to stop me. I need this." Anthony said, nearly bursting into tears by the end of his spiel.

Jane put her hands up to her face, looking on in shock.

Gye started to step forward and try to bring Anthony back, but Jane grabbed his shoulder to hold him back.

"No, this is the right thing for him. He's right, he's never truly been happy. Let him have this. It doesn't matter if it's bad for him, we just have to... let him go. That's freedom." Jane said at last.

"You know, as much as we didn't get along, him and I, I can at least understand that. I guess he's finally found what he's looking for." Gye said.

"Goodbye, Anthony!" Molly shouted out to him.

"Give my farewells to you all and to everyone I left behind. Tell them I found myself, I found happiness, I've reached my heaven. Goodbye." He said. He had turned back around to say his goodbye, and then proceeded to disappear over a hill in pursuit of the beautiful creatures.

"So... I guess, we let him go." Molly said.

"There's a man after my own heart. He took the cards life dealt him and threw them back in life's face, saying screw you, I do what I want. That's something I can understand. He rejected the dogma everyone in his life tried to feed him about how to become happy and he just found his own path. That's the point of life, you see. Your own happiness is the prize. For me it might be money and pleasure, but for him it was apparently feeling as though he was one with nature." Elicia said.

"Which is ridiculous, of course. Nature doesn't sympathize." Ray said.

"Well, think of animals, like dogs. They're part of nature, aren't they? And they can see soul-to-soul with humans." Gye said.

"Dogs were domesticated and bred to get the traits we see today." Ray said.

"By whom? By humans. And humans are part of nature, yeah?" Gye replied.

"This is all getting to be too much for me to think about. Let's just agree that he's happy now. We still have a mission to accomplish." Jane said.

They pressed on.

CHAPTER 18
FIRE & BLOOD

Vaurien Kane sat on the bench in the room, alone, breathing in and out. He had a long spear in his hand and was wearing chain mail over a kevlar vest. Over it all he wore leather armor. He was well-protected, it seemed.

But Vaurien was not so naive as to believe that mere armor could defend measly flesh against the onslaught of the fire lizard. Although no one had fought a fire lizard in many years, Vaurien still had faint memories of the creature standing on its massive haunches and landing a massive claw right in the chest of a challenger. He died instantly, and he was considered unworthy in the eyes of the order to ever receive a place of honor in their eyes, even posthumously. That was the risk of this whole business; he might fall short and receive nothing at all. This was an all-or-nothing bet, and the stakes were his life.

He did not want the same fate for himself. Death, that was. How could be respected as a god among men if he could not even escape the most human of traps— death? He needed to win.

The thin, slanted windows on the other side of the small room let in odd shards of light that meandered lazily across the room to where he was sitting. He could see the dust in the air, standing nearly motionless like sentinels guarding over his devotion. The boards of wood that made up the floor were also caked in dust— for this room was sorely underused, being specifically as a place of preparation for one to make oneself pure before challenging the fire lizard— and the whole place had a musty musk that was overpowering to the senses.

Vaurien Kane took his thick-framed black glasses into his hands. He reached into a pocket with some difficulty and retrieved the microfiber cloth that he carried around for this purpose. He used the cloth to clean the glasses and returned them to sit on his face. He looked entirely unlike himself without glasses; his eyes didn't convey the same burning— and somehow simultaneously icy— intensity that they usually did under the magnification of his glasses. His graying hair, which he kept cropped relatively short, was a testament to the fact that he was running out of time to seize power. He could not afford to back down and take the longer road; he had to act soon. And soon meant now.

He wasn't entirely comfortable dressed in anything other than a classy suit. He was used to having other people's blood on his hands when he wore his suits; he felt that his luck might reverse himself if he did not wear his suit, and his own blood would end up on someone else's hands this time. Or claws, as it were.

He stood and looked out of the open door into the empty hallway that connected the small room to the amphitheater, where he would soon do battle with the creature like a Roman prisoner in the colosseum. He could heard the faint din of noisy conversation from around the corner, where everyone was seated. But no one was watching him. He reached under the Kevlar— again, with some difficulty— and retrieved a pouch of reddish liquid. He double-checked that he was alone and then carefully dribbled the liquid all over the end of the spear. Moments after it had all been imbued into the spear, the red color faded to an un-noticeable hint of its original color. He would not be found out. He was not opposed to bending the rules to gain an advantage.

"Fire and blood." Vaurien Kane whispered. It was a promise.

He turned and walked down the hallway with a confident gait, careful not to touch the end of the spear to anything. He thought for a moment that he might look suspicious, so he adjusted the natural-ness of his walk to compensate.

He turned the corner to enter the amphitheater's stage (the viewers were seated in circular rows rising increasingly behind each other, like a colosseum) and the crowd cheered noisily. Human beings are easily excited by the prospect of bloodshed, and they care not whether the blood is human or animal.

Vaurien saw Ashara Kimeno sitting at a long table with the other Lords of the order. He nodded sharply at Vaurien, tight-lipped. Vaurien grinned, pleased to see someone who appeared to have so much power brought so much under his own influence. He held his arms up like a gladiator and smiled for the crowd. They awarded him some cheering for that meaningless gesture, but Vaurien thought that it couldn't hurt to try to get them on his side. Ashara was dressed in his signature cloak— oh, how pious he looked— and tried not to look too interested in the proceedings.

You might very well be rid of me soon, Vaurien thought, and your hands will be clean of this problem, and you can go back to leading the order of Fire and Blood into a grave of ashes and scabs; you might very well soon be free to be weak and lame, but not bloody likely. Not while I have breath, he thought, and he grinned.

He looked to the other side of the arena, which was surrounded by seven-foot high walls with two gates on either side; the gate he had just come through, and the closed gate on the other side of the arena. There were great wooden spikes protruding every three feet or so, pointed inwards along the rim of the arena. The gate on the other side was dark and shrouded in mystery.

Vaurien steadied himself and twirled his spear fancifully for the benefit of the crowd. He had actually been increasing his own strength significantly over the past few months in order to prepare for this moment, training with great diligence in order to master his own body in the pursuit of strength.

He heard a growl from behind the other gate. Ashara Kimeno rose and a silence fell over the place. Vaurien wanted that kind of respect; the kind whose mere presence could bring a crowd of people to silence, all ears, ready to hear his words.

Ashara raised his arms and began to speak.

"Ancients, we seek your judgement upon your servant, Vaurien Kane. By our consent he comes before you to prove his worthiness in your eyes, to serve you in a place of honor and lead your people. Let him live or die by your grace." He incanted.

After letting the silence draw out (perhaps to show Vaurien who held the power in this situation), Ashara Kimeno ordered the gate to be opened. With a series of creaks and squeals from the mechanism that opened it,

The crowd leaned in and sat in absolute silence, straining for a glance at the horrendous creature. The four large fires spread around the arena of the amphitheater were the only lighting in the indoor space.

A growl shook the ground. Vaurien squinted into the darkness, suddenly having some very serious doubts about this plan. He was separated from the now-opened gate of the creature by about a quarter of a football field.

Everyone waited in tense silence for what felt like an eternity but could have been just a few seconds.

Someone whistled to the creature from the stands, but nothing happened. Vaurien looked at Ashara questioningly. Was he behind this?

But Ashara looked just as confused as everyone else. When a few more moments passed, people began to chatter in the stands.

"Where is the creature?" Vaurien Kane demanded loudly.

The crowd was getting restless.

Suddenly one of the younger members of the order jumped out from the stands and into the arena. He grabbed a spear and rushed towards the gate. He slowed considerably when he actually approached the gate, and came to a stop right before the edge of the darkness. The man nearly turned back before the boos of the crowd convinced him otherwise. He tentatively swung his spear into the darkness, but it hit nothing.

The man stood there for a moment like an idiot before a long, scaly neck zoomed out of the darkness and swallowed his head whole.

The creature stomped all four feet forward until the man's body was an unrecognizable sack of bloody flesh.

The reaction from the crowd was half shrieks and half cheers.

The fire lizard had four scaly feet— each with terrifying claws at the end— and a tail nearly the length of its body swinging around like a wrecking ball behind it. The creature had thin, slanted eyes and an upturned snout that made it look like a demon was glaring at the viewer. It's tongue flickered out like a Gecko's, but with much more of a terror factor. It was the height of a man and the width of a car, with a longer length. It was rather large and enormously terrifying.

Vaurien Kane had to shake his head to wake himself from his amazement. This one was so much larger than the one he had vaguely remembered seeing before, and looked like it had significantly more teeth.

Its belly had a soft orange-isn glow, as did its tail. That was probably where it got the name 'fire lizard', as it looked like it might be a dragon preparing to spew fire. But the lizard would not offer him so quick a death as that.

It began looking around once it had had its fill of the other man who had so foolishly jumped into the arena before. It locked eyes with Vaurien. He cocked his head and returned the ferocious gaze, beginning to advance with his spear well ahead of him. The creature seemed taken aback by his tenacity for a moment. Vaurien could see the ancient question of fight or flight ticking in the back of the creature's eyes. It chose to fight, and it was on.

The crowd was in a frenzy of shouting and cheering by this point. Vaurien reveled in it, even though he knew it was nothing compared to what he would eventually command from people.

"Fire and blood." Vaurien whispered under his breath.

The creature charged at him and then slowed down when Vaurien matched its moves. It began to slowly move in a great circle around him.

Suddenly, it lunged at him. Vaurien brought a ferocious uppercut slice towards the creature's neck, but only the wooden part of the spear touched it. The creature knocked Vaurien to his back with a mighty swing of its tail.

He lay there, dazed, the wind knocked out of him. He struggled to breath and righted himself to his feet just in time to jump over the lizard's tail as it tried to smash him.

Vaurien rolled forward and ducked beneath the creature, bringing the spear up to graze the creature's belly as he rolled out from under it. He immediately rolled again to avoid the inevitable slash from the creature's claw, but he was caught full in the back and right shoulder by the attack. He felt the pain of the claw digging into his back and bit back a scream. He was a god among men, he tried to tell himself, he felt no pain.

He faced the creature and pointed the spear directly at it. It reared back on its haunches— Vaurien almost expected it to breathe fire at him, but of course it could not— and eyed him. He looked at the cut on the creature's belly and realized it had barely been grazed. He would need to cut deeper to kill the thing.

The crowd was in an absolute frenzy. Even Ashara Kimeno was on the edge of his seat, looking on in excitement. Vaurien had them in the palm of his hand, if he could just survive long enough to make use of that fact.

He felt the blood beginning to ooze out of his shoulder and knew he only had so much time left before he would be doomed. He had to make this quick.

The fire lizard swung its tail at him again. This time, Vaurien waited until it was a second from hitting him before jumping on top of it— meanwhile transferring his spear from his right to his left hand, as he was beginning to feel a tingling sensation of weakness in his right hand from the cut he had received before— and quickly jumping onto the creature's back.

The fire lizard gave an enormous roar and shook him off.

As he was in mid-air, Vaurien mustered all his strength and threw this spear with all his might straight towards the heart of the fire lizard.

CHAPTER 19
SPIDERS & ICE

"Don't move." Gye whispered suddenly.

Elicia, Molly, Jane, Elicia, and Ray all froze in their tracks. They looked at him questioningly.

It was silent. Not the kind of 'silence' where birds sing in the distance and the sounds of nature are heard; the real kind of silence where no sounds are being made at all. That was the odd thing, everything had gone deathly quiet.

"That can't possibly be good." Jane whispered, brushing her long blond-streaked brunette hair behind her shoulders.

"If you just assume everything will go badly, you'll be right most of the time." Elicia whispered back.

"Shut up." Gye whispered, slightly louder.

Jane rolled her eyes but complied anyways.

Molly was peering into the woods, looking high and low for the source of the disturbance. She had changed into a black leather jacket over dark blue jeans. She had taken to walking with a wooden staff she had made out of a sapling oak tree.

Elicia and Ray had straggled behind a bit, but both of them now stood absolutely still (besides Elicia breathing a little raggedly) and tried to understand what was going on.

"I saw something move!" Molly cried out in a loud whisper. She was pointing out into the forest.

Suddenly a blur of motion whirled by and smacked Jane into the ground. It was gone before she could react.

She dusted herself off, obviously shaken.

Gye backed up and dropped his pack on the ground.

"Everyone on high alert." He said.

"What was that?" Jane asked, her voice trembling. That was the first time Gye had ever heard her give off any semblance of fear. He felt sorry for her.

"I've just about had enough of this place. It gives me the creeps." Ray Kaymar said.

"We reach the top in one more day, tops, if we keep up the pace. Let's just keep it together." Gye said. He offered Jane a hand to help her up.

The blur of motion slammed into the both of them this time, sending Gye reeling and Jane back onto the ground.

"It's an Arachnid!" Elicia screamed, and she fainted.

The Arachnid poised itself over Jane and hissed. She screamed a blood-curdling scream filled with the deepest fear Gye had ever heard.

Gye rolled and landed a punch on the creature's back. With a swipe of its powerful back legs it send him sprawling again. It turned its attention back to Jane and pinned her to the ground with two of its legs.

She was doomed.

She cried out in horror at the sight. The thing smelled so utterly disgusting this close up, and its eyes were disturbing— they looked like black marbles, with no hint of human emotion or feeling behind them. The creature was actually fuzzy all over, coated with thin hairs that brushed up against her. She felt the slight ticklish sensation on her wrists and wanted to vomit.

The Arachnid hissed again and reared up to land its fangs in her. Suddenly Molly swung her wooden staff around with all her might and slammed it straight into the creature's head, right into its two largest eyes. It screeched and tried to turn and face her, but she was already on it with her staff again, driving it deep into its midsection and then lopping off one of its legs. The leg fell, twitching, to the ground next to Elicia. She awoke at the smell of the ooze coming out of it and backed up against a tree.

The Arachnid mustered its remaining strength and slammed Molly up against a tree. The wind was knocked out of her and her staff dropped out of her hands. The creature wobbled closer to her. She gasped and went on all fours, trying desperately to reach the staff. The Arachnid, seeing her reach for the weapon, realized the connection of events that had led to it being injured and grabbed the staff in its mouth. When it couldn't break the weapon with its mouth, it slammed it against the tree and broke it in two. It dropped the pieces and returned to attack Molly.

She screamed and rolled under the jumping spider like an olympic gymnast. She landed at the base of the tree and grabbed one of the halves of her staff— the least sticky side— and lunged back at the Arachnid. It lunged at her at the same time, and she drove the sharp, broken end of the staff with all of her might through the creature's open mouth and through its brain. It squealed and twitched and fell to the ground. It finally stopped moving. The stench that came from the body was worse than rotted eggs.

Molly burst into tears and wiped her hands on the nearest tree obsessively, trying very hard to get all remnants of the Arachnid off of her person. She was obviously disturbed by the experience.

"You saved me." Jane gasped through her own teary eyes.

Molly couldn't answer through her deep, guttural sobs. She closed her eyes and rocked back and forth in place, barely breathing.

"We need to get out of here." Ray said.

Gye rose from the ground, shaken, and agreed. They hurriedly grabbed their strewn-about bags and ran as furiously as they could up the mountain. They ran until their muscles burned and then farther, still farther, in fear. When reason had finally won out over the horror of the situation, they slowed down to a halt and flopped onto the ground, exhausted.

Elicia wheezed.

"I should have given up smoking years ago. I can barely breath. Agh. Ah." She wheezed.

"Molly, you saved us back there. We would've all been killed without you." Gye said gently.

She smiled weakly back at him through bleary eyes and wiped away a tear.

"I'm deathly afraid of spiders. Even the little ones that used to run around on the hardwood floors at my old house... even the little ones, I would scream and jump up on a counter. Oh god. And now, and now there's these spiders as big as me... it's my worst nightmare. Oh god. I can't deal with this." She said, dissolving back into trauma.

"But you did. You overcame all of that, and you did it to save us. I don't have the words to thank you." Gye said.

"I was wrong about you," Jane added, sitting upright and leaning against the trunk of a massive tree, "I was so, so, so wrong about you. Please forgive me. Please." Jane said.

"I don't remember much about my father— he passed away when I was very young— but I do clearly remember one thing he taught me. Bravery is the highest thing we can aspire to in life, he said. Well, that's you." Gye interjected.

Molly just nodded weakly, head down, and brushed the leaves off her leather jacket.

"Should we just camp here?" Ray asked.

"NO. No, no I just can't do that. I need to get out of this forest." Molly said desperately.

"You heard her. Let's go." Gye said. And they trudged further up the mountain, hopefully farther away from the evils and horrors of the forest. Hopefully. Hopefully...

CHAPTER 20
FIRE & BLOOD II

Vaurien's spear found its mark, and the spear impaled itself deeply into the flesh of the fire lizard.

The creature still had some fight in it, though, and swiped at Vaurien with its mighty claw. He jumped backwards just in time, and then barely mustered the stability to roll out of the way of another attack just in time.

The poison was not working fast enough, although it was obvious that the creature was slowing down from the poison and the blood loss. He needed the creature to die quickly or he was finished, and now he was weaponless.

The creature came about with its tail and nearly flattened Vaurien. In a split second decision, Vaurien Kane mustered all of his adrenaline and sprinted towards the nearest large fire that was lighting the arena.

He felt the weight of the fire lizard's gate on the ground near him. He was running out of time.

He reached the flame and put it between himself and the fire lizard. The creature reeled back at the closeness of the flame and moved back and forth, trying to get an angle to pounce at Vaurien and end him. Vaurien knew he just needed to keep the fire lizard in place long enough for the poison to kill it. The creature swayed and nearly dropped, but roared and reared its head in defiance of death. Vaurien couldn't help but admire the creature, for it refused to die.

Vaurien sensed that the crowd would soon turn against him if he continued to hide, so he removed his chain mail quickly and balled it up.

He whistled and threw the chain mail to the right of the flame. When the fire lizard pounced at it, Vaurien dashed around the other side of the flame and jumped on the creature once again. This time, it was too weak to resist.

Vaurien reached and grabbed the shaft of the spear, which was still mostly lodged in the creature's flesh. He yanked it out, and a torrent of blood flowed out of the wound and stained the ground. He raised the spear high, eliciting a mighty cheer from the crowd, and brought the spear around the creature's neck. He yelled a mighty battle cry as he sliced across the creature's throat from behind with the spear. The fire lizard tried to roar defiantly one last time, but it only turned the torrent of blood flowing out of it into a flood, punctuated by the gurgling of its throat.

"Shhhhhh, hush now." Vaurien whispered into the creature's ear as he twisted the end of the spear. A cry of guttural pain escaped the creature's vocal cords, a last cry to be allowed to die quickly.

I guess humans aren't the only ones who do that, Vaurien thought as he twisted the spear again.

He stood and yanked the spearhead across the creature's whole head as he did so, killing it completely. The orange, glowing liquid oozed out of the creature's scales and joined the pool of blood on the ground.

"Fire and blood." Vaurien Kane said as he looked at the combination.

He stood and raised both hands into the air, like the champion he was.

Ashara Kimeno's face had paled considerably. He raised himself up, shaking visibly, and cleared his throat.

The audience was slow to acknowledge him this time. Vaurien's feat was still fresh in their minds, and it was far more exciting to them than their boring old leader who was weak and frail and fat. Vaurien reveled in his new power.

Ashara Kimeno cleared his throat again and spoke, although his voice shook noticeably.

"The Ancients have made their holy will known. Let it be henceforth known that Vaurien Kane has been found worthy in the sight of the ancients and men, and he is now and forevermore a Lord of the Order of Fire and Blood." Ashara said. He sat his great hefty weight down heavily on the chair. From that moment on, Vaurien knew, the High Lord would no longer be the real power behind the Order.

"I have proven myself beyond a shadow of a doubt. The will of the Ancients is with me. I have a new directive from the holy ones. We will rise to battle like the days of old and avenge the Ancients against the unbelievers. Rise with me, to battle!" Vaurien yelled.

The crowd's screamed response in the affirmative was deafening. Vaurien smiled from ear to ear for the first time in years. The forest of blasphemy would soon be a tombstone for the blasphemers who had dared laugh at and malign the Ancients. They would no longer be laughed at, only feared as they should rightly be.

CHAPTER 21
TOP OF THE WORLD

"Grab my hand. Come on." Gye said.

"I'm slipping." Jane responded through clenched teeth. Gye was hauling her up the steep, icy slope. The mountain was getting so steep at this point that they had to climb nearly vertically for the next fifty feet or so, trying their hardest to make any progress against the fiercely slicing shafts of cold wind knifing through their ill-prepared clothes.

With a burst of effort, Gye pulled Jane up to the edge of the outcropping of rock that the remainder of the group were already resting on. She plopped down beside him, panting heavily. Her shirt rode up her belly as she stretched out her arms on the ground like a starfish in exhaustion; she seemed too tired to care.

"I can't go on any more." Jane complained, wiping a lock of hair out of her eyes. Her eyes looked so much more steely blue in this light than Gye had ever seen them. He thought it rather an attractive color.

"We can't stop here, we'll die without some kind of shelter." Molly said.

"When did you become Ms. wilderness explorer? We'll probably die anyways." Elicia said.

"That's not a very healthy view of things." Molly replied.

"A dose of reality is always healthy. We just need to get the drone and get out, no time to dilly-dally." Elicia said.

"You're the one costing us the most time, you slow-moving beast. Can you maybe waddle a little faster?" Ray snapped angrily.

"Enough. No more of this. If we're going to get out of this alive, we need to stop squabbling and stick together." Gye said.

"I don't particularly care about that right now. This monster insulted me. If he doesn't apologize, I wont be helping him out at all, let me assure you." Elicia said.

"One thing you should know about me: I never apologize." Ray said. He grabbed his bag and slung it over his shoulder, then began climbing again.

"Let's just get a move on." Gye said.

"Help me up." Jane said, sticking out her hand to Gye from her perch on the cold ground.

He grabbed her forearm and pulled her to her feet. She grunted and dusted herself off.

"Don't worry, we're nearly to the top. You can make it." Gye said.

"We'll see about that." Jane groaned.

The wind kicked up and Gye noticed his fingers becoming less and less responsive. It was getting icy and slick this close to the top. He knew they needed to get out of these conditions soon or else they would be nothing more than skeletons, left on this mountainside to be found by archeologists a long time in the future.

Gye heard a scream from higher up the mountain and saw Molly slip on a patch of ice. She tried to maintain her balance but she fell backwards.

Gye caught the back of her shirt with his frigid right hand and screamed at the pain of the weight on his near-frozen limb. His fingers were burning, like the pain of stubbing your toe really, really hard. She was dangling from his grasp, threatening to fall away from him forever. He couldn't let that happen.

"No!" He yelled out. But it did no good. She was slipping.

The world went into slow-motion. His frozen arm spasmed and Molly Hazelwood fell out of his grasp.

He saw her brown eyes look into his, looking for solace as she fell. They never broke eye contact as she went down, dark hair flapping about her head like a superhero's cape. The ice on her leather jacket was left behind in the air momentarily by the suddenness of her fall.

He turned his gaze upward instantly. He couldn't watch this. No, no... he wasn't strong enough to see her go. Not this way.

"Molly!" Jane screamed downwards. Jane frantically began scrambling downwards. Her torn jeans were caught against a sharp rock sticking out from the face of the cliff for a moment before she tore an even larger hole by ripping them free. She was barely keeping herself from throwing herself downwards.

"What are you doing?" Gye asked.

"Look, she landed on that cliffside! There's a chance she's alive." She shouted through ragged breaths as she descended.

Gye allowed himself to look down. Yes, she was right! Molly lay on top of the cliff about twenty feet down, limbs sprawled about from the fetal position. She wasn't moving, but she might have just had the wind knocked out of her.

He carefully and quickly— more so the latter than the former— clambered downwards. He passed Jane, panting heavily, and jumped the last few feet to the ground next to Molly. The shock bounced painfully into his knees and shot up his spine— even though he had bent his knees as he had learned to do a long time ago when jumping from heights— but he brushed the insignificant sensation aside and scrambled over to Molly's side. He heard Jane land on the ground a few seconds after he did.

"Molly!" He yelled. He saw her stir as he came up beside her.

Her eyes blinked open as he shook her. She coughed and looked around wildly, not sure where she was for a second.

"Ow." She mumbled as she tried to sit up.

"Are you okay? Where does it hurt?" Gye asked.

"What, are you going to kiss it better?" She said glibly. She winced and clenched her teeth in pain.

"All joking aside, I can barely keep from screaming right now because my ankle hurts so bad." Molly said.

Jane arrived by her side.

"Molly! I'm so glad you're alive!" Jane said. Gye noticed that she was barely keeping back a flood of tears.

Molly reached out and caressed Jane's face.

"I'm ok. Mostly. I'm pretty sure my right ankle is sprained, and I'm sore all over. Thanks for trying to catch me, though." She said to Gye.

"I tried, I failed. Now you're hurt, and it's my fault." He said.

"All you can do is try." Molly said, trying to muster a smile but only barely managing to hold back the pain.

"There's no way you can climb with that ankle, and you'll die if you stay behind. You'll have to climb on my back and I'll carry you up." Gye said.

"You would do that for me?" Molly asked.

"I would do anything for you." Gye said.

"That's so sweet. You've come a long way from being the heartless scavenger I met a few weeks ago." Jane said.

"And you're still the same, mostly. Just more interesting and slightly less mysterious." He said. He wrapped her hands between his as he said so.

She looked down at her hands joined with his.

"What are you doing?" She asked.

"Just warming your hands." He said with a grin.

"Of course. Come on Molly, I'll help you get up." Jane said.

Gye could feel Molly's breathing on his neck as he pulled both of their weights upwards. No matter how often he kept reminding himself he was so close to the top, he couldn't help but see the distance and time separating him from the top as an eternity stretching out before him. Everyone else had already passed them and were well ahead of his slow, meandering pace.

Her arms were around his neck and her legs were crossed around his torso. At least it was warmer this way. He had never noticed how heavy other people— even smaller ones like Molly— were. She may as well have been a sack of lead, albeit a better conversationalist.

A wisp of her dark hair was in his eye as he looked upwards. He tried to blow it out of the way but to no avail. He couldn't use his hands, as he was sure doing so would result in them plummeting all the way down to the base of the mountain. And there would be no getting up from a fall that time.

"Sorry." She said, noticing his trouble. She flung her head back to get the hair of out his way. He heard her stifle a cry of pain from the motion. She was trying not to show any pain and be brave, but he could feel every tremor in her body as it was touching his, and he knew that she was both in pain and out of bravery.

"Are you okay back there?" Gye asked.

She couldn't answer for several seconds as she tried to stop the pain from creeping into her voice.

"I'm fine." She lied.

"It's okay to not be fine." Gye answered back gently.

She sniffled and Gye felt a tear drip onto his skin. She was crying and trying not to show it.

At least they didn't have to talk very loudly to hear each other.

"The truth is, I'm not okay. I know I signed up for this the moment I snuck into the rover, and I wouldn't trade this adventure up to this point for the world, but right now... right now, I just want to die." She said.

Gye was quiet for a moment as he pulled them further upwards.

"You can't die. Just hold on and we'll get through this." Gye said

"I have no strength left, Gye. I don't know. Maybe this is the end of the road for me. I'm on a mountainside with a strained ankle and I know you can't carry me forever." She said.

"I'll certainly try." He panted.

"I know you will. But sometimes our best isn't good enough. I've loved becoming friends with you all on this adventure, but I have a feeling that somehow this will be my last one. I don't think I'll make it through this. But you, you, at least, have the adventure of a lifetime ahead of you. Romance always is life's greatest adventure." She said.

"What are you talking about?" He asked. He could see the top now. Just a few more hefts upwards and they would be there.

"Oh please. Don't tell me you don't see sparks flying between you and Jane. You're meant for each other, I can see it." She said.

"I feel something for her, yes. I'd be lying if I denied it. But I'm not sure I believe in love, and besides, we're too young to be falling in love. That's for later in life. We don't even know ourselves yet, truly." He said. He had to stop moving to get that one out.

"To love another person before you even know yourself, and to love them even when you know them completely and the excitement fades, that's something poetic. That's something worthwhile. That's an adventure you can look back on at the end of your life and say, I had that, so at least it was all worth it." Molly said.

"I don't know. I'll think about it." Gye said.

"Oh, come on. If I don't make it through this, I at least want to know you made it out of this with something more valuable than money." Molly said.

"I said I'll think about it." He grunted as he pulled them up over the side of the cliff.

"You've lost your family. You're afraid to love. But this could be good for you, Gye Storm. You should pursue it."

Gye didn't reply. They had finally made it to the top, and the view was beautiful.

The lush, beautiful forest spread out before them in an endless panorama. There were clouds below them, dancing effortlessly on the breeze with the birds and the trees.

"Wow. This is truly amazing. If only I had my easel and canvas and some acrylics, I could try to paint this beauty." Molly said.

"I'm sure you would do justice to it." Jane said.

"Alright, we need to find the drone. Anyone see it?" Ray asked, ever the pragmatist.

The top of the mountain was not particularly large, but was relatively flat and about thirty feet across.

"You're sure it was up here? If you made us do all this climbing for no reason, I'm going to kill myself." Elicia said.

"We traced to to *exactly* the top of this mountain. It has to be up here." Gye said.

"You're certain?" Ray asked.

"If I weren't certain, I wouldn't be qualified for the job they hired me to do. Yes, I'm certain!" Gye said hotly.

"What's that over there?" Jane asked, pointing to the center of the top of the mountain.

"It looks like... wait, is this a volcano? It's hallow!" Gye exclaimed.

They made their way over to examine the anomaly closer, with Molly still on Gye's back.

The mountain opened up into a large tunnel that was dimly lit on the inside by some faint light source deep inside.

"This must be where the anomaly that caused the existence of the forest is to be found." Jane said.

"Are you sure we should go in there?" Molly asked.

"The drone isn't anywhere else around here, so it must be inside this tunnel. We've come this far, we may as well press on." Elicia said.

They all agreed on this fact and stepped into the tunnel gingerly.

"Quite embarrassingly, though... I have to pee. I'm going back out there for a minute, don't move on without me!" Elicia said with an odd degree of cheeriness.

She went back out of the tunnel, looked around and made sure she was out of their view. She did not pee; however, she did look all around again and reach into a zipped pocket in her pants, from which she took out a small black box with a few buttons on it and an extendable antennae. She extended the antennae, turned it on, and pressed the buttons as she saw fit. The light indicator on the side flashed red in a steady pattern and the device made a few beeping sounds. Elicia wiped her hands on her jeans— ridding herself of the sweat— and then composed herself. She then looked around again and then waddled back into the tunnel to rejoin the others.

"Shall we crack on?" She said.

###

"Mr. Kane? We received the signal. The origin has been pinpointed. Awaiting your orders." The man at the door said.

Vaurien Kane smiled and set down the knife he was sharpening. "Excellent. Prepare the men. We fly within the hour."

When the man had left, Vaurien reached for his thick-framed black glasses and set them down on the table. He took a cloth out of his pocket and wiped the lenses, then put them back on his face.

His heart had been aching lately. No, he was not feeling some kind of ephemeral emotion or desire for someone; merely, his physical heart was running out of time before it would need to be replaced. Again. What was this, the twentieth time already? He turned and jotted down a note on his pen pad—'need new heart', he wrote, in oddly casual, all-lowercase print. He would have to remember to acquire a new one upon his inevitable triumphant return.

The thought made him look over to the letter he had kept in the desk for the past two decades or so. It was still his favorite to read, because it was so full of hope and promise despite what was happening — the man had been lied to, of course. He would receive no payment, and his family would crumble without him.

"Eggs and promises are easily broken." Vaurien Kane muttered to himself.

He came to a sudden realization, and smiled. The way things all seem connected, he remarked to himself, it is such a small world indeed.

He stood and looked out the window behind him, at the relatively peaceful city.

"The lion has laid down with the lamb because the lion had had its fill. But now the lion is hungry again, and peace will turn to bloodshed."

CHAPTER 22
INTO THE DARKNESS

Thankfully, the tunnel was not a steep descent, and was large enough for two of them to stand side by side and still be able to move forward. It sloped gently downwards like an enormous spiral staircase — unfortunately, minus the stairs.

It was dim, but not too dim that you couldn't see your hands right in front of you. The walls seemed mostly smooth but oddly scratched in some places. Gye didn't think that boded too well for their journey.

"I have a bad feeling about this." Ray said.

"I have bad feelings about most things. Those feelings, however, are usually caused by intoxication and should not be taken seriously." Elicia said glibly.

"You never cease to disappoint me with your immoral approach to life. What, did you strangle your conscious to death?" Ray said.

"Smoke poisoning would be more likely." Elicia replied deftly.

"For the both of us, then." Ray said.

"At least that's one thing we have in common." Elicia said.

"You're still an annoying twat." Ray said.

"I know." She replied.

"Keep it down, guys. We don't know what could be listening in." Gye said ominously.

"He's right. Spiders don't live underground, do they?" Ray asked.

"Insects can live in surprising locations. You never know." Jane replied.

"That's not very reassuring." Molly said. Gye had to crouch down slightly while walking to avoid hitting her head against the ceiling of the tunnel. It was not exactly relaxing.

"I can't help but feel that we're walking into a trap." Jane said.

"What do you mean?" Elicia said, rather more aggressively than Gye expected.

Jane was slightly taken aback.

"This whole thing… we're going into this unknown lair to find something we want. We're like a mouse hunting after cheese, enticed into a mouse trap…" She said.

"I've rather had my fill of traps." Molly said.

"What if we're the cheese?" Ray Kaymar asked.

"It's not important." Elicia replied.

There was a faint crackling sound from further down the tunnel. But it was enough to stop the group dead in their tracks.

The hair raised on the back of Gye's neck. He could feel Molly holding him tighter.

"What was that?" Jane whispered.

"Well, there's no turning back now. Onward." Gye said, keeping his voice remarkably steady despite the fear he was feeling.

###

Hours passed by, and the tunnel floor was beginning to level out. The ceiling had gotten progressively shorter as time went on, and Gye practically had to crawl along with the others— with Molly on his back— just to keep from scraping the ceiling. She had been feeling pain less often, although whether that was a good thing or a bad thing, Gye couldn't tell.

They came upon a section of the tunnel where the ground was covered in liquid. Elicia was the first to discover it.

"What's that splashing sound?" She asked.

"Let's just hope that it's water." Ray commented.

"I hope so. I'm thirsty and I've run out of water." Jane Silver said.

"I've got some! Here." Molly said.

"You should save your provisions for yourself, Molly." Elicia cautioned.

"It wont hurt to share a little." She replied.

"How adorable. You haven't become cynical yet. That's the most fun about watching new generations of young people become older-you get to watch their optimism die." Elicia said.

"You depress me." Gye grunted as he sloshed through the deepening liquid. It seemed thicker than water, although perhaps that was just the effort of carrying the weight of two people. He couldn't tell the color of the liquid due to the dimness of the lighting, which reduced their surroundings to various shades of gray.

Jane took just a sip from Molly's water and then handed it back to her gratefully.

The tunnel suddenly lead to an abrupt end. It merely ended, with no explanation, with a dirt wall.

"Well, this sucks." Ray said.

Elicia fumed.

"I thought you said the drone was down here." She said, her voice dripping with icy tones.

"I did. We knew that the coordinates were on top of this mountain, but the drone wasn't on top, so the only explanation is that its inside the mountain somewhere." Gye said. But his voice no longer held the brick certainty that he had once had.

"You incompetent fool. This is the end of me, then." Elicia said, sitting heavily against the wall of dirt. Some of it collapsed onto her hair.

"Figures." She mumbled, wiping it out as best she could with the modicum of light.

"Wait. If we know its inside the mountain, and this is the only way in, then the trail can't end here. Maybe we can dig through the dirt!" Molly suggested.

"It could be miles long. We could die down here waiting and waiting to break through, always thinking we were on the cusp of discovery." Elicia said.

"Well, its cold as all get out in here, so we're more likely to die of hypothermia than all that. Come on, let's give it a shot." Molly said.

Gye set her down gingerly— making sure her ankle never touched the floor— and walked over to the dirt wall.

He began clawing into it (although he was already nearly exhausted from the journey) and removing dirt.

"Ray, Jane, Elicia, come on, help me out here." He said.

They joined in and the pace of dirt removal quickened remarkably.

"It's a shame I have to ruin a perfect white blazer with this much dirt." Elicia complained.

"Wow, that sounds like something Anthony would say." Ray said.

"I'll give the boy one thing, he did have marvelous fashion sense. Can't say the same for any of you clowns." Elicia muttered.

"Can we focus, please?" Jane asked.

The dirt wall was beginning to cave in. They were making progress.

With a final savage kick to the center, the dirt wall crumbled to the floor into a heap of rubble. The sudden presence of orange-ish light surprised them, and Gye had to cover his eyes for a moment to recover.

"We broke through!" Jane exclaimed.

"Hey! Don't forget me." Molly said.

Gye went back for her and picked her up. She resumed her perch on his back, but Gye thought that she weighed him down much less now. They dipped low to get through the small hole through the dirt wall, and then stepped gingerly into a large, cavernous room.

They could see ahead of them that the ceiling was about forty feet high, but blocking the way forward were two long, twelve foot high walls that came from the distance and converged into a square opening in front of them. That was the only way in.

"Now this is unusual." Jane said.

"I'd consider most of what we've done so far on this journey to be unusual." Elicia said.

"Let's press on." Gye said, readjusting Molly's position to be more comfortable, and taking the first steps forward himself.

They passed through the opening to find several passages branching off from it.

"My, it's like a maze in here!" Molly said.

"So how do we solve it?" Gye asked.

"These walls aren't stone. This mountain was bored into by some creature— probably a *hive* of creatures... and these cells that branch off from each other have to have some kind of purpose in their colony. I presume, at least." Jane said.

"But the colony could have died out many years ago, yes? It might be as easy as walking in, getting what we want, and walking out." Ray said.

"But then how would the drone have gotten down in here in the first place?" Gye asked.

"I guess we'll find out." Elicia said curtly.

"Well, I suppose we have to decide in fairly short order how we are going to go about searching this... maze, as you called it." Gye said.

"We could split up. You and Molly, myself and Jane, and Elicia... can go by herself." Ray Kaymar said.

"Not unless hell freezes over." Elicia quipped.

"With your personality, I'm sure it will when you get there." Ray said.

"That's not funny. And no, here's what I propose: myself, Gye, Jane, and the lovely Ms. Hazelwood will all go searching as a group, being sure to stay very close together, while Ray can take the time alone to go—" Elicia started.

"There's no need for that. We're all staying together." Gye said, readjusting again.

"I agree. I don't think splitting up has ever gone well for anyone, ever." Jane said.

"We would cover more ground if we split up, is all I'm saying." Ray Kaymar said.

"Perhaps we'd best listen to him. Remember the last time we let him get angry and he shattered a glass? Maybe this time he'll combust and blow this whole bloody thing up for us." Elicia taunted.

But Ray remained surprisingly composed.

"Are you finished?" Ray replied contemptuously.

"I have an idea." Molly interrupted.

"Do tell." Elicia said flatly.

She continued on.

"If we take just the leftmost or rightmost opening every time we come upon a split in the pathway, then we can always trace our way back and try a different route if we end up at a dead end." She said.

"That sounds like the best option we've got." Gye said.

"We may as well give it a try." Jane said.

"Well, do we choose left or right?" Ray asked.

"Anyone have a coin we can flip?" Molly asked.

"Yes, because I was certain the one thing I would need in a forest untouched by human hands in millennia would be human currency. Right, okay." Elicia snapped.

"I was just trying to help." Molly said.

"You aren't being very helpful just now." Elicia replied.

"She slipped and twisted her ankle, it could've happened to any of us." Jane said defensively.

"Sure, whatever. That's not important." Elicia said.

"Well, since Molly hurt her right ankle, we should go left." Gye opined.

"I enjoy your whimsical approach to decision making." Elicia said.

"Come on, it's as good as any other way of deciding." Gye said.

"Fair enough. Let's go left, then." She said.

They took the left tunnel. Gye began whistling a tune from a song he had once heard, some old song from a retro club that wanted to pretend it was from a few decades ago. Ray recognized the tune and began humming along.

"What are you going on about, eh? Cut it out." Elicia said.

"Why so pessimistic? We need a bit of a war chant going into battle, don't we?" Ray Kaymar said.

"I wish you had been eaten by the Arachnid instead of that lovely Spanish cook. And I never even got to seduce him. What a waste of a pretty face." Elicia muttered.

"Too soon." Gye said, rolling his eyes.

"What? You people need to wake up and face reality. Royce is dead, Captain Walker is probably dead, Anthony is probably dead. Then he'd truly be one with nature." Elicia mused.

"Cut it out, would you? You might not have liked him, but we were good friends. He was with me through the hardest time in my life. You might not have respected him, but he was the best of people when it really counted." Jane Silver said.

They came upon another divergence in the path.

"Left again, I presume." Jane said.

"That would be the most logical. Although sometimes what's most logical is not what's best. But I suppose we'll see." Elicia said.

The ground in the left tunnel was riddled with dust and black particles strewn about like a world war two minefield. The tunnel on the right seemed overly clean by comparison, and all the more inviting because of it. Gye found it almost tempting enough to choose the right tunnel, but in the end he decided it was best to just stick to the plan.

"This isn't exactly ideal." Molly said when she noticed the dingy nature of the tunnel they were about to go through.

"It would be best just to keep cracking on." Jane said.

Hours later, after many left turns upon left turns upon left turns upon left turns… et cetera, they had reached the point of exhaustion. The air was getting hot and stuffy and nearly unbreathable in its humidity.

Even after all of the ways they had come, they still didn't feel as though they had made any progress. They had gone fully all the way down the leftmost route and found a dead end; then gone back a ways and tried the nearest from the left and come upon a dead end, and then repeated the process until they weren't even sure who they were any more.

Sleep was tugging at Gye's eyelids and whispering for him to succumb to its pleasures. All he wanted to do was fall over and sleep for hours and hours and hours... but he could not. They had a mission to accomplish, and they couldn't be caught with their pants down, as it were. The drone wasn't going to find itself.

The walls of the 'maze'— as they had unanimously designated it — were not made of stone, as Jane had pointed out, but were made of a waxy yellow-ish substance that left residue on the fingers of anyone who touched it. The act of touching it, in fact, left a perfect fingerprint in the material, like a forensics team had left fingerprinting dust on a future crime scene and was now coming back to collect it. Elicia even tried tasting it, and had concluded that it was far too waxy for her taste but would suit any patron just fine at an American restaurant. Gye was too tired to take umbrage at that comment.

They were sitting together, knees bent, backs against the walls of the tunnel where they had decided to take a break from their seemingly endless journey.

Jane was sitting across from Gye, her ankles intertwined with his due to the lack of space in the tunnel. No one wanted to venture too far from the others, for fear that some creature would snatch them out from the midst of the darkness and they would never be heard from again. Ray, at least, had found a small flashlight in his backpack. It had long ago ran out of batteries, but it was able to emit at least a small amount of light by using the energy of the heat of a human hand. Ray took almost an hour of their voyage to speak about the scientific principles that went into it and its construction.

While no one was paying any attention when Ray Kaymar rambled on about Peltier pads and the Makosinski principles, the group conversation was, at least, the only thing keeping them sane in this claustrophobic environment.

Suddenly a sharp buzzing sound from far down the tunnel to their right— which they had not gone down before— awakened them from their ephemeral reverie.

It was over in seconds, but they were sure they had heard something.

"We have to go down there. It's our only shot." Gye said.

The others reluctantly agreed and they started off, getting the blood in their veins to move around with some difficulty.

After a long while of walking, they came across a sudden corner. Gye turned it first and gasped at what he saw.

CHAPTER 23
THE BEES' KNEES

In front of him— and the rest of the group as they joined him— were rows upon rows of hexagonal structures filled with honey, each one about a foot across and almost a foot tall. The place was lit with a faint orange light, the source of which Gye could not ascertain.

"Guys," He said in a low whisper, "we're in a bee hive."

Molly squeezed him tighter, obviously not relishing the prospect of encountering enormous bees.

"Well, there is good news, at least. At least it's not a wasps' nest." Jane said.

"Always seeing the bright side, how quaint of you. What do we do now?" Elicia asked.

"Well, the bees— or whatever they are— must have taken the drone into their hive for some reason. Do bees horde things, Jane?" Gye asked.

"I don't remember if they do, but I see no reason why a… bee-like creature with increased size wouldn't. Perhaps at this size it is more suitable for them to horde things to help build their hive." She said.

"And, um, what size are we talking about here?" Molly asked. There was no mistaking the fear that was creeping into her voice.

"Judging by the size of the honeycombs… probably about a foot long on average." Jane said.

"Heh. A foot long. Now here's one of those they wouldn't sell at Subway." Elicia said.

"That's not funny. If there's one thing I hate more than spiders, it's bees. They'd all better be out gathering pollen or whatever bees do." Molly said.

"Well, I have some bad news for you. Fewer than ten percent of a hive is ever away from it at one given time, so it's not likely that they'll all be gone." Jane said.

As if on cue, they heard a buzzing in the distance. They quickly shrank behind the corner and peeked out, wanting to see the grotesque thing for themselves.

True to Jane's prediction, the bee was about a foot long. Its stinger glistened like a carbon fiber knife— surely getting stung by one of them would be fatal— and its wings buzzed furiously to keep it upright. The bee's fuzzy, almost cloth-like exterior was coated with pollen in places. Its black, emotionless eyes were terrifying— mostly because it was impossible to tell where the bee was looking at any given time. And there was certainly no soul behind those eyes. It looked like a monstrous doll that someone had made as a prank to scare the living daylights out of someone. But no, this was reality, and it was nothing short of traumatizing.

Gye felt Molly shuddering violently at the sight, and she turned her head and clenched her eyes shut. She would rather not see this atrocity, it seemed.

"Why's it moving so slow?" Ray Kaymar asked, apparently less taken aback by the creature's existence that the rest of them.

"Good question." Jane said, and she squinted to see the creature better.

It was returning to add some pollen to a nearly empty honeycomb. It used its feet to scrape the pollen off of its hairy body and its antennae and into the honeycomb. Then, its mission accomplished, it waddled away into an opening on the nearest wall.

"Holy…" Gye said.

"I'm literally shivering right now." Molly said.

"I think that most of the hive is in hibernation because they are inside this cold mountain. I'm guessing it's only seasonally snowy, then. But that increases our chances of success dramatically, I think." Jane said.

"Well, that's good news. One of the few things that are good news right now, I guess. We're all alive, that's good news. Well done, all." Molly said.

"Don't pat yourself on the back just yet. Who's to know if we'll survive or not? I might die just of fright, myself." Elicia Cantor said.

"Let's just hope we all make it out alive. Now, the only way further into the hive is through that opening where the bee went. How do we get over there? Any ideas? I don't want to swim through honey." Gye said, shifting to balance Molly's weight better. She grimaced as her ankle brushed against the wall.

"We could try to walk on the edges of the honeycombs. That might work." Jane said.

"It's worth a shot. You first." Gye said.

Jane acquiesced and walked up to the edge of the field of honeycombs. The others followed quickly behind, Molly still on Gye's back. The first several dozen rows of honeycombs were empty, so they were easy to traverse, but that easy of transport disappeared when the encountered honeycombs that were actually filled with Honey.

Gye was exceedingly careful to keep both of his feet on more than one side of the honeycomb at a time, so that his and Molly's combined weight did not crush the wall of the honeycomb and practically glue them to the floor of the hive.

"Everyone doing alright?" Gye called out.

Almost on cue, Jane slipped and fell. Both of her feet landed in separate honeycombs— she was covered up to her calves in honey— but thankfully, she caught her hands on the edges of some other honeycombs and steadied herself. She stood back up and tried to brush the honey off, her face as red as a tomato in embarrassment.

"This sucks so much. And these jeans were so cute. Ugh." She muttered as she squeezed the honey out of the fabric as much as she could. She ended up borrowing Ray Kaymar's knife to cut the honey-soiled parts of her jeans off. She ended up looking like she was wearing stained capris. Her black tank top was splattered as well, and the liquid-infused fabric clung to her body, revealing her form. Gye couldn't help but admire it.

"Bee pants, a new product coming this fall from Levi's. Pre-order now." Jane said, trying to be self-deprecative.

"Don't be embarrassed. I would've fallen twice by now if Gye weren't carrying me." Molly said.

They walked the rest of the way to the entrance, and no one else fell into the honey, thankfully for them.

They entered into the next cavernous room and looked at the sight before them.

To their left, rows upon rows of bees sat dormant, like a plethora of cars parked in a parking lot. They were even spaced out with an unnatural regularity. There were less than a dozen active bees among the many, many of them laying there in hibernation; the active ones were going in and out of another cavernous room Gye could see from his perspective. He guessed that that must have been the room where the larvae and eggs were kept. None of the bees appeared to notice their entrance.

To their right, there was another whole room apart from the main room, and in that room there was the largest collection of natural junk Gye had ever seen. Although that wasn't saying much.

"There it is! The drone!" Ray Kaymar said, pointing to the edge of the pile. Gye followed his pointing finger and looked in that direction.

Sure enough, there was the drone; the only metallic object among the junk pile of enormous leaves, the occasional rock, and other miscellaneous objects.

Gye finally saw where the orange-ish light was coming from. The bees had created a gel substance, which was probably mostly wax, and used it to seal off this part of the hive from the outside world. It seemed that the bees had collapsed the wall between their hive and the outside world, and then had re-built it to protect their home when they realized what they had done.

"There it is. Our whole mission, the money... it's all right there." Elicia said. She was practically salivating at the mouth upon seeing the prospect.

"Do you see the wax wall over there? If we can cut through it without getting killed, we can get out scott free!" Gye exclaimed.

Suddenly a bee perked up and moved its head to look in their direction from across the room.

"Don't... move." Gye whispered.

The bee waddled closer— apparently flying was too much effort — and then examined them closely for a moment. It seemed particularly interested in Jane. Then it seemed to do the Bee equivalent of a shrug and moved on.

"It smelled the honey on me! I think it thought we were just honey. The scent must have blocked our pheromones." Jane whispered.

"I don't know what that means, but let's grab the drone and get out." Gye said.

They practically tiptoed towards the drone, trying to make as little sound as was humanly possible.

Jane nearly dropped her bag onto the floor. Gye looked at her ferociously, as if that would stop their demise from happening. But thankfully, none of the giant bees stirred

They arrived at the pile of junk. Ray Kaymar moved ahead of them to the wax wall and began gingerly cutting away at the place where the wax met the stone of the mountain. He worked with swift and careful effectiveness.

The drone was about a meter long. Its outside was packed with an array of sensors and equipment, the purposes of which Gye could not begin to ascertain. There was one blinking LED light on the side of it, pulsing at about twelve times per minute.

Elicia actually hugged the drone and smiled widely.

"Enough with the PDA, please." Jane joked.

She then helped Elicia grab the other end of the drone and carry it towards Ray.

By the time Gye (carrying Molly), Elicia, and Jane had reached Ray, he was about to push out the panel of wax that he had cut out of the wax wall. It was about a meter and a half tall, just enough room for them to step through.

Ray tried to push it out, but it wouldn't budge.

A deep whirring sound penetrated the air. It wasn't coming from inside the hive, if Gye could tell correctly.

"Hurry." Molly whispered over Gye's shoulder.

"I'm trying! It wont budge." Ray said.

"Try kicking it in." Jane urged.

Ray took her advice and backed up a bit. By now the deep whirring sound had reached a fever pitch. There was a stirring among the ranks of the bees, and some were beginning to awaken.

"Come onnnn." Gye said.

Ray ran forward and gave a massive kick to the wax. It splintered across like a thick alloy of metallic glass.

The bees heard this disturbance to their hive, and several of the nearer ones began crawling slowly in their direction.

Molly took one look into their deep, soulless black eyes and stifled a scream.

The ground shook like a small earthquake had taken place.

Gye, tired of waiting, walked towards the splintered wax. Then, with a single savage kick, the wax splintered to pieces.

"Let's move!" He yelled.

They tumbled out of the opening like captured ants out of an empty jar of jelly that some kid had used to capture them with for fun.

"Let's get out of here." Jane said. Her black tank top was now grimy with the dirt of their escape.

The ground shook again, and again it was like a small earthquake had hit. But now that they were outside, Gye could hear the the sound was coming from the sky.

He looked up slowly from the base of the mountain and looked upwards, dreading what could be there.

Gye heard Jane gasp as he saw it himself.

There, flying above the mountain, was an enormous octocopter. It had eight vertical propellers, like a helicopter's; they were laid out with six on each long side of the ship and two on each shorter side, like a family dinner table, except the chairs were propellers. The thing was at least a football field long, although Gye could not quite measure accurately from his current position.

A cannon fired from the broadside of the octocopter and the projectile smashed into the side of the mountain. In seconds, the area surrounding the impact had burst into flames.

"Take cover!" Gye shouted as the ship fired again. He followed Ray as they made for the relative safety of the nearest massive tree. He was breathing heavily, as Molly's tight grip around his chest constricted his breathing.

Gye looked up as he ran. Dozens of bees were streaming out of the hive, buzzing about angrily at the ruckus that had become the ambience of their home.

A shot boomed heavily out of the octocopter, and Gye saw one of the larger bees splatter into many pieces upon impact. Shot upon shot fired and machine gun fire strafed the air until most of the bees lay decimated on the ground. Gye turned his attention fully to escaping; he could not spare the time to watch the rest of the carnage that was unfolding behind him.

A bullet— fifty caliber if Gye estimated its size correctly— whizzed past his head (and Molly's) and slammed heavily into the trunk of the tree nearest him. Gye dove for cover and barely escaped a stream of likeminded bullets, each one seemingly hell bent on his destruction.

When the spray of machine gun bullets had subsided for a moment, Gye got back up and sprinted to catch up with the others.

In moments they were at the base of the tree. Ray had his knife out and ready, as if that would help.

Gye looked around.

"Where's Elicia and Jane?" He asked. They were nowhere to be seen.

"I see... Jane's lying on the ground over there." Ray said, rather more unconcernedly than Gye would have preferred. He spotted her, set Molly down at the base of the tree, and ran towards her.

He found her laying in the fetal position, with one arm strew out behind her, and a large bruise on her forehead.

Gye shook her until her eyes fluttered open.

"Oh, thank God." Gye said, falling to his knees next to her.

"Elicia... she betrayed us. She hit me in the head and stole off with the drone, waving at the Octocopter." Jane reached for the wound on her forehead and grimaced.

"I'm so dizzy right now." She said.

"That ship… why were they here? How would they know where to find us?" Gye asked.

"I'm sure Elicia had a tracker. And I heard her say, right after she hit me, I heard her say… 'Vaurien Kane sends his greetings.'" Jane said.

It dawned on Gye what had happened. Of course. Gye had refused Vaurien Kane's offer, so he had instead gone after Elicia. And Elicia, with her relentlessly immoral views on life, had seen no problem with selling out to the highest bidder.

The Octocopter had, indeed, flittered out of sight (probably to land and take Elicia aboard), but its deep, synchronized whirring sound could still be heard plenty loudly.

"Help me up." Jane said, reaching a hand out to Gye.

Gye took it and pulled her up to her feet. She nearly fell over from the dizziness, but Gye caught her in his arms.

She looked into his eyes like they were the deepest pools on earth, and she was trying to see if she could see the bottom of them. She got lost in her journey.

Gye snapped out of it and carefully lead her towards the tree where they were hiding out, step by step.

They all collapsed at the base of the tree, exhausted and spent.

"What on earth do we do now?" Molly asked.

"There's nothing to do! We've lost, it's over!" Jane practically yelled at her. But she wouldn't give up.

"We've thought so before, but we always made it through. We always find a way." Molly said.

"Wrong. Wrong, wrong, wrong. All we were trying to do to save the world from itself through that knowledge, it's all down the toilet now. There's nothing to be done. First I lose Anthony, now I've lost what we were fighting for. I can't seem to catch a break. And Elicia's betrayed us, although I guess I should've seen that coming. Who's to know who's next?" Jane said, eyeing Molly probingly.

"Me? I would never-" She started.

"—She did sneak aboard the rover. Whoever was on that ship, whoever was behind this, they got to Elicia. Who's to say they didn't get to this mysterious stow away as well? We could be walking into another trap." Ray Kaymar said. He spoke with scientific clarity, never allowing a hint of personal feeling to enter his voice.

"I wouldn't. I just wouldn't. Why don't you trust me?" Molly said, holding her ankle tight. Gye felt a pang of sympathy for her.

"If she were going to betray us too, why would she still be here?" Gye asked.

"I don't know. I don't know much of anything at this point. This is why I have trust issues." Jane said.

"Trusting people in the first place is, I think, the only real trust issue." Ray Kaymar said bitterly.

"Let's not get carried away here." Gye said.

"What do you mean?" Jane asked.

"Molly's not the problem here." Gye said.

"Whatever. I'm done." Jane said, plopping down on the ground resignedly.

Molly struggled mightily to stand on one leg.

"You don't want me around? Fine." She said, whipping her dark hair around to cover her eyes. She hobbled away ridiculously.

"Let her go." Ray Kaymar said.

But Gye couldn't do that, so he went after her.

Molly turned her head when she saw Gye approaching. They were out of sight and earshot of the others by this time.

"Please, I just need... I just need to be alone." Molly said, trying desperately not to sniffle as a silent tear streamed down her cheek. It was a heartbreaking sight.

"It's no good to be alone. No matter what happens between all of us, we have to stick together. It's the only way, it's the only way for us to get out of here alive." Gye said.

"I just, I just can't. I can't be near you all, I just tear you apart. I'm no good. I thought I could get aboard the rover and tag along with you on the greatest adventure of a lifetime but… I just ended up being another piece of cargo, another thing weighing you down as you did something important with your lives. I'm just a deadweight, I'm just… I'm nothing. I'm just, I'm just… empty. I'm holding you back, you need to go on without me. Let me at least die on my own two legs." She said.

"You're not going to die, Molly, I promise. I won't let it happen, not to you. And you're staying with us. We can make it through this. You were right, we can still press on. We may have lost what we came here for, but that doesn't mean there's no more life to be lived. I just means we have to try harder next time. Together, as a team." Gye said.

She was quiet for a moment, not looking him in the eye. She picked up a giant green leaf that had fallen from the tree, and she held it in her hands.

"This is what I am. This leaf looks like it's alive, it might even think it's still part of the tree. But it's not. It's going to die, it's already dying. Its fate is sealed, there's no way out. There's no way out for me either." She said. And she tore up the leaf in her hands.

"You're wrong. That's all I have to say, is you're wrong." Gye said.

"I wish that were the case, but it just isn't." Molly Hazelwood said.

"Come on, you can't expect me to just leave you here and let you die." Gye said.

"I know you wouldn't do that. Maybe you're right. Maybe I'm just stuck in tunnel vision and I can't see what's right in front of me. Maybe Jane doesn't hate me, and maybe I still have a place in the world." Molly said, her voice trailing off into a mutter.

"That's the thing about love, is that sometimes it looks like hatred. Love isn't just the happy feelings you get around someone when you're feeling okay and they're feeling okay. Love is more than a feeling. It's how you live alongside others, even when they're at their darkest and you are too, when you can't seem to get along. That doesn't mean you don't love each other, that just means you're at a low point— a valley— in that relationship. The view from a mountain means nothing to someone who's never seen that mountain from below. If you've taught me one thing, it's to just not give up on love, even when it's hard." Gye said.

"I know deep down that you're right. But I just need to be alone right now. Can you give me that, at least? Please?" She said, staring directly into his eyes as she said so.

"As much as I hate to, I guess if that's what you need, we'll have to let go." Gye said.

She turned without another word, and he was left standing there in the woods, practically alone. He sighed heavily and began making his way back to where he had last seen Ray and Jane.

He had to lose this battle, but perhaps the war was still winable.

CHAPTER 24
CAPTURED

"What are we going to do now?" Gye asked. Ray and Jane were sitting next to him, against the trunk of the great tree.

"I guess we have to try to make our way out of here." Jane asked.

"I just need a minute. To get over all of this." Ray Kaymar said.

They sat in silence for more than a minute. For half an hour, in fact, silently allowing themselves to process their thoughts.

"It was wrong, what we did to Molly." Jane said at last.

"It was misplaced anger is all." Ray Kaymar agreed quietly.

"We have to find her." Gye said.

Suddenly Gye noticed the deep whirring sound of the Octocopter that had slowly been moving in from the distance.

"Do you hear that?" Gye asked.

"Oh dear. We'd best find her quickly." Jane said, standing up.

"She's crippled at the moment. It's not like she could've gotten far." Ray said.

"This way, come on." Gye said, leading them.

The sound of the octocopter's whirring blades resonated against the trees and echoed back into itself, creating a dissonant cacophony of sounds. The sound rose like a wave on a beach and crashed down, creating a disorientating discord.

"Molly!" Gye shouted, hoping against hope that she could hear him.

He could see the octocopter through the tops of the trees. They slowed down as they approached, not wanting to give any indication of their presence.

Jane gasped.

"We're too late." She said despondently.

Gye looked over to where she was pointing and felt his heart sink.

The octocopter was spinning down to land in the clearing, with several ropes hanging off of it where men had descended. Gye saw Molly in the middle of a group of five or six of them, each one having a rifle strung over their shoulder. They were forcing her to walk on her sprained ankle despite the pain, and he heard her cry out after only a few steps.

A ramp extended out of one of the doors on one of the long sides of the octocopter, and Vaurien Kane stood in the doorway. He was instantly recognizable. He was wearing a long black trench coat, and his signature thick-framed black glasses were squarely set on his narrow face. His ghoulish but also somehow faintly charming smile was visible even from this distance. Gye shuddered at the sight of him.

Gye, Jane, and Ray peeked out from the tree they were hiding behind, powerless to help their friend.

"Oh no." Jane said helplessly, her voice a flat monotone of despair.

They took her aboard and the party disappeared into the enormous ship. The great eight propellers slowly wound down into silence.

"What are we going to do?" Jane asked, clutching Gye's forearm as she looked towards the enormous vehicle.

"We'll have to... think of a plan." Gye said helplessly.

###

"What is your name?" Vaurien Kane asked.

"Why am I here?" Molly Hazelwood asked.

"What is your name?" Vaurien Kane asked again, unperturbed. He reached into the bowl of grapes on the table in front of him and placed one on his lips; he held it there for a second before inhaling it into his mouth and chewing it. He repeated the process every few seconds with a new grape, never once breaking eye contact with Molly.

The black desk between them looked, at first glance, as though it was suspended in mid air. But it was not. Instead, incredibly thin strands of carbon fiber kept the desk upright. The other items and furniture in the room gave off much the same impression, but each one, upon close inspection, was not as it first appeared.

Molly was bewildered by the sight of the crazy designs in the room. Everything appeared to be trying to say that it was defying the laws of nature and rising above them, but that was not, in fact, the case. It was all a facade.

"What is your name?" Vaurien Kane asked again.

Molly sighed.

"Molly Hazelwood. Now you tell me yours." She said.

"Vaurien Kane. Or God, if you prefer to call me by my professional title." He said with an easy grin. There was something odd about his smile; it never reached his eyes. His mouth made the motion of smiling, but the look in his eye remained exactly the same. Molly was reminded sharply of the Arachnid she had killed, the way its eyes kept the same eerie stoniness even after death. A chill flew up and down her spine, and she shivered involuntarily. The room suddenly felt very, very cold. Vaurien's gaze never wavered through this, but she could tell that he had her figured out to a T already, and was playing with her like an expert musician with their favorite instrument.

"God, huh? I don't remember reading about you in the Old Testament." Molly said, mustering what courage she could to be adversarial to him despite her fear.

"Don't you remember? 'When the people complained, it displeased the lord. When the lord heard it, his anger burned, and so the fire of the lord burned among them and consumed some of the people.' I have quite a reputation, if you were not yet aware." Vaurien Kane said.

"That's odd. They never said God was a creepy old german guy who needs glasses when I was in Sunday school." Molly said, trying to casually flip her hair over her shoulder. Instead, she ended up fumbling her fingers and looking rather nervous. Again, Vaurien Kane's eyes took it all in without the slightest indication of change.

"That's an unfair description of me, I think. Come on, we don't even know each other yet. I think you might quite like me, actually. But enough about me. I want to know about you. Why are you here, in this forest of mystery?" Vaurien Kane asked.

"I know why *you're* here. Because Elicia Cantor is a traitor. You should keep an eye on her, you know. Once a traitor, always a traitor. She's just as likely to turn on you as she did on us." Molly said. She tried to be strong, but her voice broke at the end. She faked a cough to try to cover it up.

Vaurien Kane popped another grape into his mouth, again without ever breaking eye contact.

"Elicia Cantor did what was right for herself, that is true. But you'd be wrong if you think I trust her. I trust her, pardon the cliche, about as much as I could throw her. And you know how far it's possible to throw her. By which I mean, it isn't." Vaurien said.

"So what? What do you want from me?" Molly asked.

"I want information. You'll understand soon. Why are you here?" He asked.

"If Elicia betrayed us to you, then you already know all about our mission, so why are you asking me? I stowed away anyways. I wasn't even meant to come along in the first place." Molly Hazelwood said.

"Ah, clever girl. I see that we can skip the formalities and go right to the meat of the issue. You're intelligent, I'm sure you can figure out what I want." Vaurien Kane said. He adjusted his glasses and stared deeply into her soul. She could feel her resolve crumbling under the weight of his glance.

"I don't know what you mean." She said.

"Ah, perhaps not so clever after all, eh? Pity." Vaurien Kane said.

"Well, sorry I don't fit in your little view of intelligence, Mr. God." Molly said, her voice dripping with sarcasm.

"Oh please, just God. Mr. God was my father." He intoned.

"I'm sure that's hilarious to you, but I still want to know why you're raining down fire on a whole forest that, if I recall correctly, has done exactly nothing wrong to you." Molly Hazelwood said.

"You are surprisingly perceptive. You are right, the forest has committed no crime; by the laws of man and nature, it ought to stand. But if your little friends have their way, all sorts of malicious lies will be spread, maligning the Ancients and speaking as though the discoveries of this forest prove anything for your, shall we deign to call it, *science*. It is a necessary sacrifice, to give a few lives that perhaps others might find their ways to the light." Vaurien Kane said.

"Most of that went over my head, but I get the general idea. You're insane." Molly said.

"Again, you are so needlessly harsh. And Elicia had said you had a reputation as being rather likable." Vaurien said.

"What do I care what you think of me?" Molly asked.

"I think you ought to. Because I hold your life in my hands. And you're going to need to start proving yourself very useful, very quickly. Your friends. Where are they?" Vaurien Kane asked.

"You think I would tell you?" Molly Hazelwood asked.

"I know you will." He said.

"Don't be so cocky. I may be small, but I took a self-defense class in college, and I'm pretty sure I could hold my own against the likes of you." Molly said.

"Now who's cocky? But please, enough with the hyperbole. Your friends will never know you betrayed them, so what's the harm? Your life will be spared, and more than likely they'll die anyway. I plan to sacrifice them on a pyre of fire when I return from this blasphemous forest. If you prove yourself useful, I may be able to hide you away from all that. Come on, what do you say?" Vaurien Kane implored.

"Why would you sacrifice them? And to whom? I can't make heads or tails of what you want." Molly Hazelwood said.

Vaurien Kane smiled thinly and put the pen in his hand into his breast pocket before shifting in his seat and leaning forward, steepling his hands under his chin. Even this small movement forward was enough to instantly cause Molly substantial discomfort from his presence.

She tried to steeple her hands under her chin as well, but her hands were too shaky to hold the position, and she sat backwards, obviously defeated in this battle of body language.

"Molly Hazelwood, there is much you have to learn, apparently." He said, his german accent coming out thickly into his voice, adding another layer of coldness to his persona.

"Well, I'm not exactly going anywhere at the moment. Do tell." She said. She found that if she tried her hardest to imagine that she was talking to someone less frightening— for instance, the dark lord Satan — she could hold her own.

"Very good, Ms. Hazelwood. Very good. Well, since you are apparently quite keen on knowing, I shall deign to tell you. The Order of Fire and Blood, as you might expect, has a great deal to do with fire and blood. We are of the belief that the true creation of the world is unknowable, but we do know that the first inhabitants of this world were the Ancients. They had many mystical powers, and their feats of might and wisdom are legendary. In our order, it is possible to learn these abilities by paying your dues and leveling up. The most coveted level is, of course, becoming a Lord, which I am now proud to call myself, although I am sure it will take me some time to unlock the abilities of this level." Vaurien Kane said.

"What, ah, abilities... have you already unlocked?" Molly Hazelwood asked.

"A large multitude, but I am forbidden to discuss any of them with anyone outside our sacred order." Vaurien Kane said.

"Your cult, you mean. You're part of a cult, and they're just using you." Molly Hazelwood.

Vaurien's strong jaw clenched shut, and she could see a strong anger rising up in his eyes. She flinched but tried not to show it.

"You are wrong about that, my dear. Rather, it is you who has been used and brainwashed by science." Vaurien Kane said.

"I'm not a scientist, but even I know that you need proof to make a statement like that." Molly said.

"That is the essence of the fact that they have brainwashed it, is it not? To say that proof is required when only truth is. But nonetheless, we are deviating from the point. One way or another, you're going to help me capture your friends." Vaurien Kane stated matter of factly.

"I won't, and there's no way you can make me." Molly replied.

"There is absolutely nothing I cannot make you do. But I tire of these games. I give you only this last chance, right now, to help me of your own will and be rewarded, or else... go down the less pleasant route." Vaurien said.

"No. I will never betray my friends." Molly said.

Vaurien sighed and reached into the bowl of grapes to pick out the very last one. He held it between his thumb and finger, looked Molly straight in the eye, and squished it. He rubbed his fingers together until the pieces had all fallen to the floor.

Vaurien Kane stood up abruptly and began to pace around the room. He nodded to someone behind her and suddenly her arms were being fastened to the arms of the chair. She tried to struggle, but was too weak. She tried to bite the arm nearest her, but that only resulted in a painful kick to her sprained ankle. She kept quiet and still after that.

Vaurien turned to face her again, and this time, he had a long white syringe in his hand. He leaned in very close, his face just inches from hers, and he smiled. Molly noticed that this time, his smile was truly genuine; it reached into his eyes and beamed back the truth. She couldn't breathe from the terror.

"Molly... Hazelwood, was it? Yes, I believe that's right. I would like to thank you in advance for helping me catch your little friends, and I wish you a safe journey to the other side." He said, his german accent coming in thickly to his voice. He smiled another genuine smile, grinning more to himself than anything else, and pushed the syringe into Molly's neck.

"The wages of sin is death, and payday is here." He said, pushing in the back of the syringe as he injected the liquid into her veins. She fought with all her might, but she barely managed to move at all.

Everything lost color. Vaurien's face turned to a skull, and then his eyes were the only thing with color in her existence; a horrible, flashing red... and then everything was white.

Vaurien Kane wiped his hands and motioned to the attending man.

"Set her body up in the plush chair in the library. Make it look like she's reading, and face her mostly away from the door." Vaurien instructed curtly. The man saluted and began going about his work.

"Be ready, for soon, we tempt bees with honey." Vaurien Kane called out as he left the room.

CHAPTER 25
DE-BAITING A COURSE OF ACTION

Gye used Ray's knife to peel off the skin of the orange-like fruit he was attempting to eat. It stubbornly refused to give up its contents, however, so he was forced to use force. He pushed too hard and ended up slicing his thumb. He grimaced and sucked the wound until it stopped bleeding. And then he tried again, as he always did. It gave way, as most things do, and surrendered its contents.

It had been several hours since Molly had been captured, and in that time, Gye, Jane, and Ray had nothing to do but become increasingly restless.

"If this Vaurien Kane fellow succeeds, we'll have lost both Molly and our mission. Who knows what he's capable of doing to this world of ours if we don't stop him." Ray Kaymar said.

"Nothing good, obviously. We're truly carrying our weights in gold here." Jane Silver said.

"And it is a heavy burden, truly. I guess I shouldn't have had those extra donuts last week." Ray Kaymar joked weakly.

"Look, there's some people leaving the octocopter!" Gye whispered. Ray, Jane, and Gye all crouched down lower and spied on them.

Gye could make out Vaurien Kane, Elicia— who didn't look the least bit remorseful about having just sold out her so-called friends— and perhaps a dozen other fellows, each one armed with a handgun, and one woman with a sniper rifle. They looked around carefully before marching off, in the direction Vaurien was pointing. He led the party away from the octocopter and into the forest. Several shouts could be heard, but Gye could not distinguish what any of them were saying.

"They've sent out a search party!" Gye said.

"Did you see Molly with them?" Jane asked.

"No. Ray?"

"I didn't either. She's either already dead or we're unbelievably lucky." Ray said.

"I'd rather believe the second one. It seems the wolves have left the den unguarded in their lustful search for prey." Gye said.

"Should we risk it and try to search for her in there? Not to mention the drone, of course, but Molly's more important. They almost certainly left someone behind to guard her." Jane said.

"Well, we'll just have to risk it. I'm sure we can overpower one or two guards. Ray has a knife, so that should make it easier." Gye said.

They ran from tree to tree, observing the surrounding area carefully to make sure the search party did not close in on them unexpectedly. When the cover of the trees had run out and the clearing had began, they began to army crawl across the field. They decided to prioritize speed over sneakiness, however, and got up to run the rest of the distance. Panting and wheezing they arrived at the still-extended metal stairs leading to the boarding door of the octocopter.

They stopped for a moment to catch their collective breath.

"This is, if nothing else, absolutely exhilarating." Jane commented.

"I'm guessing you don't often get to rescue your friends when you're couped up in a lab for hours ever day, do you?" Gye snarked.

"Slow down there, cowboy. No one's been rescued yet." She retorted.

They made their way up the grated metal stairs— taking care to make as little noise as possible as they did so— and reached the door.

It wasn't locked.

"How unbelievably arrogant of them." Ray Kaymar mused.

"We'd best not press our luck. Inside, quickly." Gye said.

They entered in and shut the door behind them.

The inside decor of the octocopter was stunningly old and ill-kept. There was red wallpaper curling off the walls at the corners of the small entrance room. It had faded to pink and even white over the years in certain places. The floor boards were decrepit and seemed stunningly out of place for such a contemporary vessel. The whole ship was dimly lit, from small LEDs spread out in a line on the walls. They were poorly installed, and the craftsmanship of the whole thing was abominable to say the least.

The entrance room opened up in two directions. On the left Gye could see several crates stacked in rows; one of which was left opened and had a bag of grain sticking out.

"That's their food supply." Ray Kaymar noted. He looked around distastefully, obviously not a fan of the architecture and design of the place.

He looked over at the frame of the octocopter, which was visible through the cracking wall in places.

"Impure aluminum. What a horrible material to choose. Would it have killed them to spring for a nice alloy? My god, this is atrocious. I've seen homes in the ghetto with better interiors than this." Ray said.

"Ray, I don't think evil people are much concerned with the aesthetics of their equipment. I think they care a great deal more about how it gets them from point A to point B, where point A is whatever hellhole they grew up in and point B is destroying as much of everything as they can." Jane said.

"They should be a great deal more concerned with aesthetics, although I admit I may be biased… I mean, if you're going to rain down destruction on people, would it kill them to do with with a little *style*?" Ray asked.

"That's not exactly our concern at the moment. New plan. We stick to the left, like we did in the bee hive, and hopefully we'll eventually find what we're looking for." Gye said.

"Sounds like a plan." Jane said.

"That's because it is one." Ray Kaymar said.

"Whatever. Let's move." Jane replied.

They crept along, as silently as they were capable of being, and went into the food storage room. Gye pressed himself up against the opened door first, trying to look inside as much as possible before entering. He then suddenly and forcefully rushed inside, ready to take out anyone who might have been loitering inside. But there was no one there.

"All clear here." Gye whispered.

Ray and Jane entered slowly behind him, looking around the room as they did so. This room was just as decrepit as the last, although the crates at least looked newer than rock and roll music.

"Do they have anything edible? I haven't eaten in so long, I just realized it." Jane said.

"Have a look in the crates. I'll guard your back." Gye said.

She walked over to the nearest one and placed her hands under the heavy top to try and open it. It creaked loudly with every touch, sending each minuscule sound reverberating through the spaces of the octocopter like a pin dropping in a perfectly silent room. She cringed at every sound and looked around with an expression of terror. Her face was a canvas for the splashes of crimson embarrassment that jumped up from her psyche to claim space on her skin.

Finally, many awful, skull-rattling creaks later, Jane had removed the wooden top from the crate. She grunted as she gingerly placed it on the floor. It made an awful thunking sound on contact, and the resulting echoes were like a gong loudly played in a massive cathedral. Or at least it seemed that way, from their perspective.

"Well, if there are any guards here, we know where they'll be pretty soon." Gye quipped.

"I had no idea it would be so loud. But look, there's dried fruit in here! Score!" Jane said. She hurriedly tore open the plastic bag and grabbed a handful of dried apples. She tossed them into her mouth.

"Mmmmh! I never knew food could taste so good."

Gye realized at that moment how hungry he was. The thought of food enticed him.

"Care to share?"

Jane tossed him a bag of dried carrots in response. He tore them open greedily and ate them with hurried gusto. Ray had his own snack and was finished with it by the time Gye was done with his.

"I didn't realize how hungry I'd become. Just caught up in the moments of what we were doing, I forgot about... man, I'm so thirsty too." He said. He looked around until he found a container of bottled waters. He grabbed one and slammed it down in what must have been record times.

"What is it about traipsing about in the middle of an insane forest that really puts the hunger and thirst in ya? Man." Jane said.

"Don't forget going through a beehive and getting attacked by an octocopter. Exciting times, this." Ray Kaymar said.

"You never know what'll happen to you in this day and age. Especially poor Molly. I don't think she had any idea what was coming to her when she snuck on the rover with us. Life is full of all kinds of surprises." Jane said dryly.

"Speaking of whom... we'd better get a move on. That door over there looks promising." Gye said.

They entered in through the door. Its frame was painted white, but the underlying ugly green color was visible through the chipped paint.

There was a walkway in the center of the room, stretching from one end to the other. The floor was hard, chipped cement in this room, with an occasional piece of carpet haphazardly spread about, as was the case with the substance of the walkway. On either side of the walkway were stacked bunkbeds. It was modeled after a military barracks, but obviously was nowhere near the cleanliness level required by a respectable military. Nonetheless, evidence of menacing intentions was visible strewn about; there was a faded green hardhat left on the pillow of one bed, and each bed was, to the credit of whoever was in charge, made and kept in clean order. There was a box labelled 'AMMUNITION' on a shelf which was between two bunkbeds on the left side of the walkway.

Ray shook the supports of one of the beds— it was a cheap, hallow cylinder.

"I wonder if this is legally able to be called a metal? How pathetic." He muttered.

Gye noticed a blue light coming from one of the walls. Upon closer inspection, he found that it was a tank of water stretching from floor to ceiling all along the outside-facing side of the octocopter. It was about three feet deep and appeared to be empty, save for the water.

"This is an oddity. It's like… a giant fish tank." Gye noted.

Jane shrieked and Gye turned quickly towards her. She was holding her hand to her chest, breathing as she looked eye to eye with the aquatic creature in the tank.

It was five feet long, looked like a shark with antennae, and had pure black, marble-esque eyes. Its bared teeth looked like they were stuck in a permanently evil grin.

"Jeez! What in the world is that?" Ray asked.

"I don't recognize it. But it doesn't look particularly friendly." Jane said, backing away from the glass.

"It's definitely from the lake we explored earlier. I remember a baby one of these floating by. I'll dub it the *Formidulosus*." Gye said.

"Formidulosus, I like it. Not too creative, though." Jane Silver said.

"Looks like this Vaurien Kane has a taste for the exotic." Ray said, his tone almost one of admiration.

"There's nothing else here. Let's move on." Gye said.

They breezed through the dead room and walked through the open door on the other end of the walkway.

It opened up into a small hallway, with two doors on the left side before the hallway turned at an angle away; with nothing but a blank wall on the right.

Gye gingerly placed his hand on the door and looked into the window. It was too gritty to make out much detail, but he could see that there was a large amount of natural light in the room.

"I don't think they've had a janitor in this thing in at least a decade. Goodness, I can't even see through this window. What've they been doing, going mud racing? Jeez." Jane said.

The white specks of dust slowly drifting down from the disturbance of their presence were visible on Jane's black tank top, which he had not noticed before.

Noticing Gye's attention, Jane smirked.

"I wear my heart on my sleeve. That's why I only wear tank tops." She said.

Ray interrupted by opening the door carelessly and stepping inside.

There was no one inside, thankfully for them.

"You should be more careful, Ray." Jane cautioned.

"What does it matter? I was inside watching the two of you anyways, a gunshot to the head would've just sealed the deal. But look, there's a giant gun here anyways, I might as well just use that." Ray Kaymar said.

There was, indeed, a cannon mounted in the small room. It was pointed out of a window just large enough to accommodate a range of motion of about sixty degrees horizontally and vertically, judging by the distance from the base of the cannon to the window.

There was one shelf on the left wall, with several rows of shells strapped down to it. Each one was longer than Gye's hand span, as he quickly checked.

"They're packing some serious firepower up in here." Jane said.

"Gye, if you make a joke about your guns being bigger, I swear to God, I will kill myself right now." Ray said.

"I wasn't even going to say that! You're all kinds of rude today." Gye said.

"Guys. Let's focus. Molly's not in this room." Jane Silver said.

"Neither is the drone. So we must keep looking." Ray said pointedly.

They backed out of the room— single file, thanks to the small door— and regrouped around the second door on the left in this part of the hallway.

"This time, we enter more carefully." Gye said. But there was no window on this door, so he had to just quickly open the door and rush in anyways.

Again, there was no on inside. But there was an access door (made of plexiglass) directly inside which led to the engine powering one of the octocopter's eight massive propellers keeping the whole thing flying.

"It's like a giant blender." Jane noted.

"Too bad Anthony's not still here, or we would have a fruit to put in that blender." Ray joked.

Jane ignored him and they walked out of the room and back into the hallway.

They crept up to the corner and quickly turned it to surprise anyone who might have been there, but of course, there wasn't anyone present.

"I'm beginning to think they were stupid enough not to leave a guard behind." Gye said finally.

Around the corner was a hallway that stretched all the way to the other end of the octocopter and turned to the right sharply again. The only door on either side of this hallway was on the left side, in the middle of the hallway.

The massive fish tank was visible again on the outside-facing wall, and the Formidulosus was following them around like a creepy stalker.

"Every time I look at that thing, I get the shivers." Jane said.

"Let's hope it stays in there." Gye commented.

They walked quietly down the hallway, padding their steps to reduce noise, although they were beginning to doubt whether that would be any kind of beneficial.

The door to this room didn't even have a handle, but was a slab of wood hung loosely onto two rusty hinges, all of it painted a dull army green, which was more chipped away than it was present.

With a magnanimous, protesting squeak, the door easily swung open.

The room was roughly a triangle in shape, with the longest side being connected to the hallway, and the two opposing sides meeting opposite at the corner opposite the door.

On each of the two shorter walls that formed the triangle, there were two large circular windows which let in a great deal of light, which was a pleasant contrast to what they had thus far seen. The frames of the windows were stainless steel, and were bolted into the metal walls with titanium bolts.

The room was split in half, in terms of contents. On the left were various stacked, unlabeled crates; on the right were strictly neatly aligned and stacked boxes, each one black and labeled 'FUEL' in bright yellow layers. There were six rows of the fuel, all of which except for the row closest to the door were full. Obviously, the voyage had taken up some fuel already.

"Well, I'd say it's fairly obvious what's going on here." Ray Kaymar said.

"And still no Molly." Gye said.

"And still no drone." Ray said.

They trudged slowly out of the room and walked down the hall, barely even looking around the corner before turning it and continuing.

This side of the octocopter seemed to be almost a mirror image of the other side, with the exception that the hallway on this side had three doors on the right (from their current perspective) that evidently led into rooms which were in the center of the octocopter. There was additionally a door on their immediate left which did not have a corresponding door on the opposite side.

"Well, this is at least promising. We should've come this way in the first place." Jane said.

"It was a fifty fifty chance. Sometimes you get the outcome you want, sometimes you don't, that's life." Ray Kaymar said.

"How poignant of you to say." Gye said, rolling his eyes subtly at Jane. She cracked a smile, hiding it before Ray looked her way.

"Let's try the door on the left first." Ray said.

The door was heavy, metal, and thick. There were bars on the top half, so they could see inside. It was apparently some kind of holding cell.

"Is Molly in there?" Jane asked. She couldn't see from her perspective.

"Nope. It's empty. And dark. And cold. Essentially, we're done here." Ray Kaymar said.

Gye tried to open the door anyways, but it was locked. He rattled it a bit, but it still wouldn't budge.

"Well, I guess we'll try the door on the right then." Gye said.

This door was slate gray all the way, and had a brushed nickel handle. It was a rather stark contrast to the decrepit nature of the other facilities in this ship. Gye felt a creeping macabre sensation flittering up his spine. The hair on his arms raised.

He gulped as he pushed the door open.

It was Vaurien Kane's office. Or, rather, it was a replica.

Ray Kaymar looked around in awe. He ran over to the mighty 'floating' desk and touched the nearly invisible carbon fiber supports.

"My, this is amazing! Psychopathic, yes, but incredible engineering. Props to whoever thought of this." Ray Kaymar said appreciatively.

There was a chair which, in accordance with the rest of the design of the furniture, was designed to look like it was in the midst of imploding against some great external force.

"Ray, we don't have time to admire the scenery. They could be back at any second, and this is the last room I want to be in. I don't know if you've ever had the pleasure of meeting Mr. Vaurien Kane, but he's… not exactly fun." Gye understated.

"You've met him?" Ray Kaymar said inquisitively.

Gye suddenly became very self-conscious. He hadn't revealed his little meeting with Vaurien yet…

"Yes, yes I have." He said casually.

The fish tank ran along the outside-facing wall and continued into the next room. The Formidulosus had followed them yet again, and was still looking at them as if they were a delectable meat that it had not yet had the pleasure of tasting.

"Let's move on to the next room." Jane said, disturbed by the sight of the Formidulosus. It followed them.

Thankfully Vaurien's working room was directly connected to the next room, so they didn't have to venture back out to the hallway in order to move on to the next room.

As they stepped in, they had to move upwards on a ramp about six feet long, which took them up about five feet in height. It was a rather steep ascent. It made Gye flash back to when they were scaling the top of the mountain, and he had failed to catch Molly…

He snapped out of it and walked ahead.

"The cabin. Where the pilot controls the flight of this aircraft." Ray Kaymar noted.

In the center of the room was a large black leather chair, which was situated behind a massive desk with many controls on it.

In front of the desk was one large floor-to-ceiling window, out of which the forest and the top of the octocopter was visible. The pilot's cabin was above the rest of the octocopter, obviously to increase visibility for navigation.

Gye sat in the chair for a moment and looked out.

"Well there, Captain, what now?" Ray Kaymar joked.

"Look, that hatch leads to the top deck of the octocopter. You can walk out onto it, see the guard rails on the sides?" Ray noted. They could see the dull metal top of the octocopter stretching out before them. It was not a particularly interesting sight.

"What's this?" Jane asked, referring to a large metal-reinforced wooden crate with a black cloth over it that was on the nearest table.

Jane impatiently whisked the cloth off and gasped.

It was the drone.

"Hooray!" Ray Kaymar shouted. He looked around self-consciously, not meaning to have let out such an outburst.

"Looks like we didn't do this whole thing for nothing after all." Jane said appreciatively.

"Well, let's get out of here!" Ray said.

"Aren't you forgetting something? Or, rather, someone?" Gye asked.

"You're referring to Ms. Hazelwood, of course. Of course. Yes, we must continue to risk our lives for that unfortunate individual." Ray said.

"Do you realize how badly you hurt her? And how badly *we* hurt her. We abandoned her and let her be taken captive by a psychopath. I think we owe her just a little bit of an apology, don't you think?" Gye said pointedly.

"Alright, alright, take it easy there cowboy. Help me lift this, and let's keep looking." He said.

They went back down to the hallway and continued.

###

Vaurien Kane stood, one arm propped against the massive trunk of the tree, his posse of followers surrounding him. In his hand he held a tablet computer, which was currently displaying the security camera footage from inside the octocopter. They laughed as they watched the three adventurers stumble around idiotically around the octocopter, like a bug trapped in a window pane; too stupid to realize the truth of the situation. They were walking right into the trap.

"Oh, we're getting to the good part! He's about to approach the library, where we placed Ms. Hazelwood. Watch carefully, this is going to be great." Vaurien Kane said. His comment was met with a chorus of laughter.

"That door ahead is open. Careful, if there's a guard anywhere in this ship, it's in there, I'd bet my life on it." Gye cautioned.

"I'll go on ahead and check it out. I'll signal you if it's safe." He continued. They nodded their agreement and stayed back as he crept forward down the hallway.

The open door was on his left, and yellowish light was spilling out into the dim hallway. He could see a case of books from where he was... was it some kind of library? He supposed that even villains needed to keep themselves educated.

He put his hand on the wall, right behind the door hinge, and used it to balance himself as he peeked his head around the corner. He squinted as the light hit his face, and looked around as quickly as he could.

There were rows of books— it was a library after all, it seemed — all set against the walls of the room. There was one circular window, but it was smudged and dirtied by so much use that Gye couldn't see through it at all. The floor was a shining hardwood, and it was curling up at the edges where the floor met the walls.

There was a plush green reading chair in the center of the room, angled away from the door. In that chair was a girl. And that girl was Molly Hazelwood.

Gye gasped when he saw her. The whole place was eerily quiet. She had a book in her hands, and was apparently casually reading to pass the time.

He wanted to shout to her and scream for joy, but he knew he had to fix some things first.

He looked around to make sure no one else was in the room before standing in the door frame.

"Molly, we're here to rescue you. But first, I just need to straighten this out, between you and me, and between this group of ours. We wronged you. Don't turn around, this is easier to say when it's not to your face." He said. As he spoke, Jane and Ray joined him. They were taken aback by the scene as well.

"I'd just like to say I'm sorry. I'm sorry I let you get hurt, that was my fault. I'm sorry we turned on you when things went badly... there's no excuse for it. We did you wrong, and all I can do is ask for your forgiveness. You're an amazing human being, and I've treasured getting to know you over the course of this journey. It pains my heart that we have wronged you, and I just want you to be happy, and we haven't made you happy at all." Gye said. It was a rush of emotion.

Jane joined in.

"Molly... I'm sorry. We were so, so wrong. If you can find it in your heart to forgive us, please do. If not, I'll understand." She said.

Ray Kaymar spoke reluctantly.

"I'm not good at apologies. I'm not good at emotions. But I do know when I've done an injustice to someone, and that's what happened. So.. I'm sorry." He said.

They looked at her, expecting some sort of response. But she just sat there, book in her hands, face looking down at it in despondence.

"Maybe she was more devastated by what we did than we even thought..." Jane started.

"Molly. Please talk to us. You don't have to forgive. I mean, it would mean the world if you did. But at least acknowledge that we're here, and we're here for you. Please." Gye said.

She still didn't move, still didn't respond.

Gye moved closer in the room. He began to have a sick, sinking feeling in the pit of his stomach. Something wasn't right here. He walked forward tentatively.

Ray and Jane set down the drone and joined him.

Her skin looked awfully pale, and her usually neatly-kept hair was a mess.

He touched her arm, and it was cold.

"Oh… oh my god." He said. He fell to his knees, and the force of that action knocked the book out of her cold hands and onto the floor. Her head slumped forward, and the truth was revealed.

"Oh. Oh no, oh no no no no no. This can't… this can't be happening. No." Jane whispered.

Ray walked forward hurriedly and placed his fingers on her neck, checking for a pulse. He checked again, and tried again, and tried once more again.

In a shaky, trembling version of his usually unnaturally calm voice, Ray Kaymar spoke.

"She's dead." He said.

"She can't be dead. She just can't. She was our survivor, the glue of our group… she can't be dead. She's not dead." Gye said.

"What sick bastard did this?" Jane asked.

There was a slow clap from the doorway behind them. They turned around quickly, horrified.

"Very convincing performance. Very convincing, indeed. I almost, for a minute there, believed that love was real. But of course, let's not be silly. You may drop your facades now." Vaurien Kane said.

"You killed her!" Jane screamed, tears streaming down her face. She sobbed, and her face descended into her hands.

"Did I? No, no no. You're mistaken. It is you who has caused her death." He said, his chilly german accent sending a train of shivers up Gye's spine. He wasn't by any means a tall man, but his stature seemed a mountain in that moment.

"Why? Why did you put an arrow through the heart of an angel?" Gye asked, his voice cracking. Several guards entered from behind Vaurien and surrounded them, but it wasn't as if they would've been able to resist anyway. They were beyond devastated.

"Why? You ask such disappointingly simple questions. To catch a bee, I set out the sweetest of honey. To catch one would've been enough, but this honey has delivered three bees to me. Now that's efficiency!" Vaurien Kane exclaimed.

"Got to give the germans one thing. They're an efficient folk." Ray Kaymar muttered. A guard took his knife from him.

"Now, if you would wrap up this sob show quickly, I'd like to get you to a holding cell in short order. I plan to sacrifice the lot of you— and Ms. Hazelwood's body— to the Ancients upon my triumphant return. And that precious drone of yours will be the explosion to light the pyre, I think. Oh, how the mighty have fallen so low…" Vaurien Kane incanted as he walked out.

"Alright, move along." The female guard with the rifle ordered.

"Will you at least bury her? Please?" Gye yelled out as they dragged him to his feet.

"You heard the boss. She goes on the pyre with the lot of you." A man replied. He had dark skin, an extremely wide girth, and was wearing a red cape. At least he sounded somewhat sympathetic in comparison to the icy cold Vaurien Kane.

Gye noticed one of the larger guards grabbing the drone and bringing it out of the room through the other door.

They were marched away down the hallway to the holding cell, where they were unceremoniously dumped.

235

CHAPTER 26
ELICIA

Elicia sat in the large chair with legs folded in front of her, trying to give off the impression of collected calm whilst inwardly ceding consciousness to calamity. She twiddled her thumbs against her will and chewed her lip as she looked on uncomfortably at the man across the table.

His chiseled face, plastered with an uncanny smile, beamed back an unconcerned expression not all that different from that of a wolf sitting plump and contented after consuming a fresh kill, licking its chops clean of spurted blood.

Elicia swept her blonde, straight hair back with practiced experience and cleared her throat softly.

Vaurien blinked mechanically and turned his attention towards her.

"I am so glad you decided to take my offer in the end, Elicia. I was beginning to worry that I wouldn't get my way. And I think we both know the world is a less painful place for all involved when I do get my way." He said, chuckling emptily at the end of his remark.

Elicia's heart began to pump so hard against her ribcage that she thought it might shatter the bones in her spine. She fought back a shiver as she realized Vaurien Kane had gotten under her skin.

She hadn't expected it to be this difficult. It was a mere business transaction, wasn't it? Money for services. But this wasn't like every other time she had turned the tables in the favor of someone who had paid her to do so. This wasn't the usual game of chess that always ended in her playing the players themselves and benefitting herself in the process. No, this time it had gotten personal. She had let her heartstrings be played by this motley crew of flawed but lovable people, and now her heart began to recoil against the feeling of the strings being cut. Love was music in matters of the heart, and the pursuit of power was silence. Perhaps, for once, she preferred the music.

Perhaps Vaurien Kane saw this sad melody flash across her eyes as he shifted forward, eyes steeling in preparation to do damage.

He laughed suddenly and jerked backwards, flinging his hands casually behind his head and slouching into the chair. With an air of nonchalance he plopped his feet onto the desk between them and grinned.

Elicia was no stranger to body language and understood without hesitation what he was trying to establish. I'm in control here, he was saying, and even if the entire universe joined you against me, it would all be for nothing. So don't even think of trying to get out from under my thumb.

Vaurien shifted to get more comfortable in the chair.

"Elicia, you seem a little down. Why don't—" but Vaurien's speech was cut short by a very sudden and severe bout of coughing. The sound of it echoed into the echelons of the room and bounced back as cannon blasts upon Elicia's ears. She winced at the sound.

When the coughing attack had finally subsided, Vaurien took his sleeve away from his mouth and winced slightly. The sleeve was splattered with blood. Without hesitating, Vaurien reached into the desk drawer, withdrew a lighter, and set the sleeve on fire.

Elicia jumped to her feet, but by the time she had even done that, Vaurien had already put out the fire and nonchalantly patted the sleeve to remove the ashes from it.

"I'm sorry. I have a medical condition. It seems I'm due for a replacement heart soon." Vaurien said without emotion.

Elicia sat back down in the chair and allowed a short silence to elapse before responding.

"Well, with medical science the way it is these days, that sh— ah, that shouldn't be a problem." She said, stammering.

"For others, perhaps. But I'm not so lucky. It seems the Ancients have seen fit for me to endure the imperfections of this form more so than others for now. But worry not, all will be redeemed in sacred time to come. All will be redeemed, you will see. But not yet. Do you want to know a great coincidence I have recently become aware of? Do you?" Vaurien said, a tinge of excitement creeping into his voice. But even excitement for Vaurien Kane seemed tinged with malice.

"Of course, Mr. Kane. Coincidences are lovely things, aren't they? Why, a few days ago I believe we had a spirited debate about whether it was possible to be late to a coincidence. Which is ridiculous, of course, considering—" Elicia said, the words beginning to flow from her mouth outside of her control as she tried to fill the uncomfortable silence with anything but Vaurien's steely gaze.

Mercifully, he interrupted her.

"This Gye Storm of yours. You are surely familiar with him, yes? Of course you are. He is one of those who you betrayed today. Let's not mince words. A contract is a contract, we both know this. One rather poetic coincidence between myself and this career adventurer named Gye Storm is that I killed his family. Again, let's not mince words. His father was found to be a compatible heart donor. I promised him that his family would never want for money if he gave it to me. We completed the transaction and I kept my word. They didn't want for money, and they don't now, obviously. It's kind of hard to want money when you're dead. But that's a topic for another time. Or, I suppose, I would've kept that promise if it weren't for the fact that Gye Storm escaped my reach that day. And now he has come back, and once again I will have a chance to fulfill my contractual obligations. And I will, of course. He will be sacrificed to the Ancients like the others. What a beautiful gift the Ancients have given me, though, that I may see everything come full circle this way. They are gracious with their small favors like these." Vaurien mused.

Elicia felt tears forming at the corners of her eyes. This man was insane. She had known instinctively that he should not be trusted when she made her deal with him. But she hadn't known she had made a faustian deal with the devil. She just hadn't known.

CHAPTER 27
IN THE CELL

"She's gone. I can't believe it, but she's gone." Jane Silver said.

Neither Gye nor Ray could muster a response. They were all curled up in various positions of shock, strew about the cell like a deck of cards blown in the wind.

The cell was dim, dirty, and grimy. Occasionally they could see someone or other pass by through the bars of the door, but they didn't care much.

The octocopter's great engines whirred into action, and with a series of jerks and hefts, the ship was airborne.

"Looks like we're on our way to be sacrificed. So, that's fun." Gye said.

"What difference does it make? We basically betrayed our friend and let her get murdered. I'd say we deserve to die at this point." Jane Silver said.

"We didn't kill her, Vaurien Kane killed her. He should pay for this, don't take it out on yourself." Ray Kaymar said, his voice on the verge of breaking.

"I know, I just… I wish…" Jane started. She never finished, just looked off into the distance, her usually bright blue eyes dimmed.

"I want to kill Vaurien Kane. With my bare hands. I want to squeeze the life out of him and watch those lifeless eyes turn to fear…" Gye said.

"Wanting wont get us anywhere. We're locked in a cell, and more than likely we're doomed to die." Jane said.

"Sounds about right." Gye said.

They sat there contemplatively.

The perfect time of the whirring propeller blades was the metronome for the depressing piano music playing in Gye's head. The echoes off the hard metal walls was the violin section, coming in with sweeping statements of sadness like the feeling of jumping off a cliff… and it all coalesced into a single tear, which streamed down his face without shame or notice.

Jane sighed and turned over, facing the ceiling. It reminded her of the first time she had run away from home, in the winter time, and just stared into the abyss that was the clear, starry night sky. The sight and the feeling of being so entirely alone in the universe scared her half to death that night, and she had run back home before her parents had even noticed she was gone.

The sound of heavy footsteps was heard from down the hallway. They all sat up at the sound of a key being placed into the heavy lock and turned. A horrible squeak shattered the relative quiet, and a burning shaft of light knifed its way into the room through the door. Someone stepped inside with a hatchet in hand, a pistol at the hip, and keys in one hand.

It was Elicia Cantor.

"You." Jane said. It was a simple statement, but her tone was one of pure accusation.

She quickly shut the door behind her and came closer.

She took several seconds to gain the composure to speak.

"I'm so sorry. I didn't know, I had no idea… that they would do this." Elicia Cantor said.

"But you thought betraying us was a good idea? You chose this path. This is *your* fault." Jane said sharply.

"Yes. Yes it is." Elicia said helplessly. Jane had looked as if she were ready with a barrage of verbal fire, but she wilted at this statement.

"But I was wrong. I thought it didn't matter what I did to other people, just like I thought the same way for all these years… but I was wrong, this time. It did matter. My own life… wasn't the most important thing, anymore. And now I've realized it, and it's already too late, and I… I can't take it back, what I've done. It's just too late. But I can help you guys take revenge on the evil psychopath who really did this to her. This weighs heavily on my shoulders, to be sure. I can't make up for it, but I need to do everything I can to try. And that means freeing you, and helping you do whatever it is you need to do to stop Vaurien Kane, and get the drone back. I know you'll probably want to be just done with me, but… let me help you now." She said, hefting the hatchet in her hand.

"Alright. We have no choice but to… we have to work together. But we have to be all in." Gye said. He stood, and the others did too.

"I don't know about the rest of y'all, but I'm about ready to break a Kane. Who's with me?"

"We're in. What's the plan?" Jane asked.

"Get the drone. Make Vaurien Kane pay for what he did. And get our of here alive." Gye said.

"Well, there are a dozen guards between you and the drone, and every one of them is part of Vaurien's insane cult. You'll have to wade through them first, and we're gonna need more than just the one hatchet to do that." Elicia said.

"But you've also got a pistol." Ray pointed out.

"We fire a shot in here, and they'll know in half a second where to swarm and find us, and I know one thing, they'll be much more inclined to make do with sacrificing our bodies than sacrificing us alive." Elicia said.

"She's right. We need to strike hard and fast so they don't know what hit them, and we need to cut off the head of the snake as quickly as possible." Gye said.

"What's this about a snake?" Ray Kaymar asked confusedly.

"It's a metaphor, Ray. Jeez, try to keep up." Gye said.

"One more thing, Ray. You might want this back." Elicia said. She reached into her coat pocket and retrieved the knife that had been confiscated from him earlier.

CHAPTER 28
REINFORCEMENTS

The green forest stretched out for miles ahead. At the shore of this sea of green was an unceremoniously constructed building with several landing pads and one large glass entrance. The only living thing in sight was a lone guard, standing at casual attention with a rifle strapped to his back, occasionally pacing back and forth along a painted black and bright yellow hazard line lining the perimeter of the establishment.

The guard was wearing a faded baby blue helmet with scratches and one questionable dent in it. He wore deep green army fatigues with a subtle camouflage pattern, and light tan combat boots.

A plodding, clunking, thudding mechanical sound interrupted the relative solace of his existence. He squinted and looked out at the forest. There was a rustle of trees, moving slowly in his direction.

He pulled out his binoculars and looked through them, but from his distance away, he could not make out what it was.

"Alpha one one three, base, do you read me? Over." He said into his radio.

After a few seconds of silence, the reply came.

"Go ahead, Indigo three."

"Disturbance noted eight hundred meters from post. Seeking direction, over."

"We'll send reinforcements immediately. Stand by."

The disturbance grew ever closer as he waited impatiently for the order to be fulfilled. As it grew closer he could make out the details of the sound with greater clarity.

It sounded like a strained, tired machine on its last legs, nearing the death of its mechanical existence.

Footsteps sounded from behind, and a party of half a dozen other guards plus a woman in a suit, handgun in hand, joined him.

"Over there, do you see? Four O'clock."

The source of the strained sounds meandered closer until it broke through the tree line at last with a weak crackle.

It was the *Venture* rover. Or, what was left of it, anyways. There were enormous gashes on the sides, the glass was shattered, one limb was missing entirely, and one limb was half contorted, dragging along like an injured animal's.

"My god, what's happened to it?"

The machine nearly ran into the building, but it came to a painful, screeching halt just in time.

"Get a medical team to the *Venture* right away." The woman in the suit said, holstering her pistol.

"Any sign of life?"

"Sending in medical now. Send status report immediately."

They reached the ravaged machine. The ladder to the entrance of the *Venture* had long ago been torn asunder, so they had to improvise and bring out their own step ladder. It cost several seconds. The heat of the day beat down heavily on them as they tore open the *Venture*'s door and charged in.

It was dim except for the places where harsh light knifed into the gashes in the sides of the *Venture* and the resulting rays cast hard light shapes onto the damaged floor. The high-quality wood paneling of the inside walls was shattered, and large sections had fallen onto the floor.

The lights in the room flickered harshly every few seconds, and large cables were drooping down from the ceiling. Blue electricity was visible in some of the wires as each pulse of electricity went through the dying lights, and the whole place gave the impression of a mechanical version of a creature that was on its last dying breaths, like a beached whale slowly accepting death.

The most shocking sight in the room was the man in the chair in the corner, slumped over, bandages covering the stump of his shoulder where his arm used to be. A first aid kit lay open on the table next to the couch, and there was an uncomfortable amount of blood pooled up in a dent in the wood floor, where some if it had clotted into a nasty scab. It smelled like death.

The man's face was extraordinarily pale, and the faint rise and fall of his chest was the only indication that this incarnation of death was, in fact, not dead.

The medics rushed to his side in a split second. His eyes slid open and the fear, the endless valley of fear behind each pupil was a terrifying sight. His mouth let out a tired, crusty croaking sound, like one would expect the sound of wind passing through a cracked, dusty valley to sound like. He must have been exceedingly thirsty.

"Rescue… need… rescue… my friends…" was all he could get out before they whisked him out and into the med center of the building. The guard looked at the dripping trail of blood that marked their path, and shuddered.

Hours later, Inspector John Mendes stood in front of the Captain, who, at least, had some color returning to his cheeks at last. He was sitting down, with a fresh bandage at his arm.

"It's good to see you alive, Captain." Inspector Mendes said.

"Just barely. I've never felt so close to death. I could taste hell on the tip of my tongue." Captain Walker said.

John Mendes shifted uncomfortably, squinting his eyes in that perpetually anxious way of his before mustering the courage to speak.

"What, ah,… what happened to your arm, good Captain?"

"Oh, that. I had almost forgotten, thank you for the reminder. Sometimes I still feel the pain of sawing it off, even through the dulling effect of the opiate painkiller… just a few minutes ago I tried to reach for my water, and I was wondering why my hand wasn't working, and I looked down, and I... I screamed." He said, his face taking on a painful twist.

"But, ah, what *happened* to it?" John Mendes tried again.

"Have you ever stared death in its many eyes, John? I have. The devil is a massive spider, I think. Or the memory if it. I fought the devil that night, wrestled with him through the hallucinations. The recurring, inescapable scarring of the attack just came back again and again to me, and I had to feel the pain so many times... it was less than an hour after I set off alone, as I saw the pale green and white streaks creeping up my arm and felt the evil venom coursing through my veins — I was lucky, I'm sure I would've died if it had more than scratched me— that I knew it was amputation or death. So far, I am regretting my choice immensely, but it will be worth it to save my friends..." He said. A strange look of confusion crossed his face, and he looked around quizzically.

"Did you send in a rescue team after them yet?" He asked, his voice hardening.

"That would require the requisite authorization—" Mendes started.

"Are you insane? GET A MOVE ON, we don't have any time to lose!" Captain Walker said, summoning an unnatural strength to rise to his feet.

CHAPTER 29
DIVERSION

"If we don't make it out of this alive…" Jane said, searching for the words to say. She was standing with Gye behind the open door; they were the last two remaining in the cell, giving Ray and Elicia enough time to set up their diversion.

"…then we'll have lived lives worth living, and ended them with a bang." Gye replied.

"I mean… if we don't make it out of this alive, there's something I want you to know." Jane said, her blue eyes shifting back and forth as they scanned his face. What she was looking for, he could not say.

She broke eye contact and half turned away.

"We'd better get in place…" She started, turning to walk away.

Gye grabbed her hand and spun her around so that she was facing him, and they were close.

They looked into each other's eyes wordlessly for several seconds. Gye could feel the possibilities slipping away as time seemed to grind to a near halt. He almost spoke just as he heard three clanging metal sounds; the signal to get in position.

"That's the signal." He said weakly. They parted awkwardly and looked both ways before exiting into the hallway.

There was a faint buzzing sound that was different in pitch from the one emitted by the octocopter's blades.

"Do you hear that?" Gye asked.

Jane stopped to listen.

"Out the window, do you see?" She asked, pointing.

He looked, and was surprised at what he saw. Four helicopters, each one painted dull green or black, were inbound.

"Who…?"

"Captain Walker must've made it back! They're coming to our rescue!" Jane exclaimed, a little too loudly for his comfort.

A loud crashing sound was heard from inside the octocopter. The diversion.

Boots pounding metal was the next thing they heard, followed by an indistinct yelling.

"We're not in position yet!" Jane exclaimed as they ran.

"Thanks for that fact, genius." Gye replied. Not exactly his best comeback.

As they rounded the corner, they saw three armed guards putting Elicia and Ray up against the wall. Each one held what looked like a 9mm pistol. When they turned around at the sound of Gye and Jane running, Elicia and Ray immediately split and ran.

"Stop right there!" The leader of the group commanded. They heeded his command for a split second before turning and rushing back the way they came.

A single shot was fired, and the bullet ricocheted off the wall and sliced across the back of Gye's left shoulder at an angle. It felt like a hard shove at first, and he stumbled to the ground. When he tried to use his left arm to jump back to his feet, he yelled and fell back. Every nerve in his left arm felt like it was on fire and vibrating at the same time, until a calm numbness set in.

Jane pulled him to his feet somehow and they rounded the corner again. His vision was a blur until they reached the inside of a dim room, with a faint illumination of blue light. He didn't recognize the other two people inside for several seconds before he realized they were Elicia Cantor and Ray Kaymar.

"You've been shot!" Elicia exclaimed.

"Man up, it was only a 9mm. And I would say grazed, not shot." Ray said derisively.

"No gunshot wound, no opinion." Gye said through clenched teeth. It felt like someone had taken a butcher knife and slashed across his shoulder with it.

"Here, take a painkiller." Elicia said, tossing him two white pills.

"The fact that you just have these on hand is concerning." Gye said. She shrugged and winked.

"I don't judge the ways you have fun, my dear."

There was an attempt from the hallway to open the door, but it was bolted shut. They moved on, but every few seconds the sound of someone running past could be heard.

"Well, we're screwed. There's no way we can get to the pilot's room now." Elicia said. She was backed up against the back wall, where the water tank was. She looked behind her and screamed.

"What is that thing?!" She asked, referring to the aquatic creature that had been following Ray, Jane, and Gye around earlier.

"Oh, that. He's our pet fish. I named him *Formidulosus*." Gye said, letting go of his shoulder as the painkillers started to kick in.

"Such a cute name. I had no idea that thing was in there." Elicia said, recovering her breath. It looked on with its beady black eyes, opening and closing its maw as if to declare its appetite for those on the other side of the glass.

"I've dated men smaller than that thing, jeez. It's like a demented satanic seahorse when it cures up like that. I can't stop shivering, is that normal? How strong is that glass?" Elicia rambled, backing away slowly as she spoke.

"Looks like we're trapped in here with that thing for company." Gye said. His bullet wound only vaguely ached at this point.

There was a collective pause.

"Unless we were to join it on the other side of the glass…" Jane said slowly.

"Are you out of your mind? Or just suicidal?" Elicia asked.

"That's our only chance. We open this door, we're screwed, and getting sacrificed by a psychopath is a certainty for us. But if we use the *Formidulosus*'s water tank to get into the pilot's room…" Jane said.

"Then we at least have a chance." Gye finished.

"It's crazy. Impossible, probably. But it just might work." Ray said.

"Aren't you all forgetting something? We can't just chill with Frankenfish up in that tank and expect nothing to happen." Elicia said.

"Frankenstein was the scientist who created the monster, not the monster itself, but point taken." Ray said.

"Whatever. No way in hell I'm facing up against that thing." Elicia said.

"Do you have a better plan?" Gye asked.

The only answer was an uncomfortable silence.

"I didn't think so."

"Fine. That's all well and good, but I hope you've got something up your sleeve to get Frankenfish out of our way. Unless one of you is some kind of fish whisperer." Elicia said.

"Have you ever tapped on a the glass of a fish tank? The fish almost always swim away. Maybe when we break the glass to get in, he'll swim away." Gye said.

"Elicia, your hatchet, please." Ray asked. She gave it over to him gingerly, stepping back quickly afterwards as if she half expected to be cut in half by his residual anger. But no such thing happened. She was visibly relieved, and wiped her brow with the cuff of her long white shirt.

"Stand back, everyone." Ray said calmly, stepping up next to the glass and cracking his back and arms in preparation.

"This room will flood fairly quickly, yeah?" Elicia said nervously.

"There is already a half meter or so of air space at the top of the tank. The increased total water-holding capacity of this ship, which will be increased by the inclusion of this mostly water-tight room, will then cause a lowering of the water levels, which should allow us enough room to breathe." Ray said, stretching and grunting between words as he prepared.

"Could you maybe get on with it? You're not competing in the olympics here." Jane said, eying the *Formidulosus* as it shifted back and forth like a snake preparing to strike. An involuntary shiver and shot of adrenaline shot down her spine at the sight of being so close to it.

"Fine then, you do it, O' ye impatient one." Ray said, handing the hatchet abruptly to her.

"Ray, is that really—" Gye started.

"No, it's fine. I've got this." Jane interjected.

She got into a stance like a baseball player preparing to hit a home run. With a sudden WHACKing sound, the metal hatchet was stuck in the glass and a spider web of cracks was spreading around it. A trickle of water began sloshing out rhythmically. The *Formidulosus* hissed repeatedly, and after several more intimidation attempts, swam away quickly as the vortex of outpouring water began to exert pressure on it. Jane grinned as she admired her handiwork.

"Not bad for a… scientist." Ray said.

Jane grabbed the handle of the hatchet and pulled it out. The glass shattered into the room, and the sloshing water began to cascade. In seconds the water level in the room was up to two feet.

"Follow Elicia! She knows the way." Jane said.

Elicia seemed somewhat surprised by this, but accepted the charge immediately and took up a position at the front of the group.

"I'd just like to apologize in advance if this ends up with any of us dying." She shouted out in lilting syllables before plunging into the water tank through the now-massive hole. Jane followed, then Gye, and Ray Kaymar brought up the rear.

CHAPTER 30
FORMIDULOSUS

There was no sign of the *Formidulosus* as they first entered. The space was more cramped than Gye expected, and his grazed bullet wound was stinging in the presence of the acidic water. He pushed forward, walking on the bottom of the tank (which was occasionally littered with a decomposing substance which he assumed was excretion from the tank's resident, and thus he attempted to avoid the aforementioned) and pushing to to top for air every forty seconds or so. He was not the best of swimmers, and his wound only aggravated that fact.

They neared an area where the tank could be viewed from a room, and Elicia slowed to peak around the corner to make sure the coast was clear. They had to wait for what felt like an eternity until her bulk could flounder to the top, take a gasping wheeze of an inhalation, and blunder back down. She looked around the corner and signaled to the others that the coast was clear.

They made a 'run' for it— as much as it could be called running, as the water made them move in what felt like slow motion— to try to take cover in the next section of the tank which was not visible to observers inside the main body of the octocopter.

Gye had to go up for a breath about halfway through, and by the time he came back down, he could see the others looking back at him and motioning various inscrutable hand signals. Confused, he looked into the room, and he froze.

There were four men walking in lockstep, chatting among themselves. Gye froze, not even exhaling a little bit to depressurize his ears and nose as he was accustomed to doing. When they each appeared to be looking away for long enough— he had not yet been spotted— he shoved himself to the top of the tank, where he floated, face-down, hands and feet pushed against the glass to prevent any kind of movement from happening. He could tilt his head in this position to take a breath, but he dared not do so yet. His heart was beating frantically— life and death were held in his hands at this moment— and he noticed his arms and legs trembling.

He noticed a flurry of movement from the direction in the tank that he had just come from, but when he tried to look over and ascertain the source of it, he could see nothing.

When he looked back into the room, the men were gone. Gingerly, he lowered himself to the ground and ran to join the others.

"That was a close one. We need to be more careful." Elicia said between gasps as they floated together, heads and arms above the water level of the tank.

"I thought I saw something from behind me. I don't want to stick around any longer, so shall we crack on?" Gye said.

Jane, Elicia, and Ray agreed and plunged underwater. Gye started pushing against the sides with his hands in order to move faster; the others noticed and began to adopt the same technique.

They reached the last blind spot before the pilot's room. They surfaced again at Elicia's signal. Gye panted for oxygen; he hadn't noticed how long he'd been holding his breath. His wounded shoulder ached, and the arm was beginning to feel the burn.

"The maintenance door is immediately inside the room. It's at the top of the tank, so we'll have to jump to the ground, seeing as we didn't come in this way and didn't put the ladder up before going in." Elicia said.

Gye felt a buzzing, tingling sensation in his nerves. He shivered involuntarily, rubbing his shoulders. He noticed a similar state in the others.

"Don't look now, but I think our fishy friend is back." Ray said.

Gye looked anyway.

It was obviously surprised to see them in its abode, and was hissing and flailing its antennae at them tentatively. It was slowly and carefully moving towards them.

Waves of blurry blueness were emanating from the *Formidulosus*, and as it got closer, the stinging sensation in Gye's nerves intensified.

"It appears to have some sort of electrical defense system. Similar to an electric eel, I think. Quite fascinating, considering the differences in their evolutionary pathways..." Jane said.

"That's all rather well and good, but if you're quite finished, my dear, I'd like to get the hell out of here." Elicia said curtly.

They drifted back to the bottom and pressed on. Gye did not want to look back, for fear that the *Formidulosus* would see his action as threatening and rush at them.

The tingling sensation continued to intensify, feeling extraordinarily similar to the sensation of hitting one's elbow nerve against something hard, with the resulting fuzzy pain. Except this pain rippled through his body like a pebble thrown into a pond, emanating forth into his body.

They reached the area just below the door. Elicia and Jane were already banging on the door by the time Gye floated up to join them. Gasping for oxygen, he slipped when he tried to lend them a hand. The electric feeling in his nerves was beginning to make his muscles tremble.

He finally looked back, and the *Formidulosus* was eye to eye with him, sticking out of the water like a demented mermaid seeking to send into damnation the souls of passing sailors.

Gye instantly flailed and kicked at it. From this close, the pure blackness of its creepy eyes bored into his soul, and the metallic appearance of its scales was frightening, looking like an impenetrable suit of armor, protecting the *Formidulosus* from any threat.

It backed up slightly and hissed, sending a particularly harsh wave of electricity at him. Gye could taste a bitter metallic taste on his tongue, like the taste he vaguely remembered of sucking on a battery as a child.

He inhaled involuntarily, and water got into his lungs. He began to panic and flailed to the surface, violently coughing out a stream of water. The fringes of his vision darkened, and he seemed unable to speak or hear anything. His whole existence was tunnel vision. All he saw was a hand from above reaching, grabbing onto him, and then the hard sensation of falling from a height onto a hard floor.

The wind was knocked out of him.

"Quick, seal the doors!" He heard a voice say as he came to.

He was so thirsty, and barely managed to open his eyes. He suddenly remembered where he was and what was happening.

He was in the pilot's room. Out the massive window he could see a helicopter flying by, and heard a cannon discharge. The helicopter swerved to avoid it, and machine gun fire strafed across the octocopter.

He stood slowly, coughing up water, and looked around. A puddle of water lay around him, and his clothes were sopping wet. He tried to wring them out as he stood.

Jane, Elicia, and Ray had piled everything they could against the entrance to the room. They did nothing about the exit onto the top of the octocopter, as there was no one out there, and so it was unnecessary. There was an unconscious body lying on the floor. It was an oriental man with black slacks and a white dress shirt, with a shiny black hat to match. His shoes were worn and had obviously been repaired several times. Gye looked at the macro detail of the texture of the man's clothes in a daze before snapping back into the present.

Ray was standing at the controls of the octocopter. Ray, Elicia, and Jane were just as sopping wet as he was. Jane's black tank top stuck to her form through the wetness. She didn't notice his gaze, as she was moving something across the room to block the door.

"What's going on?" Gye asked.

"Did you have a nice nap, princess? Oh, good. Now if you wouldn't mind helping out a little bit, we're barring the door and trying to maneuver the octocopter so the helicopters can land someone on this thing to help us out." Ray explained in a hurried huff.

"Right, okay." Gye said, still dazed. It felt similar to what he used to feel after sprinting for several minutes; the way his eyes almost felt like they were popping out of his head, and the world wouldn't stop spinning at the edges.

He made eye contact with the *Formidulosus* through the glass. There was a large pool of water at the base of the glass below the door where they had escaped.

He shivered and banged on the glass, as if that would do anything to set the situation right. The *Formidulosus* actually shrank back, which was at least somewhat satisfying.

Gye finally noticed the furious banging and knocking that was going on at one of the doors. It sounded like they were trying to knock down the door, but thankfully for them, this was one of the few well-constructed facets of the entire structure.

There was a booming sound, and he saw one of the helicopters light up into a furious blaze of orange and reds. A piece of shrapnel from the explosion embedded itself into the windshield, sending one long, thick crack racing across it. Three parachutes opened up in the sky as the remains of the helicopter fell, and one of them was hit by an ensuing blast from the octocopter. Gye watched with unnerving clarity as the bleached white parachute was sprayed with red before turning to black and falling as ashes, a cloud that was slowly drifting downwards. Surely it would become fertilizer for the growth of something new once it hit the forest floor.

The other three helicopters were retreating.

"No, no! They can't abandon us!" Gye yelled, louder than he intended to.

"They won't risk it." Elicit said forlornly.

There was a clicking sound, and the door to the top deck of the octocopter opened easily.

A man with a clear, chilling german accent spoke with ease.

"I see you have become quite accustomed to this cozy little fortress you have constructed in here. Unfortunately, I am the landlord here, and I have come to evict you." He said.

"Vaurien Kane." Gye stated.

"And you are... *an idiot*. Surrender this hopeless resistance immediately, for there is no hope that you should prevail." He said. He casually reached into his pocket and brought out a handheld watch, which he glanced at, muttered something indistinct, and replaced it back into his black blazer's left inside breast pocket.

"Why so anxious about the time, Vaurien? Counting down the seconds before we cut off your head for what you did to Molly?" Ray said, nearly shouting by the end.

"Calm down, Mr. Kaymar. I had hoped you would remain the calm intellectual. It seems I was mistaken. No, I am trying to make sure we stay on schedule for the sacrifice. If we do not make it back in time, the lunar patterns will not be in proper alignment, and we will have to wait another month before the sacrifices. A small inconvenience, to be sure, but my time is valuable." Vaurien explained.

"So should we kill him now, or later?" Jane asked.

Vaurien Kane pulled out a pistol and aimed it at Elicia.

"I know you stole the pistol, you treacherous woman. If you so much as flinch wrong and lead me to believe you are making the mistake of reaching for it, I will kill you instantly. But I should hope not. The Ancients are most pleased by living sacrifices, as it is the holiest of rites to make them, so I would prefer not to kill any more of my lambs. Now. The pistol." Vaurien Kane said.

She reluctantly reached into her pocket and produced the sopping wet pistol. Not that it would have done them any good anyways, in the state it was in.

"Ah, so you had a little swim, did you? It's a pity we fed my pet earlier today. You would have made the prettiest fish food." He said, directing the comment towards Jane.

"Would you have made the same kind of comment about a man? I don't think so." Jane said. Upon seeing Vaurien's confused look, she kicked his hand holding the gun and immediately ran out the door. Gye didn't stop to see if he had lost the gun or not and ran out to join her, followed by Elicia.

He heard the door slamming shut behind him and picked up the pace.

"What now!?" He shouted over the loudness of the propellers and the wind.

"Keep running!" Jane shouted back. He heard three gunshots, but none found their marks.

As they reached the outside edge of the octocopter's top deck, they had to grab onto the shaky metal guardrails to avoid being swept off the metal top of the octocopter like a speck of dust on a linoleum tile.

They were hidden from the door they had just left by a jutting out block of metal, which was emitting exhaust from the other side.

Gye signaled for the others to stay put and gingerly looked around the corner.

Vaurien Kane was on the top of the octocopter, slowly making his way towards them. He didn't see where they were, and was looking all around, panning his pistol around in all directions like in a war video game.

"New plan." Gye said as loudly as he dared.

"What?" Elicia asked, unable to hear what he was saying.

He motioned for them to get closer to him— uncomfortably close in his personal space, in fact, but that was necessary— and he tried again.

"We wait for Vaurien to come around this exhaust stack. When he starts coming around, we stay on the opposite side until we are facing the door. Then we run back into the pilot's room and try to land this thing." Gye said.

"We can't land it, I couldn't figure out the sequence to deploy the landing gear." Ray said, annoyed.

"Then we're crashing this thing— as gently as possible— and hoping for the best. Understood?" He said. They nodded.

When Vaurien Kane was just close enough, Gye signaled to Jane, Ray, and Elicia, and they ran as quietly as possible.

The octocopter was tilted by this time— a result of being left without a pilot for the past while— and they had to run somewhat uphill to compensate. The helicopters were watching from a distance, and they were holding their fire, apparently realizing that the people they were trying to rescue were on top of the octocopter.

A shot fired and whizzed overhead. Gye looked back. Vaurien Kane was aiming at them.

"Down!" He shouted. They listened, and two bullet holes appeared in the metal in front of them. Gye and Jane would both have been hit square in the torso.

"He's reloading! Go!" He screamed at them.

They made it back inside and locked the door.

"The drone, where is it?" Gye asked Elicia.

###

Vaurien Kane looked at the piece of paper in his hand and laughed sadistically. So that was why Gye Storm had seemed so familiar. Like father, like son.

"Perhaps it's time..." Vaurien muttered aloud, "to see what Gye Storm is made of."

CHAPTER 31
AS THE WORLD BURNS…

"Vaurien's room. He's a power-hungry monster. Where else could he possibly keep it?" Elicia intoned.

The banging at the door had stopped, as the guards had apparently realized the reality of the chase on the roof of the octocopter.

Gye moved the items away from the door and took Ray's knife in hand. He opened the door quickly and jumped into the room, ready to slay an attacker.

There was only one guard in the room, who was awakened from his reverie rather quickly and unpleasantly. Gye gave the man a swift uppercut right cross to the jaw and he was out like a light. Gye grabbed the man's rifle, swung it over his own shoulder, and looked around.

"Over there!" Elicia said, waddling in from the door. Their clothes had been mostly dried by the fierce wind outside, but they still made loud sloshing sounds every time they moved. Elicia's once-white jacket was gray with streaks of bluish green. Jane joined them, placing a hand on Gye's shoulder.

He noted where Elicia was pointing and looked over. It was a small, drone-sized brown coffin, with the word 'BLASPHEMER' written in psychotic red letters across the side. It looked like it had been written in blood, although whose blood, Gye could not begin to guess.

"It's in there?" Gye asked.

Elicia gulped involuntarily, suddenly aware of the depth of the seriousness of their adversary.

"Uh... yeah." She said, pushing the thought away and waddling over to it. Gye, Jane, and Elicia worked together to pop the top off of the coffin— it was a finely-worked, detailed design— and set it aside. The drone was inside, the one light on the side still blinking at its soothingly steady rate.

"There they are!" a man shouted from the hallway. It was the large, heavyset man with dark skin and a red cape who they had noted earlier.

"Elicia, get the drone to the pilot's room!" Gye shouted, grabbing Jane's arm and bringing her with him as he charged to the door. The man at the forefront was taken aback, and his surprise gave them just enough time to slam the door shut. It had no lock, so they had to push and shove against it with all their mights to keep it closed.

Elicia struggled and called out to Ray, who ran over to her and helped her heft it into the pilot's room.

A particularly painful push on the door sent a wave of pain into Gye's shoulder. He could not see the helicopters anywhere near from his perspective.

"Are you sure we want to do this?" Ray asked, poised at the control seat.

"Do it! It's our only chance. Crash this thing!" Gye shouted.

Gravity seemed to fall away as the octocopter fell towards earth. It was like floating in one of those photos of astronauts in space, free and happy.

Gye and Jane locked eyes through the madness. He pulled her in quickly, caressed her cheek, and kissed her.

"What was that for?" She yelled through the mayhem.

"Luck!" He returned.

She shrugged and pulled him back in, kissing him back much harder than he had done to her. He briefly saw stars as their lips separated.

The moment of unexpected solace ended as abruptly as it had began.

The octocopter smashed with a horrendous violence into the ground, and their blissful flying was cut short. The metal structure screamed as pieces were torn off by the pressure, and an explosion sent the world to black.

Black, black, black… surely there was more to the world than this? Oh, there was the high ringing sound. A banging feeling of pain in his temples. The world suddenly came into focus. It was loud, bright, and, most of all, painful.

He stood to his feet. Someone took his hand. He looked over. It was Jane Silver.

They worked together to gather Elicia and Ray. The glass holding in the *Formidulosus* had shattered, and the water had spilled out and pooled around them, probably saving them from some rather serious burns. The *Formidulosus* lay, twitching and helpless, on dry land. It seemed frail and not nearly as evil as it had before, in this state. Perhaps death does that to every creature, not just humans, he reflected. Gye took the hatchet from Elicia and, with one well-placed blow, put the creature out of its misery. Its once-terrifying black orbs of eyes faded to a light gray as its last muscle relaxed into death.

The wreckage of the Octocopter lay strewn about in every direction. Piles of scraps obscured the landscape. Gye winced as he noticed a man impaled onto the ground by a jagged beam of metal, his arms dangling limply in the air like one of those inflatable colorful statues waving in the wind.

A terrifying whoosh burned through the air and a line of flames sprang up from the edge of the wreckage. The heat became unbearable in seconds.

"Run!" Jane yelled, grabbing Gye's hand as she led him, Ray, and Elicia towards the edge of the forest.

The helicopters landed and the sounds of gunfire erupted behind them. Men shouted and bullets whistled through the air.

They laid huddled against a tree, heads down against the whirlwind of chaos surrounding them.

Jane yelled out as a bullet thudded against the tree, sending a shockwave of force rippling through their huddle. Gye was between Elicia and Jane, trying to hold his hand steady as it trembled against Jane's shoulders.

"The forest is catching fire!" Elicia screamed, pointing towards an enflamed tree close to the wreckage.

"Let's hope not. You can't outrun a forest fire." Gye said.

"Maybe not. But a helicopter might be able to. Let's go." Jane said, pulling them up together and stepping forward.

Before she could move forward, the nearest soldier was hit square in the chest by a powerful round. He sank to the ground with a muffled cry and died.

Stepping over him, Jane led the others forward. Gye tried not to look down as they went over the dead body.

They moved forward as bullets whizzed by in the air above them, pounding through Gye's head like the twisted drum rhythms of a heavy metal song.

Nothing truly came into focus. Perhaps his brain was simply trying to process so much information at once, or perhaps it was mere sleep deprivation. Whatever it was, Gye found himself shaking his head wildly as he ran, following in Jane's footsteps.

With a whoosh, the fire sliced across their path, separating them from the helicopters on the more open part of the wreckage site.

With this sudden stop, Gye finally could begin to understand the area around him. Massive propellers of the octocopter lay strewn about like seeds in a field, spread about rather diffusely with the hull of the aircraft broken into larger chunks in the area between them.

"Back!" Gye yelled, finally fully in control of himself again. They turned around.

And came face to face with Vaurien Kane.

Vaurien spread his arms wide, cane in one hand, pistol in the other. On either side of him were guards in full black uniform, machine guns at the ready. One of them popped off a round into the distance, the muzzle flashing through the gathering smoke like lightning through clouds.

"Blasphemers! You have maligned the Ancients for the last time! This will be—" He began.

Jane cut him off mercilessly.

"Hold up, you sociopathic prick. Save your monologue for when you're exchanging stories with Lucifer in hell. I'm sure it'll help you pass the time. Not that it'll help, considering you'll be there for eternity. And you'll deserve it too, after what you did to Molly. I don't care what you're about to say about your spiritual mumbo jumbo. It's all a lie, and you're just a rich, privileged sucker."

Vaurien was completely stunned for several moments after this unexpected verbal barrage.

Suddenly a round exploded overhead and everyone dropped to the ground.

An enormous rumbling sound permeated the ground and a buzzing feeling began vibrating their bones.

"What...?" Elicia said.

Gye looked up into the distance. Perhaps a mile away was the mountain where they had recovered the drone. A few dark shapes were visible against the sky...

Gye gasped as he realized what was happening. The hive was awakening. He felt a sinking feeling in his chest as every childhood memory of being stung washed upon him at once.

"Gye Storm!" Vaurien Kane called out, rising from his crouched position.

"We're about to have much bigger problems, if you don't mind —" Gye began.

"I slaughtered your family all those years ago. I am the man you've been searching for. I owe a debt to your father— and I will repay it with your death." He said, walking over purposefully, his tattered suit swaying in the breeze. He grabbed his cracked glasses and threw them carelessly into the dirt.

Gye could have sworn his heart stopped beating for several seconds. But where he expected to feel a torrent of rage pour through his veins, he only felt tired. Deathly, bone tired. This had been the focus of his life for so long, to finally have the culprit in his grasp should have felt like the greatest opportunity for vengeance and purpose he had ever felt. But it wasn't. It wasn't as if he could hate Vaurien more, after what he had done to Molly. He could only watch apathetically as Vaurien walked closer.

Vaurien's guards were nowhere to be found, lost to the ether of dust and smoke.

"Get the drone," Gye called out to his companions, "and get to a helicopter. If we don't have that, all of this was for nothing." His voice was flat, emotionless. He flexed his shoulders and popped his back, pulling his fists forward.

With a flash, a knife was in Vaurien's hand, and half a second later it was jabbed halfway into Gye's forearm.

Gye yelled out mightily and grabbed Vaurien's neck with his other hand. He squeezed as hard as he could, enjoying the sight of Vaurien's eyes bulging out like a frog's. His face turned purple and his throat pulsated like living jello.

Vaurien quickly yanked the knife out of Gye's arm and slashed it across his other forearm. Gye's grip was broken and blood began to discolor both of his sleeves.

Gye suddenly felt dizzy and woozy. Vaurien recomposed himself and held the knife in front of him menacingly.

Gye backpedaled and turned around, hobbling into as good of a sprint as he could manage in his condition.

He dove behind a piece of wreckage as a massive bee buzzed past him. Gye shuddered deeply and rolled back to his feet, grabbing a piece of metal from the ground that could at least work somewhat as a weapon.

Gye turned around just in time to use his makeshift weapon to block Vaurien's knife jab. Vaurien's ordinarily perfectly calm face was curled into an unstoppable rage, and his eyes somehow gave off the impression of a volcano nearing eruption. Gye winced as he noticed the steady dripping of blood from his arms onto the ground below.

Vaurien suddenly coughed with enormous force, spewing blood from his mouth all over Gye's face. Reeling backwards, Gye managed to land a swift kick to Vaurien's groin before falling flat on his back.

Rolling to his left just in time to dodge Vaurien's attempt to jump onto him, Gye lunged forward and managed to smack Vaurien's head into the wreckage behind him.

"Gye!" He heard Jane call out, muffled.

He saw her hanging out of a helicopter, twenty feet or so away, sweeping low near the ground. Somehow the steady thudding sound of the helicopter's blades had escaped him. The drone was visible in the helicopter. At least that much was secure.

He tripped over some rubble as he tried running towards her, falling flat on his face. A giant bee landed on his back and Gye convulsed out of sheer revulsion, surprising the creature enough to cause it to take off again.

Launching supernaturally to his feet, Gye took off at a full sprint and in seconds had jumped straight into the waiting helicopter.

"Oh my god. I've never seen anyone run so quickly in my life. Whoa— what happened to your hands?" Elicia exclaimed.

Before he could answer, Jane wrapped her arms around him and hugged him close.

The helicopter shot skyward and immediately swerved downward again to get out of the way of two oncoming bees.

"Let's get out of here!" Ray yelled from the cockpit. He was yelling at the pilot from the co-pilot's seat to go faster, as if that would help somehow.

There was a thudding sound, and suddenly Vaurien Kane had jumped into the helicopter as well.

"We have unfinished business, Gye Storm!" He yelled over the noise, holding the knife in front of him menacingly.

Jane brought a heavy bag around and swung at him, but he ducked and in a flash was behind her with the knife.

Holding the knife to her throat, Vaurien smiled at Gye triumphantly.

The helicopter shook as the pilot swerved to avoid another rampant bee.

Noticing the hive, Vaurien chuckled softly.

"It's over, Gye Storm. Those blasphemous creatures will be the death of us all. There's no stopping fate. But you're going to skydive straight into that hive, or your darling princess in distress here is gonna bleed out through the jugular. Instruct the pilot to fly over the hive." Vaurien said.

Jane wiggled in protest to his statement, but Vaurien only pressed more tightly with the knife until a small stream of blood trickled weakly from her neck. She was quite silent after that.

Ray instructed the pilot to do so and the helicopter lurched forward.

The view seemed oddly serene in that moment. The fire was dying down, and all that remained of the octocopter was a smoldering wreckage. Gye choked on the smoke as he looked on helplessly at Jane, looking into her wild blue eyes as if to assure her that everything would be okay. Although it almost certainly wouldn't be.

In moments they were over the hive and Vaurien stepped aside, Jane under his knife, and motioned nonchalantly for Gye to dive out of the helicopter.

"Gye… I love you." Jane said. And she shoved all the weight of her body out of the helicopter, bringing Vaurien with her.

All at once, rage overtook Gye's composure and he screamed a demonic scream of unearthly rage at Vaurien as he fell. His neck veins popped dramatically and he was fleshly red.

How dare he take everything Gye had ever loved? First his family. Then Molly Hazelwood. And now Jane.

Without thinking, Gye lunged out the window as well, diving fearlessly into the spinning vortex of bees.

In a flash he was holding onto Vaurien's collar, screaming pure rage and vitriol incoherently into his face as they fell.

With a splat they crashed on top of and squished a bee. The stench immediately caused Gye to throw up, but he was at least alive.

He rolled off of Vaurien and sprang to his feet. His bloody forearms had left splotches on Vaurien's coat. Vaurien stared, barely conscious from the pummeling he had just experienced, into the dozens of bees overhead and around him.

Frantically, Gye looked around for Jane. She was nowhere to be found. A bee knocked him to the ground in an instant, and for one terrifying moment he felt its furry leg touching the back of his neck. He shuddered at the sensation and sprang back up.

He came face to face with Vaurien Kane, who promptly shoved his knife into Gye's abdomen. Gye stood still, in complete shock. For some reason, all he noticed in that moment was the horrifying stench of the dead bee that was wafting off of Vaurien. That, and the cloud of bees that was hovering overhead but would not come closer. Perhaps they feared death like any other creature alive… like Gye should have. Should have. But he didn't. In that moment, he relaxed, and everything slipped into blurriness. For a moment, the blurry faces of his family once again flashed in front of his mind. But they passed away, for at last they seemed to have no more power. They couldn't save him. He thought of nothing, and he was nothing.

Vaurien Kane stood, triumphant, watching the life force drain from Gye's eyes with the blood from his arms and abdomen.

"For the glory of the Ancients!" He yelled into the cloud of bees overhead. He noticed that there was one bee that was almost twice as large as any of the others, with a wider abdomen and longer wings. Must have been the queen.

A shuddering feeling permeated the hive and the crack in the side widened. Another shudder and a bomb fell through, blasting the area into a crater.

Vaurien fell to his knees over Gye's body and held his hands to his ears. Everything was one high-pitched squeal. He grimaced as he held back the pain.

He noticed that his knife was no longer in his hand and looked around frantically for a moment before looking down. It was sticking through his chest from behind.

"This is what happens when you take what's mine, you overgrown brat. You were never destined to be anything greater than bee food." Jane said from behind, and she yanked the knife out of him.

He fell to the ground, gasping as he watched his own blood spurt out of his chest. No, this couldn't be. This wasn't the prophecy. He was to rule, to win, to conquer… the world would respect the Ancients once more… everything would…

Jane brought the knife up and slashed Vaurien's head clean off his shoulders. She kicked it like a soccer ball into the mass of bees to the side, and it soon became so filled with stingers that it looked like a porcupine. Jane grimaced and turned to Gye, lifting him up and half-dragging him towards the cavernous exit. Vaurien's body finally toppled over on its own.

She looked back and was surprised to see one giant bee, larger than all of the others, following closely behind. It was the queen. She looked on with emotionless, glassy eyes at the straggling humans, and seemed almost robotic as she buzzed closer.

Gye coughed up blood, and snapped to some form of consciousness. The first thing he saw was the macro face of the queen bee, with all of its tiny hairs and multi-faceted eyes. It's antennae probed within inches of his face, and it seemed to recoil when its antennae was near his bloody abdomen. It stopped and stayed in place as Gye and Jane hobbled out, the rest of the bees staying behind her.

"Gye Storm, you had better stay with me, or I swear to God I will haunt your ghost for all eternity." Jane said as they walked out.

Soldiers rushed to them and immediately whisked Gye to the closest helicopter. The mass of smoldering wreckage below fell out of focus and Gye could only see the faces of Jane, Elicia, and Ray around him.

"Vaurien Kane... what happened? Did you finish the bastard?" Gye asked.

"He won't be promoting any dangerous cults any time soon, thank God." Jane said.

Gye only sighed in response and half-closed his eyes. His journey was complete.

Jane hesitated before leaning in and kissing Gye softly on the lips.

His eyes fluttered open and he was met with her diamond-like gaze. Perhaps his journey had only begun.

Ray was toying with the drone in the background and Elicia merely smiled vaguely into the distance.

"I'm done with adventuring. After this, I'm going into politics. Much less intrigue and backstabbing there." Elicia said.

"Politics would suit you well, Elicia." Gye mumbled.

"What about you, Gye?"

"What will I do with my future? I suppose... God only knows." And he smiled as he looked into Jane's eyes.

CHAPTER 32
NOTHING IS EVER QUITE FINISHED

The noisy, buzzing classroom slowly wound down to silence as the teacher tapped a ruler like a baseball bat against her other hand. When at last the students had quieted, she cleared her throat and began the lecture.

"Students, as I'm sure you've all heard, the very foundations of our knowledge of biology and life itself have been shaken to their core by the Hazelwood Forest findings. Your assignment tonight will be a four-page report— no less than four pages, mind you— on the scientific and political consequences of this finding. As the identities of the expedition members are still classified, I don't expect you to do the usual personal profiles as we usually do for current events. Now, according to this illustration…"

The teacher droned on. A girl with brown eyes and brown hair, sitting in the back row, glanced up sharply. The wheels of adventure were already churning in the back of her mind. Surely they couldn't have discovered everything in that forest… surely the story was as of yet incomplete. She smiled to herself. The history books would not forget her, she thought as she leaned back in her chair, suddenly paying very, very close attention to the subject at hand.

CHAPTER 33
PARIS, BENEATH THE STARS

It was one year later.

"Here's to the world knowing the truth." Gye said, clinking his glass with Jane. They were trespassing on the roof of a famous French restaurant in Paris.

"To Molly Hazelwood, who died for who she loved. To Anthony Lafayette, who died doing what he loved. To love, adventure, and a life worth living." She replied. They drank to that.

They looked out over the city, at the famous Eiffel Tower, and at the endless sea of stars above them. Gye looked ponderously into her eyes.

"Is it so odd, under so many stars, to believe ours were destined to cross?"

EPILOGUE

She watched them from a distance, and she sighed. She had found them at last, and she was only a few steps away from... but no. Perhaps it was better this way.

Her brown eyes reflected the stars brilliantly as she looked out into the abyss of galaxies, and she pushed the equally brown locks of hair out of the way of her vision.

No, perhaps it was better this way.

ABOUT THE AUTHOR

BRANDON HELMS

Brandon Helms is an up and coming YA novelist who loves science fiction and romance stories, and often tries to combine the two.

Thank you for reading my debut novel. Please leave an Amazon review and share on social media so this book can receive a broader audience.

Made in the USA
Middletown, DE
19 April 2017